国家出版基金项目
NATIONAL PUBLICATION FOUNDATION

赵晶 选编 张瑛 吴长青 英译

南方民间创世神话选集（上）

"十三五"国家重点图书
中国南方民间文学典籍英译丛书
丛书主编 张立玉 丛书副主编 起国庆

ANTHOLOGY
OF THE
CREATION MYTHOLOGY
IN SOUTH CHINA

出品单位：
中南民族大学南方少数民族文库翻译研究基地

WUHAN UNIVERSITY PRESS
武汉大学出版社

· 汉英对照 ·

**图书在版编目(CIP)数据**

南方民间创世神话选集.上:汉英对照/赵晶选编;张瑛,吴长青英译.—武汉:武汉大学出版社,2021.7(2022.1重印)
中国南方民间文学典籍英译丛书/张立玉主编
"十三五"国家重点图书  2020年度国家出版基金资助项目
ISBN 978-7-307-22377-6

Ⅰ.南…  Ⅱ.①赵…  ②张…  ③吴…  Ⅲ.少数民族—神话—作品集—中国—汉、英  Ⅳ.I277.5

中国版本图书馆 CIP 数据核字(2021)第 102905 号

责任编辑:郭  静    责任校对:李孟潇    版式设计:韩闻锦

出版发行:**武汉大学出版社**  (430072  武昌  珞珈山)
(电子邮箱:cbs22@whu.edu.cn  网址:www.wdp.whu.edu.cn)
印刷:湖北恒泰印务有限公司
开本:720×1000  1/16    印张:18.75    字数:225 千字
版次:2021 年 7 月第 1 版    2022 年 1 月第 2 次印刷
ISBN 978-7-307-22377-6    定价:55.00 元

# 丛书编委会

**学术顾问**

王宏印　李正栓

**主编**

张立玉

**副主编**

起国庆

**编委会成员**（按姓氏笔画排列）

| | | | | | |
|---|---|---|---|---|---|
| 邓之宇 | 王向松 | 艾　芳 | 石定乐 | 龙江莉 | 刘　纯 |
| 陈兰芳 | 汤　茜 | 李克忠 | 杨　柳 | 杨筱奕 | 张立玉 |
| 张扬扬 | 张　瑛 | 和六花 | 依旺的 | 保俊萍 | 起国庆 |
| 陶开祥 | 鲁　钒 | 蔡　蔚 | 臧军娜 | | |

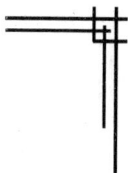

# 序

近年来，民族典籍英译捷报频传，硕果累累。韩家全教授等人的壮族系列经典翻译陆续出版，王宏印教授等人的系列民族典籍英译研究著作已经问世，李正栓教授等人的藏族格言诗英译著作不断在国内外出版，王维波教授等人的东北民族典籍英译著作纷纷付梓，李昌银教授等人的"云南少数民族经典作品英译文库"于2018年年底出版，其他民族典籍英译作品也在接踵而至。

近日，中南民族大学张立玉教授传来佳音：他们要出版"十三五"国家重点图书——"中国南方民间文学典籍英译丛书"。虽叫民间文学，其实基本上都是民族典籍。这一系列包括十本书，它们是：《黑暗传》《哭嫁歌》《哈尼阿培聪坡坡》《彝族民间故事》《南方民间创世神话选集》《十二奴局》《召树屯》《娥并与桑洛》《金笛》《梅葛》。其中，好几本是云南少数民族的。只有一本是汉族典籍，即《黑暗传》。很有意思的是，这些典籍展示了不同民族的创世史诗或诸如此类的东西。

《黑暗传》以民间歌谣唱本形象地描述了盘古开天辟地结束混沌黑暗，人类起源及社会发展的历程，融合了盘古、女娲、伏羲、炎帝神农氏、黄帝轩辕氏等众多英雄人物在洪荒时代艰难创世的一系列神话传说。它被称为汉族首部创世史诗。《哈尼阿培聪坡坡》是一部完整地记载哈尼族历史沿革的长篇史诗，堪称哈尼族的"史记"，长5000余行，以现实主义手法记叙了哈尼族祖先在各个历史时期的迁徙情况，并对其迁徙各地的原因、路线、途程，各个迁居地的社会生活、生产、风习、宗教，以及与毗邻民族的关系等，均作了详细而生动的辑录，因而该作品不仅具有文学价值，而且具有重大的历史学、社会学及宗教学价值。《南方民间创世神话选集》包括一些创世神话，主要是关于世界起源和人类起源的神话。《十二奴局》是一部在哈尼族广泛流传的民间诗歌，它通过"哈尼"（传统歌）的形式在民间演唱，世代流传。"奴局"是哈尼语，相当于汉族著述中的"篇""章"或汉族曲艺中的曲目。"十二奴局"即十二路歌的意思。译著表现了远古哈尼先民奇特的想象，涉及天体自然、人类发展、哈尼历史、历法计算、四时季令、农事活动等各个方面的知识，完整地反映了哈尼先民对天地形成、人类起源、民族迁徙的认识，具有创世神话与英雄史诗的合集之性质，可以说是哈尼族最为重要的文学经典之一。《梅葛》是彝族的一部长篇史诗，流传在云南省楚雄州的姚安、大姚等彝族地区。"梅葛"本为一种彝族歌调的名称，由于人们采用这种调子来唱彝族的创世史，因而创世史诗被称为"梅葛"。

其余几本书展示了一些少数民族的风俗习惯、恋爱故事、斗争故事等。《哭嫁歌》是土家族文化典籍。"哭嫁"是土家族姑娘在出嫁时进行的一种用歌声来诉说自己在封建买办婚姻制度下不幸命运的活动，指土家族姑娘的抒情歌谣，富有诗韵和乐感，融哀、怨、喜和乐为一体，以婉转的曲调向世人展示土家人独特的"哭"文化。《彝族民间故事》是一部以流传于云南楚雄彝族自治州彝族人民中间的民间故事为主体，同时覆盖全省包括小凉山等彝族地区的民间故事集。这些故事丰富多彩，从中能看到民族民间故事的各种形态和生动、奇妙而颇具彝族民族特色的文化特征。《召树屯》是傣族民间长篇叙事诗，叙述了傣族佛教世俗典籍《贝叶经·召树屯》中一个古老的传说故事。这部叙事诗一直为傣族人民所传唱，历久不衰。《娥并与桑洛》是一部优美生动的叙事

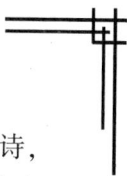

诗，一个凄美的爱情悲剧。《金笛》是一部苗族长篇叙事诗，富于变幻性和传奇性，尽情铺叙扎董丕冉与蒙诗彩奏的悲欢离合，热情赞颂他们在与魔虎的激烈斗争中所表现出来的坚贞不屈、英勇顽强的精神，许多情节含有浓郁的民族特色。

这些故事都很引人入胜，都很符合国家文化发展需求，向世人讲述中国故事，传播中华文化，并且讲述的是民族故事，充分体现了党和国家对各民族的关怀。

民族典籍英译是传播中国文化、文学和文明的重要途径，是中华文化"走出去"的重要组成部分，是国家战略，是提高文化"软实力"的重要方式，在文化交流和文明建设中起着不可或缺的作用，对提升中国国际话语权和构建中国对外话语体系以及对建设世界文学都有积极意义。

中国民族典籍使世界文化更加丰富多彩、绚丽多姿。我国各民族典籍中折射出的文化多样性极大地丰富了世界多元、特色鲜明的文化。人们对多样性形成全新的认识角度和思维方式，有助于开阔视野，丰富思考问题的角度，挖掘这些经典中的教育价值和文化价值，对世界其他民族都有指导和借鉴意义，并且有助于建设我国的文化自信。

民族典籍翻译与研究事业关乎国家的稳定统一，关乎民族关系的和谐发展，关乎世界多元文化的实现。在中国，民族典籍资源极为丰富，有待进一步挖掘、翻译，仍有许多少数民族典籍亟待拯救，民族典籍翻译与研究工作任重而道远，民族典籍翻译事业大有可为。

李正栓①

2019 年 7 月 19 日

---

① 李正栓，中国英汉语比较研究会典籍英译专业委员会常务副会长兼秘书长；中国中医药研究促进会传统文化翻译与国际传播专业委员会常务主任委员。

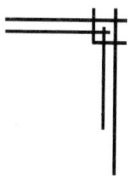

# 前　　言

创世神话是人类思维发展到较高程度，社会发展到较高阶段形成的对于文明发展具有承前启后意义的关于文明创造的神圣叙事。创世神话体现了一个民族文化的统一性、社会的整合性、思维的系统性、伦理的规范性。创世神话具有文明奠基的意义，是民族自我认同核心的文化符号。同时，创世神话具有文明传播力量，是各种文化交流、文化竞争的核心场域。

我国南方民间文化资源极为丰富。各民族都有独特的创世神话，传承了民族的历史文化观念、传统习俗、生产生活经验等，具有普及性和神圣性。这些民间创世神话是人类不可再生的非物质文化遗产，也是后世文化创造的丰富原型和具有明显文化记忆和记忆再现功能的活态宝藏。

南方民间创世神话在当代仍然具有生命力和重要价值。门巴族和珞巴族的神话都讲述了猴子变人的故事；怒族和傈僳族都有射太阳和月亮的故事；基诺族、拉祜族、傈僳族、德昂族、景颇族等都有开天辟地、人类起源的神话；诺巴族、怒族、拉祜族、傈僳族、德昂族、景颇族等都有兄妹成婚的传说。这些神话与传说无一不向人们展示了各民族之间的相互交流和融合。佤族神话《七兄弟》中说，七兄弟的孩子分别是汉族、白族、彝族、傣族、爱伲族、拉祜族和佤族的祖先，这七个民族世世代代和睦相处，相亲相爱。其他民族的民间创世神话大多数表达了类似观念。独龙族神话《洪水滔天》中提到，兄妹俩的子女是汉族、怒族、独龙族和其他六个民族的祖先；侗族神话《兄妹成亲》中讲到汉族、侗族、苗族、瑶族在很久以前都是一家人，同是一个老祖母。这类神话对于多元一体的中华民族文化的认同建构，对树立中华民族"五十六个民族五十六朵花，五十六个兄弟姐妹是一家"的民族观，对增进中华民族向心力、凝聚力，对建构人类命运共同体等具有积极的影响。

因此，《南方民间创世神话选集》的出版，既是讲好中国故事的需要，也是与世界分享这份珍贵遗产，让民族的文化成为世界共享的文化。

本书分上下两册，中英文对照，主要对南方的门巴族、珞巴族、怒族、基诺族、普米族、拉祜族、傈僳族、毛南族、德昂族、景颇族、阿昌族、布朗族、佤族、独龙族、水族、仡佬族、侗族、布衣族、仫佬族、高山族等民族的民间创世神话经典进行翻译。本书的中文原文来源于中国国际广播出版社赵晶选编的《南方少数民族创世神话选集》。英译本在对汉语原文进行细微改变之后，尽量将原文中的意思忠实地表达出来。在中南民族大学外语学院张立玉教授的大力支持和帮助下，本书终于得以完成。但由于译者水平有限，书中肯定存在诸多疏漏之处，敬请广大读者朋友批评指正。

2021 年 4 月

目

录
**Contents**

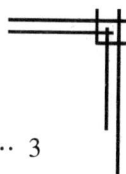

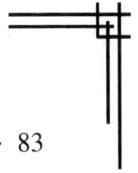

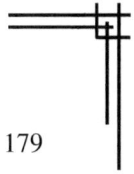

# 第一章　门巴族

## 猴子变人（一）

　　很久以前，地上没有人，但已有了猴子。有一次，姑鲁仁布切神①在嘎格多节胆这个地方召集猴子讲经，想把它们变成人。在讲经前，姑鲁仁布切对猴子说："你们应邀前来听经，听时务必紧闭双眼，不许睁开眼看我。"猴子听后，个个都很听话，立即闭上眼。姑鲁仁布切接着说："现在地上没有人，今天要把你们变成人。"正当姑鲁仁布切讲到这里时，一些猴子急切地想看一下自己怎么样变成人，高兴得忘记了神的叮嘱，把眼睛睁开了。神未制止这些猴子的举动，继续讲经。神愈往下讲，那些闭目听话的猴子眼睛愈是紧合，以致想睁开眼也睁不开了，只好静坐在原地。

----

　　①　姑鲁仁布切：门巴语，神名。

# Chapter One    Moinba Ethnic Group

## Monkeys Became Human Beings（1）

Long long ago, there was no human being but monkeys on the earth. Once in Gageduojiedan, the God Gulurenbuqie① summoned the monkeys, gave them a sermon, and tried changing them into human beings. Therefore, before giving the lecture, he said to the monkeys, "You are invited to listen to the sermon. Close your eyes and you are not allowed to open them when you are listening." Hearing the words, the monkeys were obedient and closed their eyes immediately. Then Gelurenbuqie said, "Now that there is no human being on the earth, today I am going to make you human beings." Just as he was speaking, some monkeys opened their eyes for they were so eager to see how they could become human beings that they forgot the God's words. The God did not stop them and continued his sermon. The more the God said, the closer the other monkeys' eyes became. At last, the other monkeys could not open their eyes no matter how hard they tried, and had to sit there still.

---

① Gulurenbuqie is a god of the Moinba ethnic group.

不久，姑鲁仁布切叫那些不听吩咐、睁开眼的猴子去拾柴草，采集树果、根块来。神把这些猴子采来的柴草烧着，投入树果、根块，烧熟后喂养那些未睁开眼的猴子。不经几天，这些猴子不但眼睛睁开，而且身上的毛也脱落了，从此变成了人。那些被派去拾柴，采集块根、果子的猴子，姑鲁仁布切没有给他们喂食，因而没有变成人，这些猴子就是现在猴子的祖先。

地上有了人后，人又受到专门吃人的九头怪鲜波的威胁，人类得不到繁衍。于是，姑鲁仁布切神就钻进九头怪的肚子里，把那些被九头怪吃掉的老年人、青壮年人、小孩分别集中起来，给他们讲经，保佑他们，然后把青壮年救了出来，并限制九头怪吃人的数量。人从此渐渐多了起来。

时间又过了很久很久。有一天，姑鲁仁布切又来到人间，他对人说："现在人多了，很好，但不组织起来，还不能抵抗九头怪的威胁。你们要想生存，繁衍后代，就要选出自己的首领，组织起来，这样你们才能过安宁的生活。"

Soon, Gulurenbuqie asked those disobedient monkeys who had opened their eyes before to pick up firewood and collect trees' fruits and root blocks. The God burned the firewood and put the trees' fruits and root blocks into it, and then fed the obedient monkeys with the burned food. After a few days, the obedient monkeys not only opened their eyes, but also lost their hairs, and became human beings. Those who were sent to pick up the firewood and collect the roots and the fruits were not fed. Thus, they did not become human beings, who were the ancestors of the current monkeys.

Since the human beings lived on the earth, they were threatened by Xianbo, a human-eating monster with nine heads, and could not reproduce their offspring. The monster ate many old people, young men and children, so the God burrowed into the monster's stomach, called them together respectively to sermon and bless them. Later, the God saved the young men from its stomach, and limited the number of the people eaten by the monster. Gradually, there were more and more people on the earth.

Long time passed. One day, the God Gulurenbuqie came to the human world again. He said to the human beings, "It is good to have more and more people in the world, but you can't resist the threat of the monster if you are not well-organized. You should choose your own leader and organize your people if you want to survive and breed offspring. Only in this way can you live a peaceful life."

　　人们听从姑鲁仁布切的教导，选举首领，组织起来。

　　又过了很久很久。有一天，首领向姑鲁仁布切申诉说："我们有了首领，又组织起来，人比以前多了，可吃的东西太少了，人们生活困难，头领难当，怎么办？"

　　姑鲁仁布切听后说："我把猪给你放在山上，你们将它猎杀，食它的肉；我把牛给你们，你们可用它种田，收取粮食，它撒谎时，你们就把它杀了，吃它的肉；我把鸡给你们，这些鸡偷吃神的药酒了，人病了，身体虚弱，就用它祭鬼后吃掉，补养身体；你们爱吃野兽肉，我把狗给你们，它帮助你们猎获野兽；我把鱼放在水中，你们就用投毒、鱼钩、鱼叉、弓箭和网捕捉它们……"

　　姑鲁仁布切为庇护人类的安全，经常隐藏在九头怪的肚子里。有一次，姑鲁仁布切对住在"门奔当"①的门巴人说："你们从北方来到这里住。你们希望我经常保护，就要天天早起来，对太阳念'白什姑鲁'真言，晚上睡觉前也要念。这样做了，就会平安，死后灵魂进入天堂。"

----

　　①　门奔当：远古时期门巴族的居住地。

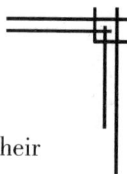

Following the God's words, the human beings chose their leader and began to organize themselves.

Long time passed. One day, the leader appealed to the God, "Now we have a leader, we are well-organized, and we have more people than before, but we haven't enough food to eat and we are in poor living conditions now. It's really difficult to be the head, and what can I do?"

Hearing this, the God answered, "I'll make the pigs live on the hill, and you can kill them and eat the meat. I'll give you the cows, and you can raise them to plough the farmland and harvest the crops. If they lie, kill them and eat them. I'll give you the chickens which were punished for drinking God's Medicinal liquor. When you are sick and frail, the chickens can be eaten to nourish your bodies after they are sacrificed to the ghosts. Since you love eating the meat of wild animals, I'll give you the dogs, which can help you hunt the wild animals. I'll put the fish in the water, and you catch them with poisons, fish hooks, harpoons, bows and arrows and nets..."

The God often hid in the stomach of the nine-head monster in order to protect the human beings. On one occasion, the God said to the Moinba people who lived in the "Menbendang"①, "Since you came from the north and lived here, you should get up early every day, say the mantra of 'BaiShiGuLu' to the sun in the morning, and repeat it before going to bed at night if you want me to protect you regularly. Only when it is done will you be safe and will your souls enter the heaven after death."

①　Menbendang is a place where the Moinba people lived in ancient time.

从此以后，门巴人就有了早晚念经的习俗。

流传地区：西藏自治区墨脱县
讲述者：嘎玛旺秋贡嘎
整理者：刘芳贤
翻译者：张永红

# 猴子变人（二）

远古时，在茫茫的大地上没有一个人，在冥冥的天空中也没有太阳和月亮，一片混混沌沌，分不出白天和黑夜。

在天的上方是天宫。天宫像飘动的白云悬浮在天空中。

有一天，天神从天宫中俯视下界，只见下界是一片滚沸的雾海，浩浩渺渺，把大地遮蔽得严严实实。

天神思忖，下界如此荒无人烟，空洞寂寞，应该去创造一个快乐世界才是。天神悲悯无限，决定派遣他的侍臣支乌①·江求深巴到下界去建立一个人的世界。

于是，支乌·江求深巴奉天神的旨意，离开了天宫，穿过滚沸的雾海，来到茫茫的大地上。

---

① 支乌：门巴语，猴子。

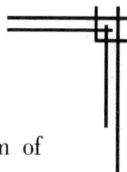

Since then, the Moinba people have formed the custom of reciting scriptures in the morning and in the evening.

Spreading area: Motuo County, Tibet

Narrator: Gamawantyu Gonga

Collector and editor: Liu Fangxian

Translator: Zhang Yonghong

## Monkeys Became Human Beings (2)

In ancient times, there was no human being on the vast land, nor were there sun and moon in the dark sky. The whole world was chaotic and there were no days and nights.

Above the heaven was the welkin, which suspended in the sky like floating white clouds.

One day, the God of Heaven looked down at the lower world from the welkin, seeing the vast land covered with a boiling sea of fog.

Then he thought that the lower world was so desolate and empty that it was quite necessary to create a happy one. With the compassion for the human beings, he decided to send his courtier Zhiwu① Jiangqiushenba to the lower world to build a world of human beings.

Following the words of the God of Heaven, Zhiwu Jiangqiushenba left the welkin, and crossed the boiling foggy sea to the vast land.

---

　① 　Zhiwu means monkey in Moinba dialect.

支乌·江求深巴离开天官不久，天神又派遣了他的另一个侍臣名叫扎深木的女神来到下界。扎深木本领高强，善于变化，能够变幻成各种动物模样。扎深木来到大地上，首先遇到了一只老虎，她就变成一只老虎，要和老虎结婚。可是，老虎不搭理她。扎深木又遇见一头狮子，她又变成一头狮子，要和狮子结婚。可是狮子也不搭理她。扎深木又遇见一只狗熊，她又变成了一只狗熊，又要和狗熊结婚。可是狗熊也不搭理她。最后，扎深木碰到了一群猴子，她就变成了一只猴子，混进了猴群。但是，扎深木变成的这只猴子，相貌丑陋极了，猴子们见了都十分厌恶，把她冷落在一边，离她远远的。扎深木开始还没有摸清是什么原因，没有觉察到自己的丑相，看到猴子都不理她，觉得很奇怪。

一天，扎深木来到河边玩耍。猛然间，她从平静如镜的河水中发现了自己的丑相，连她自己也感到十分恶心，这才恍然大悟。扎深木寻思了半晌，把身子一晃，又把自己变成了一只十分俊俏的猴子。她又去接近猴群，可是猴子们对她仍然冷淡。扎深木终于技穷，无可奈何，只得重返天宫。

不久，最初来到下界的江求深巴，也返回天宫去了。

天神召见了扎深木和江求深巴，对他们说：

"我还要派你们重返下界，不得再回到天宫来！你们在那里结为夫妻，生儿育女，在大地上创造一个人的世界吧！"

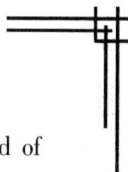

Just after Zhiwu Jiangqiushenba left the welkin, the God of Heaven sent another courtier, a goddess named Zhashenmu, to the lower world too. The goddess was powerful and good at transforming, and could change herself into all kinds of animals. When she came to the earth, she first became a tiger as she met it, and tried to marry it. But the tiger did not care. And then she became a lion when she met it, and tried to marry it. But the lion did not care, either. And next she became a black bear when she met it, and tried to marry it. But the bear did not care, either. Finally, she became a monkey when she met a group of monkeys, and pretended to be one of them. However, the monkey she turned into was so ugly that other monkeys didn't like her very much, staying far away from her and leaving her alone. Unaware of her ugliness, Zhashenmu felt confused and wondered why the monkeys took no notice of her.

One day, Zhashenmu went to the river bank. Suddenly, she saw her face in the river which was as smooth as a mirror. She herself felt sick and suddenly realized something. Thinking it over for a long time, she shook her body and turned herself into a very handsome monkey. Then she tried to approach the monkeys again, but the monkeys remained aloof from her. At last, she had to go back to the welkin.

Before long, Zhiwu Jiangqiushenba, who went to the lower world earlier than Zhashenmu, returned to the welkin too.

The God of Heaven summoned them and said to them,

"I will send you back to the lower world, and you are not allowed to go back again! You two must get married there and give birth to enough children to create a human world on the earth!"

扎深木和支乌·江求深巴遵从天神的旨意，又重返下界，立即结成了夫妻。不久，他们生了许多孩子，有男的也有女的，虽然浑身长毛，还长着尾巴，却能够用两条腿走路。可是，他们的孩子们，仍都是猴子模样，森林里的动物们都不愿同他们的子女成婚，扎深木和江求深巴只好让他们互相婚配。他们生下的孩子还是猴子模样，仍然不会狩猎，也不会种地，只会两条腿走路，攀岩爬树觅食。人的世界还是没有创造出来，扎深木和江求深巴不知怎样是好，迫不得已，再一次返回天宫去询问天神，请求天神指示。这次，天神赐给了他们一些鸡爪谷、青稞、玉米等粮食种子。天神对他们说：

"你们把这些种子撒在大地上，你们就会得到你们需要的东西。"

天神还教给他们制作工具、播种和耕地的方法。

扎深木和江求深巴又回到了大地上。他们按照天神的话，教给孩子们学会了种庄稼，从此，大地上有了各种粮食。他们还学会了造石斧，造出了世间第一把石斧。用石斧猎获了野猪、狗熊、獐子、岩羊等许多动物。

有一天，扎深木忽然发出了人语，说出了世间第一句话。猴子们感到十分惊奇，他们都向扎深木学习讲话。会讲话的猴子愈来愈多，愈来愈聪明了，长相也愈来愈好看。但是，他们还不会用火，仍然吃生冷的食物。

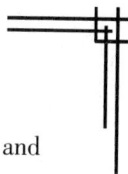

Following the words of the God of Heaven, Zhashenmu and Zhiwu Jiangqiushenba returned to the lower world again, and immediately became husband and wife. Soon, they gave birth to many children, including baby boys and baby girls. They were able to walk on two legs though they had long hairs and tails. The children, however, still looked like monkeys, and the animals in the forest were reluctant to marry their children. Zhashenmu and Zhiwu Jiangqiushenba had to let them marry each other, only to find their grand-children still looking like monkeys. They didn't know how to hunt or farm, but they could walk and climb rocks and trees for food. However, the world of human beings was still not created. Zhashenmu and Zhiwu Jiangqiushenba didn't know how to do and had to go back to the welkin and asked the God of Heaven for help. This time, the God gave them some seeds such as finger millet, highland barley and corn, and then said,

"Sow the seeds in the land and you will get what you need."

The God also taught them how to make tools, how to sow seeds and how to plough.

Zhashenmu and Zhiwu Jiangqiushenba went back home, and followed the God's words to teach their children how to do farm work. From then on, various kinds of food grew on the earth. They also learned to build stone axes and created the first stone axes in the world, with which they hunted for many wild animals, such as boars, bears, river deer, blue sheep, and so on.

One day, Zhashenmu suddenly uttered some human words, the first sentence in the world. The monkeys were very surprised, and they all learned from Zhashenmu how to speak. Then more and more monkeys could speak and became smarter and smarter. They became more and more beautiful, but they still could not use fire and just ate raw and cold food.

扎深木和江求深巴商量，决定去请求天神的帮助。他们再次来到天宫，对天神说：

"我们现在已经学会猎野兽、种庄稼、讲人话，就是我们身上的毛还是老长老长的，还长着一条长长的尾巴，这可怎么办？"

天神听着，没有说什么，只是赏赐给他们一把火种，让他们带着火种立即回到下界去。扎深木和江求深巴举着从天神那里求得的火种，回到了下界。有了火，他们学会了吃熟食。渐渐地，喜爱熟食的猴子们脱掉了身上的长毛，尾巴也都缩回去了，变成了人。

人间世界终于建立起来了。

流传地区：西藏自治区墨脱县
讲述者：伊西平措（门巴族，62岁）
搜集地点：西藏自治区墨脱县东布村
搜集时间：1986年8月
整理者：于乃昌，张力凤，陈理明

# 三兄弟和扎深木

从前，雅鲁藏布江由西向东缓缓地流淌着，像一条白练子似的。江水流到了南迦巴瓦峰脚下，就被挡住了去路，江水漫了出来，淹没了周围的大地，最后，整个世界都被淹没了，只剩下南迦巴瓦峰高高地矗立在中央。

Discussing with each other, Zhashenmu and Zhiwu Jiangqiushenba decided to ask the God of Heaven for help. They went to the welkin again, and asked the God of Heaven,

"What can we do with the long hairs and long tails now that we have learned to hunt wild animals, grow crops, and speak in human beings language?"

Hearing this, the God of Heaven said nothing but give them a spark of fire to take back home immediately. Zhashenmu and Zhiwu Jiangqiushenba went back home with the spark of fire, with which they learned to cook food. Gradually, the monkeys who loved the cooked food lost their long hairs and tails, and became the human beings.

The world of human beings finally came into being.

Spreading area: Motuo County, Tibet
Narrator: Yixipingcuo (The Moinba Ethnic Group, 62 years old)
Collecting site: Dongbu Village, Motuo County, Tibet
Collecting time: August 1986
Collector: Yu Naichang, Zhang Lifeng, Chen Liming

## Three Brothers and Zhashenmu

Once upon a time, the Yarlung Zangbo River, like a white ribbon, flowed slowly from west to east. At the foot of the Namjag Barwa Mountain, the river was blocked, which overflowed and flooded the surrounding area. Finally, the whole world was in the water, leaving the peak of the Namjag Barwa Mountain standing in the center of the world.

那时，工布地方有三个同胞兄弟，养着三头公牦牛。当大水漫到工布地方时，三兄弟急中生智，把三头公牦牛杀死，剥下牛皮做了一条小船。牛皮船就是这样来的。三兄弟乘着牛皮船，漂浮在水上。可是，船太小，水又太大，眼看牛皮船就要被水淹没了。大哥和二哥为了保住小弟弟，先后跳进大水中。大哥、二哥被淹死了，只剩下小弟弟一个人留在牛皮船上，船漂呀浮呀，一直漂到南迦巴瓦峰脚下。

小弟弟爬出牛皮船，攀到南迦巴瓦峰上。在峰顶上，他闻到了一股香火味。他四处寻找，发现香火味是从地底下冒出来的。小弟弟就挖呀挖呀，挖着挖着，突然看到一个山洞，一个仙人正在洞里闭目修行。

仙人问道：“你是什么人，到这里来干什么？”

小弟弟说：“大水淹没了一切，世界上没有一个人了。我坐着两个哥哥为我做的牛皮船漂到了这里，闻到了一股香火味，才找到了您。”

仙人说：“那么好吧，你就和我住在一起吧。”第二天一大早，仙人对小弟弟说：“你到山下去等着，水面上会出现一个怪物，你一定要抓住它。”

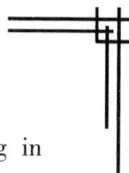

At that time, there were three sibling brothers living in Gongbu, who raised three male yaks. When the flood reached Gongbu, the three brothers responded quickly and killed the three male yaks to make a small boat with the yak skin, which became the first yak-skin boat in the world. The three brothers were floating on the water in the yak-skin boat, but the boat was too small and it was almost overthrown by the flood. In order to save the little brother, the two elder brothers jumped into the water and were drowned, leaving the little brother alone in the yak-skin boat, which floated slowly to the foot of the Namjag Barwa Mountain.

The little brother got out of the boat and climbed to the peak of the Namjag Barwa Mountain. On top of it, following a smell of burning joss sticks, he looked around and found that the smell was coming out of the underground. The little brother dug for some time, and suddenly saw a cave, in which a celestial being was practicing with his eyes closed.

The celestial being asked, "Who are you? And what are you going to do here?"

The little brother answered, "The flood had drowned everything, and nothing left. I drifted here in a yak-skin boat made by my two brothers, followed the smell of the burning joss sticks and finally found you here."

The celestial being then said, "Well, just stay here and live with me." Early on the next morning, the celestial being told the little brother, "Go down the mountain and wait until a monster appears on the surface of the flood. You must catch it when you see it."

　　小弟弟来到山下水边，等了一会儿，看到从远处的山峰上飘过来一头很大的狮子，白色的鬃毛顶到天上，牙齿插到水中，把整个水面都盖住了。小弟弟一见，吓坏了。他没敢抓。

　　小弟弟回到洞中见仙人。

　　仙人说："你没有抓住怪物，明天再去。"

　　第二天，小弟弟又来到山下。一会儿，只见一只老虎从远处天边飞来，牙齿顶着天，鬃毛长得把整个水面都盖住了。看着那吓人的样子，小弟弟又没敢抓。

　　小弟弟又回到洞中见仙人。

　　仙人看到小弟弟又没有抓住怪物，说："明天还有最后一个，你如果抓不住，就是个没有用的人，不要再回到我这里来了。"

　　第二天，小弟弟第三次来到山下，不一会儿，看见有一条很大的蛇，从水里钻了出来，盖住了整个水面。小弟弟想，不管是死是活，舍命也得抓住它，就朝着大蛇扑了过去，蛇一下子就不见了。小弟弟一回到仙人那里，仙人就对他说："从明天开始，你可以到石洞中修行了。"

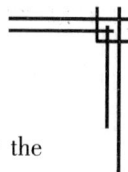

The little brother went down the mountain, waiting by the flood. A moment later, a huge lion was coming from the peak of the mountain in the distance, with its white mane up against the sky and its teeth inserting into the water, covering the whole surface of the water. The little brother was shocked and dared not catch it.

The little brother went back to the cave to see the celestial being.

The celestial being said, "You haven't caught the monster, and go to catch it tomorrow."

On the second day, the little brother came down the mountain again. A moment later, a big tiger was flying to him from the sky, with its teeth sticking to the sky and long mane covering the surface of the water. Seeing the horrible tiger, the little brother dare not catch it again.

The little brother went back to the cave to see the celestial being.

The celestial being saw him, and said, "The last monster will come tomorrow. Don't come back to see me if you can't catch it, for you are a nit."

The next day, the little brother came down the mountain again. A moment later, he saw a big snake drill out of the water and cover the whole surface of the water. The little brother thought that he had to try his best to seize it at the risk of losing his life. All at once he rushed towards the snake, and it disappeared completely.

小弟弟在洞中修行。

不知过了多少年，大水消下去了，重新露出了大地。雅鲁藏布江从南迦巴瓦峰脚下流向南方。

一天，扎深姆（罗刹女）拖着长长的头发来到正在修行的小弟弟面前，对他说："咱俩结婚吧。"

小弟弟说："没有仙人的恩准，我不能和你结婚。"

扎深姆说："你不和我结婚，我就去找参波玉①，它有九弟兄，我去做它们的老婆，让整个世界变成地狱。"

小弟弟还是不敢答应。

扎深姆让小弟弟去问仙人。

小弟弟见到仙人，说："扎深姆让我和它结婚，我没有同意，因为它是鬼，再说也没有征得你的恩准。"

仙人说："它不和你结婚就要去找参波玉，整个世界就会变成地狱。你还是和它结婚吧。"

---

① 参波玉：门巴语，阎王。

As soon as the little brother came back to see the celestial being, he said to him, "From tomorrow on, you can come here to practice."

The little brother began to practice in the cave the next day.

Many years past, the flood subsided and the earth emerged again. The Yarlung Zangbo River flowed to the south along the foot of the Namjag Barwa Mountain.

One day, Zhashenmu, with her long hair on the ground, walked to the little brother who was practicing, and said to him, "Let's get married."

"I can't marry you without the permission of the celestial being." The little brother said.

Zhashenmu threatened him, "I will go to see Canboyv (Yama)①, who has got nine brothers, and marry him if you don't, and then I'll make the whole world a hell."

Still, the little brother daren't agree with her.

Zhashenmu asked the little brother to get the permission of the celestial being.

The little brother went to see the celestial being, and said, "Zhashenmu threatened me to marry her, and I haven't agreed, for she is a ghost. What's more, I haven't got your permission."

The celestial being answered, "You'd better marry her, for the whole world would become a hell if you refuse her and she would marry Yama."

---

① Canboyv: the name of the king of Hell in the Moinba dialect.

小弟弟回去和扎深姆结了婚，扎深姆生下了许多孩子。

这些小孩子浑身都长着毛，没有饭吃，没有衣服穿。小弟弟又去找仙人。

仙人送给了小弟弟一把小刀，让他挖出窝麻的嫩叶煮水给孩子们洗澡，又给了他许多荞麦种子。

从此，西藏有了荞麦。

小弟弟听从仙人的指示，用窝麻的叶子水给孩子们洗澡，洗去了孩子们身上的毛。因为孩子们怕热水烫，都把头伸进洞里，身子露在外面，所以留下了头发。又因为孩子们都夹紧了双臂，所以留下了腋毛。从那以后，世上有了人，并且成了今天这个模样。

流传地区：西藏自治区墨脱县

讲述者：拉巴次仁（门巴族，70岁）

搜集地点：西藏自治区墨脱县墨脱区墨脱村

搜集时间：1986年8月

整理者：于乃昌，张力凤，陈理明

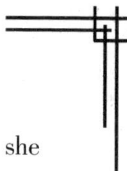

Then the little brother married Zhashenmu, and later she gave birth to many children.

The hairy children had not enough food or clothes, so the little brother again went to ask the celestial being for help.

The celestial being gave him a knife, with which he could get the leaves of the Woma and boiled them to water the children. The celestial being also gave him lots of buckwheat seeds. From then on, there was buckwheat in Tibet.

The little brother followed the celestial being's words, bathed the children with the water of the boiling leaves and washed away the hairs of the children, leaving the hair on the heads, which were put into the cave because they were afraid of being scalded by the hot water. The armpit hair was also left because they clamped their arms tightly when washed with the hot water. Since then, there were human beings in the world and become what they look like today.

Spreading area: Motuo County, Tibet

Narrator: Laba Ciren (The Moinba Ethnic Group, 70 years old)

Collecting site: Motuo Village, Motuo District, Motuo County, Tibet

Collecting time: August 1986

Collector: Yu Naichang, Zhang Lifeng, Chen Liming

# 第二章　珞巴族

## 天和地

很早以前，世上只有天和地，天是空空的，地是秃秃的，除了他们外，其他什么东西也没有。天和地商量："我们一个子孙也没有，那怎么成呢？我们结婚吧！"天不断地求情，地终于答应了，于是天就降到地上，与地紧密地贴在一起。

天地结婚后，生了许多孩子，如太阳、月亮、星星，各种动物、植物和珞巴族的祖先阿巴达尼，还有各种乌佑①。

孩子们渐渐长大了，但天和地总是挨得这么近，使他们无法生活。于是大家推选金足地育②跟天父、地母说情，请他们离开一些。天父终于同意他们的要求，离开了地母。

---

① 乌佑：珞巴语音译。泛指他们所崇拜的各种精灵。
② 金足地育：系一种蝴蝶蛹，传说中的精灵。

# Chapter Two　Lhoba Ethnic Group

## The Heaven and the Earth

Long time ago, there were only the Heaven and the Earth in the world, with the Heaven empty and the Earth bald, and except for that, nothing was there. The Heaven asked the Earth, "How can it be that we have no offspring? Let's get married!" The Heaven kept asking for love, and the Earth finally consented, so the Heaven dropped to the ground and was closely linked with the Earth.

After the marriage, the Heaven and the Earth gave birth to many children, such as the sun, the moon, the stars, different animals, plants, the ancestor Apadani of the Lhoba Ethnic Group, and all kinds of Wuyou①.

Gradually, the children grew up. The Heaven and the Earth got so close that the children could not bear it. Therefore, they chose Jinzudiyu② to persuade their father and mother to separate from each other. Finally, the Heaven agreed and left the Earth.

---

①　Wuyou refers various of angels worshipped by the Lhoba people.

②　Jinzudiyu is a chrysalis of butterfly, which is said to be an angel in the Lhoba ethnic group.

就在这个时候，地上刮来一股强风，把天吹得慢慢向上飘，天就带着分给他的孩子太阳、月亮、星星、云、雷和电等一起走了。山原来是不高的，他分给了地母。但当他见到天父离开时，急急追上去，想同天父一起走，但走了几步，又舍不得地母，追到半空后就不走了，因而成了现在这个样子。

天父离开地母时，十分伤心，眼泪扑簌扑簌地掉下来。他流的眼泪，就是雨。

流传地区：西藏自治区米林县马尼岗一带
讲述者：亚如亚崩
搜集地点：穷林村博嘎尔部落
口译者：高前
整理者：李坚尚，裘富珍


# 尼多和石奇①

尼多住在天上，石奇住在地下。有一天，他们发生争吵。尼多就统领太阳、月亮和众多的星星下来，威胁石奇。石奇见了，也不屈服，带领水下、地上的禽兽鱼儿与他们对抗。尼多见到石奇有那么多的军队，大声吼道："你兵力很强，我的也不弱，我们就拼个你死我活，血战一场吧！"

---

① 尼多、石奇：德根部落方言，指天和地。

Just as they took apart, a strong wind from the ground blew the Heaven up to the sky slowly, along with his children, the sun, the moon, the stars, the clouds, the thunder and the lightning. The mountain, which was given to the Earth, was not very high at that time, and he tried to go up with his father when he saw his father's departure, but at the sametime, he was not willing to leave his mother, and then he stopped half in the air, which made the mountain look like it now.

The Heaven was very sad as he left the Earth, and the tears he shed dropped to the ground and became the rain.

Spreading area: Manigang, Milin County, Tibet
Narrator: Yaru Yabeng
Collecting Site: Qionglin Village, Bokar Tribe
Interpreter: Gao Qian
Collector: Li Jianshang, Qiu Fuzhen

# Niduo and Shiqi[①]

Niduo lived in the heaven, while Shiqi lived on the earth. One day, they had a quarrel. Niduo took the sun, the moon and many stars to threaten Shiqi, who did not yield but took the birds and beasts on the ground and the fish in the water to fight against them. Seeing Shiqi's troop, Niduo shouted, "You are strong, and I am not weak. Let's fight to the death!"

---

① Niduo and Shiqi refer to the heaven and the earth respectively in the Lhoba dialect.

尼多说完这话后，就向石奇冲去。在他接近地面时，叫嚷要把地上所有的生灵压死。地上和水里的生灵求饶，尼多不听，继续叫嚷道："我要压下来了！我要压下来了！"一连几天都是这样。陆上、水里的生灵只好召开会议，商量对策。

正在这时，一只名叫始钦加英的小鸟飞来，询问他们的会议能想出什么对策。一个大块头的动物骄傲地说："我们正在讨论，你这个小家伙在这里多嘴多舌干什么？"

小鸟听了，生气地飞走了。

在这次会议上，大家各持己见，没有找到一致的办法，于是决定请始钦加英鸟回来，听取他的意见。

当始钦加英鸟回来后，大家都向他征求意见。小鸟回答说：

"我们要设法活下去，可你们为什么白白等死呢？"

始钦加英鸟的话，使他们清醒过来，于是决定要尼多和石奇各拿出一头大额牛，宴请大家。并且，尼多和石奇要各自待在自己的家里十天，如果谁待不住，提前跑出来，谁就变成丑八怪。尼多和石奇服从他们的调解，各自交出大额牛，宴请他们，然后回到自己的家里。

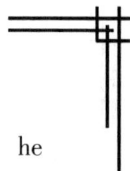

Niduo dashed towards Shiqi immediately. When he approached the ground, he shouted that he would crush all the creatures on the earth. The creatures on the ground and in the water asked for mercy, but Niduo didn't listen. He continued shouting, "I'll crush you! I'll crush you!" He shouted for a few days. All the creatures on the ground and in the water had to hold meetings to discuss how to fight back.

Just then, a little bird named Shiqingjiaying flew over and asked what proposals they could come up with. A big animal said proudly, "You little talkative bird, what are you doing here while we are discussing a problem?"

The little bird heard it and flew away angrily.

Every one held his own view at the meeting, but no solution could be found. So the little bird was invited to come back and give his advice.

When the little bird came back, everyone asked him for advice. The bird replied,

"Why do you just wait for death when we must try to survive?"

The bird's words woke the creatures up, and they decided to ask Niduo and Shiqi to feast them with a gayal respectively. Then, Niduo and Shiqi were asked to stay at their home for ten days, and the one who went out earlier would become an ugly weird. Niduo and Shiqi agreed, and each feasted the creatures with a gayal, and then went back home.

三天之后，石奇在家里待不住，走出了自己的屋子。他输了，身体随即长出大小众山，变得十分丑陋。即使现在，石奇的躯体也会不断地崩塌、震动。可尼多十天全待在家里，所以他还像过去那样漂亮。

流传地区：西藏自治区下洛渝地区
搜集地点：德根部落巴比村
搜集者：B·K·舒克拉

# 波宁和达宁

混沌初开时，世上一片汪洋，见不到别的东西。那时候，在水里生活着两兄弟，哥哥叫波宁，弟弟叫达宁，可彼此从没见过面。达宁生得像头大额牛，波宁却似一只大象。他们各自都认为自已是世界上唯一的生物，却不知道还有另一个兄弟。

波宁和达宁在水下各自潜行了很多很多年以后，有一天，他们终于相遇了。哥哥波宁见到对方，十分惊异地说："你叫什么名字？从哪里来的？"

弟弟达宁听了，也粗声粗气地问："你叫什么名字？从哪里来的？"

在世界上虽然只有他们两兄弟，但他们一见面就合不来，各自指控对方侵占自己的地盘，接着就互相动手，斯打起来，最后两人都受重伤死了。

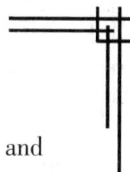

Three days later, Shiqi couldn't stay at home any longer and walked out. He lost the game, and hills of different sizes emerged from his body, which made him very ugly. Even nowadays, Shiqi's body is constantly collapsing and shaking. Niduo stayed at home for 10 days, so he was as beautiful as he used to be.

Spreading area: Lower Luoyu, Tibet
Collection site: Barbie Village, Degen Tribe
Collector: B. K. Schakla

# Boning and Daning

It was a vast expanse of water at the beginning of the chaotic world, and nothing could be seen on the earth. Two brothers, the elder Boning and the younger Daning, lived in the same water, but they had never met before. Daning looked like a gayal while Boning looked like an elephant. Either of them thought that he was the only creature in the world, and did not know the existence of the other.

Boning and Daning had been living in water for many years, and one day they finally met. When he saw Daning, Boning said with amazement, "What's your name? And where are you from?"

His brother, Daning, also asked gruffly, "What's your name? And where are you from?"

They two could not get along well with each other when they first met though they were siblings in the world. They accused each other of invading the other's territory, so they fought, and at last, both died of serious injuries.

他们死后，达宁的肉变成了大地，骨头变成了树木，头发变成了草；波宁的骨头变成了岩石，肉变成了山。宇宙就这样形成了。接着大地生下石迪麦洛，他自个儿又重整河山，改造世界，把一些地方夷为平地，把另一些地方堆成高山，接着又在山和平地之间开出了小河。人的世界就这样造成了。

流传地区：西藏自治区下洛渝地区
搜集地点：博日部落嘎升村
搜集者：维·埃尔温

# 肯　库

混沌初开时，有个叫作肯库的怪物，她到底长什么样，人们也说不清楚。

有一天，她生下一个像泥球那样的乌佑，这个乌佑随即对肯库说："我叫禅图!"

肯库对她说："你是我生下来的，你会生谁?"

禅图说："我会生阿巴达尼①!"

阿巴达尼生下后，禅图对他说："我很快就要死了，你一定要生出人来啊!"

---

①　阿巴达尼：传说为珞巴族的始祖。阿巴，珞巴语是父亲、祖先的意思。

After their death, Daning's flesh became the earth, bones became trees, and hairs became grass, while Boning's bones became rocks, and his flesh became hills, which was the beginning of the universe. Then the Earth shaped the rivers and mountains and changed the whole world, flattening some places to the ground and heaping others into high mountains, with rivers flowing out of the land between the ground and the mountains. Therefore, the human world was created.

Spreading area: Lower Luoyu, Tibet

Collection site: Gasheng Village, Bori Tribe

Collector: Victoria Erwin

# Kenku

At the beginning of the chaotic world, there was a monster named Kenku, but nobody knew what she looked like?

One day, she bore a Wuyou, who looked like a mud ball. Immediately, the Wuyou said to Kenku, "My name is Chantu."

Kenku asked her, "I gave birth to you, and who will you give birth to?"

Chantu answered, "I'm going to bear Apadani①!"

After Apadani was born, Chantu told him, "I will die soon, and you must give birth to a human being!"

---

① Apadani is said to be the ancestor of the Lhoba ethnic group. Apa means father or ancestor in the Lhoba dialect.

阿巴达尼说："我会生出人来。但你死了，到处都是黑洞洞的，人住在什么地方？到哪里去找粮食吃？到哪里去找水喝？"

禅图说："我死后，我的大腿会变成大地，你们可以搬到那里住，耕耘播种。我的眼睛将会变成太阳和月亮，把大地照亮。我的血会变成水，供人们饮用。"

禅图死后她的身体果然是这样变化的，变成了今天的天和地。

流传地区：西藏自治区下洛渝地区
搜集地点：阿帕塔尼部落日如村
搜集者：B·K·舒克拉

# 德日雅木拉

世上的万物据说都是水变的，水能使人的眼睛看见东西。很古很古以前，在水里生长出一棵名叫德日雅木拉的树。过了许多许多年后，树上又长出了一条软乎乎的虫子，这条虫子天天不停地咬树，虫子咬下的树木粉末掉到水里，天长日久逐渐变成了大地。

Apadani said, "I will. But once you die, the world will become dark, and where can the human being live? Where can he find food and water?"

Chantu said, "After I die, my thighs will become the earth, where you can move to live, cultivate and sow; My eyes will become the sun and the moon, illuminating the earth; and my blood will become water for people to drink."

After Chantu's death, her words came true, and then the heaven and the earth came into being.

Spreading area: Lower Luoyu, Tibet

Collecting site: Riru Village, Apatani Tribe

Collector: B. K. Schakla

# De Zyamula

It is said that everything in the world is originated from water, which can make people's eyes see everything. In ancient times, there was a tree named De Zyamula growing in the water. Many years later, a soft worm growing on the tree kept biting it day after day, and the tree powder fell into the water, and gradually became a vast land.

后来，这棵古老的大树倒下了。它下边的树皮变成地面，上边的树皮变成天空，树干变成岩石，树枝变成高高低低的大小山峰。

流传地区：西藏自治区下洛渝西巴霞曲流域
搜集地点：山区米里部落洛木达克村
搜集者：维·埃尔温

# 人的诞生

最初，大地是干枯的，连一滴水也没有，是火的年代。

大地上的一切都被火烧焦了，唯有一根藤子还没有枯死，只剩下一对兄妹还活着。哥哥饿得躺在地上，再也不想起来了。他看到那根没有被烧焦的藤子上还挂着一个果子，就用箭把果子射了下来，妹妹吃了一半，自己吃了一半。

天神古如仁布钦看到人间成这个样子，很是痛心，就洒了一些圣水。

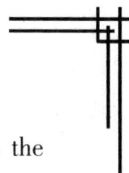

Later, the old tree fell down. The lower bark became the ground, the upper bark became the sky, the trunk became the rocks, and the branches became the peaks of different heights of mountains.

Spreading area: Lower Luoyu in the area of Xibaxiaqu, Tibet

Collecting site: the Luomudake Village, Mili tribe in the mountainous area

Collector: Victoria Erwin

# The Birth of the Human Being

At the beginning of the world, the earth was dry, and there was not even a drop of water. It was the age of fire.

Everything on the earth was scorched by fire, except for a vine and a brother and his sister. The brother was so hungry that he lay on the ground and didn't want to stand up. Seeing a fruit hung on the vine that had not been burnt, the brother shot the fruit down with an arrow, gave half of it to his sister and ate the other.

Looking at the miserable world, the God of Heaven, Gururenbuqin was very sad and sprinkled some holy water to it.

天神洒的水变成了大海，海的中间突出了一块大石头。大石头上长出了许多草，草越长越茂密，石头也越来越大，变成了陆地，并且有了山。从那以后，陆地上才有了庄稼，也有了牛羊。大海退到了陆地下面。

大海里有一头黑猪，叫"都怕那布①"。只要它一拱动，地面上就会出现地震和塌方。地震和塌方就是这样来的。

起初，陆地上没有人，天神很着急。天神想："我留在藤子上的神果被他们分食了，就让他们兄妹结合吧！"

没有多久，吃果子的兄妹成了夫妻，他们生了一个小人。这个小人站起来只有一尺高，坐下来只有拳头大。他的名字叫次列久巴②。

次列久巴一生下来就会生火、提水，还会使用石头去砍酥麻树。

天神古如仁布钦感到生下来的人太小了，他又洒下圣水，小人顿时长高了，像一棵大树。这样高的人，一次就要吃一屋子东西，力气也很大，一下子可以拔掉一棵树。

---

① 都怕那布：珞巴语，猪。珞巴人认为是家畜之首。
② 次列久巴：珞巴语中第一个人的名字。

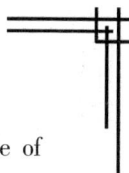

The water from the heaven became a sea, in the middle of which a big stone protruded. Grass grew from the stone, and the more grass grew, the bigger the stone became, and finally it changed into the land and hills. Since then, the crops grew on the ground, and the cattle and the sheep could also be seen everywhere. The sea then retreated from the land.

In the sea, there was a black pig named Dupanabu①. As long as it moved, the earth would quake and the land would slide, which was the beginning of the earthquakes and landslides.

In the beginning, the God was very anxious because there was no human being on the earth, and he thought, "Since the brother and sister had eaten the fruit I left on the vine, let them get married!"

Before long, the brother and sister who had eaten the fruit became husband and wife, and they gave birth to a small baby, who had only one foot height when standing and a fist in size when sitting, and he was named Ciliejiuba②.

Just as he was born, Ciliejiuba was able to light a fire, carry water, and cut the trees with a stone.

Thinking that Ciliejiuba was too small, the God of Heaven sprinkled the holy water on him and made him as tall as a big tree suddenly. Such a big person would eat a lot at a time and was strong enough to pull out a tree all of a sudden.

① Dupanabu: the name of a black pig, which was regarded as the head of the livestock in the Lhoba ethnic group.
② Ciliejiuba: the name of the first human being in the world of the Lhoba ethnic group.

天神古如仁布钦想，这样高的人，像一棵树，一次要吃那么多的东西，这怎么能行呢？他就又施展了法力。从那以后，世上的人才变成我们现在这个样子。

流传地区：西藏自治区墨脱县
讲述者：宾珠（珞巴族，70多岁）
搜集地点：西藏自治区墨脱县达木村
搜集时间：1986年9月
整理者：于乃昌，张力凤，陈理明

# 阿巴达尼和阿巴达洛

天和地结了婚以后，大地母生了很多孩子。天地间，太阳、月亮和星星、树木和花草、鸟兽和虫鱼，都是大地母生下的孩子，真是热闹极了。

后来，大地母又生了两个小儿子，哥哥叫阿巴达尼，弟弟叫阿巴达洛。

阿巴达尼聪明伶俐，喜欢在山林里活动，曾经和飞禽、走兽、昆虫结过婚，还娶过太阳的女儿冬尼海依做妻子。阿巴达尼的子孙就是现在的珞巴族。

阿巴达洛憨厚、耿直，知识渊博，生产技术高强，占据的地方广大。阿巴达洛的子孙就是现在的藏族。

讲述者：米林县纳玉乡达牛，东娘

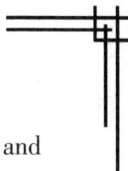

How could this be done? The God of Heaven thought and was very worried about the man, who was as tall as a big tree and with a big stomach. Thus he cast a magic spell and made the human in the world look like what we are now.

Spreading area: Motuo County, Tibet

Narrator: Bin Zhu (the Lhoba Ethnic Group, more than 70 years old)

Collecting site: Damu Village, Motuo County, Tibet

Collecting time: September 1986

Collector: Yu Naichang, Zhang Lifeng, Chen Liming

# Apadani and Apadaluo

After their marriage, the Heaven and the Earth gave birth to many children, the sun, the moon and the stars, trees and flowers, birds, beasts, insects, fish, so on and so forth, who made the world much lively.

Later, the Earth bore two little boys, the elder brother Apadani and the younger Apadaluo.

Apadani was very smart and fond of activities in the mountains. He had once married birds, beasts and insects, and even Dongnihaiyi, the daughter of the sun. Apadani's descendants are nowadays the Lhoba people.

Apadaluo was honest, upright, knowledgeable, productive and highly skilled. He was once the owner of a large landmass, and his descendants are nowadays the Tibetans.

Narrator: Daniu, Dongniang, Nayu Village, Milin County, Tibet

# 阿巴达尼的四个儿子

阿巴达尼有四个儿子：阿多东布、阿多嘎布、尼西和尼贡。

有一天，阿巴达尼把四个儿子叫到一起，对他们说："现在，你们也都大了，自己也该能够生活了。在大山的南面，有一块好地方，你们到那里去谋生吧。"

儿子们答应了。

不久，阿多东布和阿多嘎布兄弟俩告别他们的阿爸，出巴嘎山谷①，到了多嘎②。在多嘎住了一些日子，又来到了帕宗邦加。他们在帕宗邦加③立了一块大石头做标志，因为从那里开始就要远离他们的故乡了。这块大石头叫"公觉嘎马邦波"，直到现在还巍然屹立在那里呢。

---

① 巴嘎山谷：在现今米林县城以东，雅鲁藏布江南岸。

② 多嘎：在现今米林县城以东约两公里，濒临雅鲁藏布江南岸。

③ 帕宗邦加：在现今米林县城以西约四公里，纳玉沟北端，濒临雅鲁藏布江南岸。

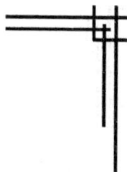

# Four Sons of Apadani

Apadani had four sons, Addo Dongbu, Addo Gabu, Nishi and Nigong.

One day, Apadani called his four sons together and said to them, "Now that you all are old enough to live by yourselves, go and find the good place at the south of the Himalayas, and make a living there."

The sons agreed.

Soon, Addo Dongbu and Addo Gabu said goodbye to Apadani, went out of the Baga Valley① and arrived at Duoga②. Having lived there for some time, they went on to Pazongbangjia③, where they set up a big stone as a mark, for from which they began to stay away their hometown. The big stone, which was called "Gongjuegamabangbo", stands there still until now.

---

① Baga Valley is located in the east of Milin County, the south bank of the Yarlung Zangbo River.

② Duoga is located about 2 miles to the east of Milin County.

③ Pazongbangjia is about 4 miles to the west of Milin County.

又过了一些时候，他们兄弟俩就从帕宗邦加地方出发，沿着纳玉沟①向南行走，穿密林，跨深涧，来到了粒山脚下。他们一直记着阿爸的话："在大山的南面，有一块好地方。"他们不肯停步，翻过了东拉山②，到了南山坡迭连班山腰平坝上。走得实在太累了，兄弟俩就坐在一块大石头上休息。肚子也实在太饿了，便从腰里掏出了从家乡带出来的糌粑。可是，平坝上一滴水也找不到，这可怎么办？聪明、机灵的嘎布就用自己的尿拌着糌粑吃。倔强、憨直的东布却不肯这样办，他坐在那里舔着干糌粑吃，一边吃还要一边说话，一下子被干糌粑噎住了，说不出话来，只是在那里"俄布俄布……"地叫。

休息完了，兄弟俩又继续往南走。他们终于到了阿爸说过的大山的南面。

兄弟俩不能总在一起呀，要划分一个地盘才是。他们俩商量着，来一场射箭比赛吧！谁的箭落到哪里，那里就是谁的属地。

---

① 纳玉沟：由米林通向洛渝的主要通道。
② 东拉山：在米林县南部，是米林县与洛渝地区的界山。

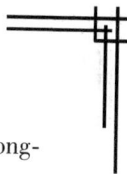

Later sometime, the two brothers set out from Pazong-bangjia, walked southwards along the Nayv Canal①, crossed the dense forest and the deep valley, and finally arrived at the foot of Li Mountain. They had kept their father's words in mind that there was a good place on the south of the mountain. They climbed over the Dongla Mountain②, and got to the dam by the side of the south slope of the Dielianban Mountain. The two brothers were so tired that they sat on a big stone to have a rest. Being very hungry, they took out the glutinous rice cake which they brought with them from the hometown. But how could they eat it without a drop of water? The clever Gabu took it with his own urine while the stubborn Dongbu refused to do so, and sat there licking the dry cake. The glutinous rice cake was too dry, and Dongbu got choked by it for he talked with Gabu while eating. He then could utter nothing but "Obu Obu".

After a while, the two brothers continued going southwards. They finally arrived at the south of the mountain which their father mentioned.

The two brothers tried to divide the territory of the land into two parts for they could not always stay together. They then decided to solve the problem with an archery competition, that is, the land where the arrow had landed would belong to the archer who shot it.

---

① the Nayv Canal is the key road from Milin County to Luoyu Region.

② Dongla Mountain is in the south of Milin County, which is the boundary mountain of Milin County and Luoyu Region.

　　射箭比赛开始了，阿多嘎布一箭射到了果洛松松，所以果洛松松①范围以内的东鸟、卡勒、达芒、协吉卡若、崩英、海奥、热玛、凌要等地，从此成了嘎布的领地。直到现在，生活在这里的人们都说自己是嘎布的子孙，称作博嘎尔人。阿多东布一箭射到了有蒂比东，所以，有蒂比东范围以内的邦斯冈底、凌布、雅布、百乐、达吉德古、斯贡克玛等地，从此成了东布的领地。直到现在，生活在这里的人们都说自己是东布的子孙，称作是凌布人、百乐人等。东布的子孙说话，前面都带有"俄布俄布"的声音。

　　阿巴达尼的另外两个儿子尼西和尼贡，听了阿爸的嘱咐以后，没有和东布、嘎布同行，他们分头谋生去了。

　　尼西出巴嘎山谷，沿着大江向南行，一直走到邦布②地方停脚了，从此在这里定居下来，这里就成了尼西的领地，他的后代就是汉宫人。

　　尼贡出巴嘎山谷，溯着大江向西行，越过三安曲林和色日洛亚两座大山，一直走到达根③地方停脚了，从此在这里定居下来，这里就成了尼贡的领地，他的后代就是达根人。

---

① 果洛松松：珞巴语地名，即现在的马尼岗。
② 邦布：珞巴语地名，在公墨脱县之南。
③ 达根：珞巴语地名，在现今西藏隆子县城境内。

The archery competition began. Addo Gabu shot an arrow and it landed in Guoluosongsong①, so Dongniao, Kale, Damang, Xieji Karuo, Bengying, Hai'ao, Rema, Lingyao and so on, which were included in Guoluosongsong, became Gabu's territory. Till now, the people living there say that they are the descendants of Gabu, and call themselves the Bogaer People. Addo Dongbu also shot an arrow and it landed in Youdibidong, so Bangsigangdi, Lingbu, Yabu, Baile, Dajidegu, Sigongkema and so on, which were included in Youdibidong, became Dongbu's territory. Till now, the people living there say that they are descendants of Dongbu, and call themselves the Lingbu People, or the Baile People. And the descendants of Dongbu had the habit of uttering "Obu, Obu" when they began to say something.

Apadani's other two sons, Nishi and Nigong, following their father's words, didn't go along with Dongbu and Gabu, but made a living separately.

Nishi went out of the Baga Valley, walked along the big river to the south, and he didn't stop until be arrived at Bangbu②, where he then settled down and made it his territory. His descendants who lived there became the Hangong People.

Nigong went out of the Baga Valley, walked along the big river to the Zangbo River to the west, crossed the two mountains, the Sananqulin Mountain and the Seriluoya Mountain, and didn't stop until he arrived at Dagen③. He then settled down there and made it his territory. His descendants who lived there became the Dagen People.

---

① Guoluosongsong is the present Manigang.

② Bangbu is a place in the Lhoba dialect, in the south of Motuo County.

③ Dagen is a place in the Lhoba dialect, in Longzi County, Tibet.

阿巴达尼的四个儿子，各占一块地方，劳动、生息、繁衍着子孙后代，这就是今天的珞巴族。

讲述者：米林县纳玉乡东娘

## 人为什么和猴子不一样

起初，有两种猴子，一种是白毛长尾巴的，一种是红毛短尾巴的。有一天，红毛短尾巴的猴子们跑到了一座大山上，把自己身上的毛都拔了下来，放到一块大岩石上，各自拿来一块石头狠劲地敲，敲出火来了。

有了火，这些短尾巴的猴子就把弄来的东西烧熟了吃，不再吃生东西了。

从此，这些短尾巴的猴子身上不再长毛了，便成了人。起初，人还有点尾巴，但是越来越短了，到后来就一点尾巴也不剩了。

讲述者：米林县纳玉乡东娘

## 虎哥与人弟

远古的时候，天地一片漆黑，什么也没有。天和地分开

Apadani's four sons, each of whom occupied an area respectively, lived and worked, and reproduced their descendants in their own territory, which formed today's Lhoba Ethnic Group.

Narrator: Dongniang, Nayu Village, Milin County

## Why Were Human Beings Different from Monkeys?

Once there were two kinds of monkeys, one with white hair and a long tail and the other with red hair and a short tail. One day, the monkeys with red hair and a short tail ran to a big mountain, pulled off their hair and put them on a big rock. They knocked at the hair with a stone until the fire sparked.

With the fire, these short-tail monkeys cooked the food and didn't have raw food any more.

Since then, these short-tail monkeys no longer grew hair and became human beings. At first, the human beings had a short tail, but it became shorter and shorter and finally nothing left.

Narrator: Dongniang, Nayu Village, Milin County

## Older Brother Tiger and Its Younger Brother Human Being

In ancient times, the world was dark and nothing was there.

以后，人就从天上掉下来，生活在地上。过了很多年，大地遭受到强烈的地震，有的人过不下去了，又飞回天上。有的人因为良心不好，只飞到半空中，就摔下地来。

那时，世上有一个姑娘和她的舅舅，他们相依为命，过着贫苦的日子。姑娘到了成婚的年龄，但找不到人成婚。有个喇嘛佛爷，让姑娘和她舅舅成亲。姑娘不肯，就躲到树上去。她刚刚爬上树，忽然感到受孕了，肚子痛如刀绞，赶忙爬下树来，刚一落地，就生下一只虎崽，后来又生下一个人。老虎出生后一落地就会跳，人生出来却动也不会动。他们就是虎哥和人弟。

人弟慢慢长大了。有一天，他们一起到森林里去打猎。虎哥毫不费力就捉到一只马鹿，人弟却连一只小兔子也抓不着。虎哥十分生气，跑过去，一把捏住弟弟的脖颈，骂他太无能了。

过了几天，虎哥又约人弟到山上去打猎。打到野兽以后，人弟拿两块石头使劲摩擦，慢慢擦出火星来。他把兽肉拿到火上去烤，烤得香喷喷的，十分好吃。虎哥却用锋利的爪子把兽肉撕成几块，张开血盆大口，狼吞虎咽地嚼起来，边吃边对弟弟说："你这个笨蛋，等我把兽肉吃光了，就要吃你的肉了。"

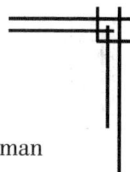

After the separation of the Heaven and the Earth, the human beings fell from the heaven and lived on the earth. Many years later, some people could not survive on the earth because of the earthquakes, so they flew back to the heaven. But some of them fell down from the mid-air because they were conscienceless.

At that time, there was a girl who lived a miserable life with her uncle. At the age of marriage, the girl could not find a man to marry. A Lama Buddha asked the girl to marry her uncle. She refused and tried to hide in the tree, but she had just climbed up the tree when she suddenly felt pregnant. Her belly was so painful that she gave birth to a baby tiger as soon as she climbed down the tree, and later gave birth to a human being too. The tiger could jump when it was born, but the human being could not move after his birth. They were the Tiger and its younger brother, the human being.

Gradually, the human being grew up. One day, they went to the forest to hunt. The Tiger caught a red deer easily, but the human being could not catch a rabbit. The Tiger was very angry, ran over to pinch its brother's neck, and scolded him for his incompetence.

A few days later, the Tiger asked its younger brother to go hunting in the mountains again. When they got their prey, the human being rubbed two stones to spark the fire and cooked the prey on it, which was roasted very savory and delicious. However, the Tiger just tore the meat into pieces with its sharp claws, opened its bloody mouth and gobbled it up. While gobbling, the Tiger said to its brother, "You idiot, I'll have your flesh as soon as I eat up."

人弟听了，吓得跑回家来，气喘吁吁地对妈妈说："妈妈，虎哥想吃我。"妈妈一听吓坏了，说："你大哥太可恶，赶紧把他除掉。"妈妈想出个主意，悄悄地告诉了人弟。

第二天，人弟假装约虎哥过江打猎。他带上了弓弩，找来一只小虫，偷偷放在虎哥背上。走到江边，人弟先渡过溜索，躲在一棵大树背后，虎哥也跟着过溜索。过着过着，小虫咬得老虎脊背痒痒，老虎忙用一只爪子去抓痒。人弟见虎哥吊在溜索上一晃一晃的，趁机取出弓弩，"嗖"的一箭，射在老虎身上。虎哥又痒又痛，抓不住溜索，"砰"的一声跌落江心，被水冲走了。

人弟高高兴兴地回到家中，告诉妈妈，妈妈也很高兴。没有老虎来吃人，人才一代一代传下来。


讲述者：腊荣老人

翻译者：明珠

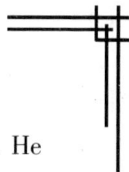

The human being was scared to hear that and ran home. He gasped to his mother, "Mom, the Tiger wants to eat me." His mother was frightened and said, "Your brother Tiger is too hateful, and We'd better get rid of it quickly." Then the mother came up with an idea and told the human being secretly.

The next day, the human being pretended to invite the Tiger to go hunting on the other side of the river. He took his bow and arrows, found a bug and put it on the back of the Tiger secretly. On the river bank, the human being first crossed the river through the suspension rope and hid behind a big tree, with the Tiger following him. When the Tiger was hanging on the suspension rope, the bug on the Tiger's back bit it and made it itchy, so the Tiger had to scratch with one claw. Seeing that the Tiger was hanging on the rope unsteadily, the human being took the opportunity to take out his bow and arrows, and hit the Tiger with one shot. Being too itchy and painful, the Tiger could not catch the rope tightly, fell down to the river and was washed away by the water.

The human being went back home happily and told the mother what had happened. The mother was very happy too. No tiger came to eat the human being, so they could live on the earth from generation to generation.

Narrator: an old man named La Rong

Translator: Pearl

# 第三章　怒　族

## 腊普和亚妞

　　古时候洪水泛滥，人类全都被淹死了。天神看到大地荒无人烟，就派了还没有成年的腊普和亚妞兄妹俩来到人间，繁衍人类。哥哥腊普很有本事，他力大无穷，特别是善使一手弩弓，百发百中，飞禽走兽很难逃脱他的手。妹妹亚妞是个善良勤劳的姑娘。兄妹俩来到大地上没有房子，就住在岩洞里；没有吃的，就去采野果，猎禽兽。

　　日子一天天地过去，兄妹俩也长大成人了，因为大地上没有其他的人，兄妹俩无法同别人成亲，哥哥心里想："现在大地上只有我们兄妹俩，若不结为夫妻生儿育女，人类就要绝灭。为了繁衍后代，我们兄妹应该结为夫妻。"腊普走到亚妞跟前不好意思地喊道："妹妹……"

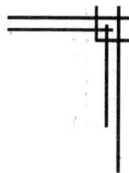

# Chapter Three  Nu Ethnic Group

## Lapu and Yaniu

In ancient times, the whole world was drowned in the widespread floods. Seeing the desolate earth, the God of Heaven sent the young man Lapu and his younger sister Yaniu to go to the earth and reproduce the human being. Lapu, a very capable and strong young man, was especially good at shooting arrows without a single miss, which made it difficult for any animal to escape from his hand. His younger sister Yaniu was a kind and hard-working girl. When the brother and sister came to the earth, there was no house but a cave for them to live in. Without food, they had to make a living by picking wild fruits and hunting animals.

Day after day, the brother and sister grew up, but they could marry nobody for there were no other people on the earth. The brother thought that, "Now that nobody but my sister and I live on the earth, the human beings would be extinct if we would not get married. In order to reproduce offspring, we'd better be husband and wife." Then the brother walked towards his sister, and said shyly, "Dear sister..."

"干哪样？"妹妹见哥哥有些害羞，说话吞吞吐吐，疑惑地问。

"妹妹，我有件事想和你商量，就怕你不答应。"

"哥哥，有什么事，你尽管说吧。"

"妹妹，你我都长大成人了，该成亲了，可是世上只有我们兄妹俩。我想，只有我们兄妹结为夫妻，生育下一代，人类才能繁衍。你说行不行？"

妹妹听了很是害羞，说："你是哥哥，我是妹妹，世上哪有兄妹结为夫妻的道理呢？"

"兄妹为夫妻虽然不合情理，但你想一想，洪水把人类都淹死完后，天神才派我们兄妹俩来到大地，为的是要我俩结为夫妻，生育下一代，使人类不致灭绝呀！"哥哥苦苦地劝说妹妹。

妹妹听了，心里想："是呀，不然天神派我们兄妹俩来到大地干什么呢？但是，我俩成亲，既无人证，又无物证，这可咋办？"亚妞想了一阵，然后说："哥哥，我们兄妹俩能不能成亲，没有人告诉我们！就是要成亲，也没有东西为凭证，如果你拿弩弓射织布架的四棵桩桩，若箭箭都射中了，我俩就结为夫妻。"

腊普答应了，拉弩搭箭，"当"的一声，不偏不倚正中织布架桩桩的中央，连射四箭都是这样。腊普和亚妞兄妹俩就结成了夫妻。

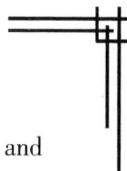

"What's happened?" Seeing her brother somewhat shy and hesitated, the younger sister asked suspiciously.

"Dear sister, I've got something to discuss with you. I'm afraid you won't agree."

"What's the matter? Just tell me, my dear brother."

"Dear sister, since we've grown up, its time to get married. But we are the only two on the earth. I think only if we get married can we reproduce the next generation. What do you think about it?"

The sister was very shy to hear that, and said, "You're my brother while I'm your sister. How can the brother and sister be husband and wife in the world?"

"It is really not reasonable. But just think for a while, the God of Heaven didn't send us to the earth until the human beings were drown in the flood. His purpose is to let us be husband and wife and reproduce the human being, so that the human being would not be extinct!" The brother tried his hard to persuade his sister.

Hearing this, the sister thought it reasonable, "Otherwise, why the God of Heaven sent us two to the earth? However, how can we get married without a marriage witness or a wedding token?" Yaniu thought for a while and said to her brother, "Dear brother, nobody could tell us whether we can get married or not. So without a witness or a token, if you can shoot the four posts of the loom with your bow and arrows, I will marry you."

Lapu agreed. He pulled the bow and shot the arrows. The four arrows shot the loom exactly in the middle of the four posts. Then Lapu and Yaniu got married.

　　几年过去了，腊普和亚妞生育了七个子女，这些孩子长大后，有的是兄妹结为夫妻，有的是跟会说话的蛇、蜂、鱼、虎交配，繁育下一代。后来人类逐步地发展起来，就以一个始祖所传的后裔称为一个氏族，与蛇所生的为蛇氏族，与蜂所生的为蜂氏族，与鱼所生的为鱼氏族，与虎所生的为虎氏族。每一个氏族都有一个共同的图腾崇拜，蛇氏族崇拜蛇，蜂氏族崇拜蜂，虎氏族崇拜虎。

　　再说腊普和亚妞兄妹俩来到大地后，好长时间，他们都没有火，不懂得吃熟食，猎取到的野兽也是生吃。后来，有一次山上燃起了大火，腊普和亚妞感到很奇怪，便前往观看，他们捡到了一只被火烧过的野兽，吃起来很香，比生的好吃多了，这样他们才懂得了吃熟食。他们想找到火种，但火已熄灭了，到哪里去找呢？兄妹俩苦思冥想了好些日子。一天，他们突然想到平时用竹子在石头上磨弩箭时，竹子会像在火上烤过一样热烘烘的。他们想，若把竹子在石头上久久摩擦，一定会发出火来。

　　于是兄妹俩找来竹子，两人轮流在石头上使力地磨呀磨，磨得竹子发烫了，他们还是不停地磨。磨了三天三夜，竹子燃起火来了，兄妹俩非常高兴，赶快找些柴棒烧起大火，把火种保存下来。从此，人们就不再吃生的动物肉了。

Some years later, Lapu and Yaniu bore seven children. When they grew up, some of them got married, and some mated with snakes, bees, fish, or tigers to reproduce the next generation. Later, with the development of the human being, the descendants of the same ancestor were called a clan, that is, the snake clan, the bee clan, the fish clan, and the tiger clan. Each clan had its own totem, the snake clan worshiping the snake, the bee clan the bee, and the tiger clan the tiger.

Long time after Lapu and Yaniu went to the earth, they had no fire and didn't know how to cook food with fire, so the animals they hunt were eaten uncooked. Later, a fire broke out on the mountain, and Lapu and Yaniu felt very curious and went to see what had happened. They picked up a burnt wild animal and found it taste delicious, which was much better than the raw meat. Until then, they began to cook food with fire. They tried to find the fire, but it had gone out. The brother and sister thought it over for a few days where to find the fire. One day, they suddenly thought that the bamboos would be hot as if they were baked on the fire when they applied them to make the bows and arrows. It would make a fire if the bamboo had been rubbed on the stone for enough time.

Then, the brother and sister found a bamboo and took turns to rub it on a stone. They didn't stop doing it for three days and nights until it became very hot and sparked a fire. The brother and sister were very glad and quickly found some sticks to burn the fire and kept it. From then on, the human being hadn't eaten raw animal meat any longer.

又过了好些年，腊普因年老死去了，亚妞把他用火烧掉。没有几年，亚妞又死了，她的子女也用火把亚妞葬了。怒族火葬的风俗，就是从腊普和亚妞开始的。

腊普和亚妞讲的是怒话，他们的子孙发展起来了，便往福贡、贡山等地迁徙，这些地方还有傈僳族，他们的人比怒族多，腊普和亚妞的子孙来到这些地方，光讲怒话行不通了。他们也就讲起傈僳话来。所以，怒话和傈僳话相差不多，而且怒族人都会讲傈僳话。

讲述者：赛阿局
翻译者：光付益
记录者：吴广甲
整理者：陈荣祥

After many years, Lapu died of old age, and Yaniu burned him. A few years late, Yaniu died too, and her children burned her either, which became the custom of cremation in Nu Ethnic Group.

Lapu and Yaniu spoke Nu language, and with the spread of their descendants, they migrated to Fugong, Gongshan and other places, where the people of Lisu Ethnic Group lived. For the People of Lisu Ethnic Group were more than the people of Nu Ethnic Group, it was not enough to speak just Nu language. Therefore, the people of Nu Ethnic Group began to learn to speak Lisu language. Nowadays, the people of Nu Ethnic Group could speak Nu language and Lisu language at the same time, for the two languages were almost the same.

Narrator: Sai Aju
Translator: Guang Fuyi
Recorder: Wu Guangjia
Organizer: Chen Rongxiang

# 射太阳月亮

古时天地相连，举手可以触天。后来，巨人将天地分开，不料洪水滔天，天地白茫茫一片，将大地淹没，只剩下兄妹二人，往葫芦里躲藏，顺水漂流。不久，水退，大地晴朗，天空出现九个太阳、九个月亮，天气十分炎热，万物无法生长，兄妹无处躲藏，于是哥哥用箭射落八个太阳八个月亮，这时气候才不寒不热。由于洪水泛滥，淹没人类，兄妹二人再也找不着人烟，兄和妹商量去寻找人类，每人各持半只木梳分别由北向南和由南向北行进，但还是找不着人烟。等返回原地兄妹相遇时，两人已鬓发斑白，互不相识，各自取出半只木梳为凭据，才认出是兄妹。由于找不到人烟，兄只好向妹求婚，妹说要一箭射中针孔才能结婚。兄一箭射中，兄妹结为夫妻，生下七男七女，第一怒族，第二独龙族，第三汉族，第四藏族，第五白族，第六傈僳族，第七纳西族。七个姑娘分别嫁给七个兄弟，住在七条江畔，繁衍了人类。

选自毛星主编《中国少数民族文学》（下），湖南人民出版社1983年版。

# Shooting the Suns and the Moons

In ancient time, the Heaven and the Earth stayed closely, and they were easy to touch each other. Later, a giant separated the Heaven from the Earth, which resulted in the flood that drowned the whole world, with only a brother and his younger sister left, hiding in a gourd and drifting along the water. Soon, the water subsided, and it cleared up, but nine suns and nine moons appeared in the sky. It was so hot that nothing could be raised on the earth, and the brother and his sister had nowhere to go. Therefore, the brother had to shot eight suns and eight moons with his arrows, and then the climate became moderate. Due to the flood that drowned the human beings, the brother and the sister could see nobody. They decided to look for the human beings respectively, with half of a wooden comb as a token for a reunion. One of them went from the north to the south, and the other went from the south to the north, but neither could find a human being. When they reunited, they almost could not recognize each other because of the graying temples until they showed the other their half wooden comb. They could not find anyone to marry, so the brother had to propose to his sister. The sister answered that she couldn't marry him until her brother shot the eye of the needle. The brother succeeded in doing so and they got married, giving birth to seven brothers and seven sisters, who became the ancestors of seven ethnic groups. The first ethnic group was Nu, the second Dulong, the third Han, the fourth Zang, the fifth Bai, the sixth Lisu and the seventh Naxi. The seven sisters married the seven brothers respectively, living along the banks of seven rivers and reproducing the human beings.

# 祖先阿铁

阿铁与妻子伊娃住在丽江，门前有一棵结满黑色果子的大树，人说是鬼栽的，果子不能吃。阿铁夫妇不相信，吃了果子，妻子伊娃死了，树变成了人，并把自己的姑娘嫁给阿铁为妻，送给他们竹篾筐。不久洪水爆发，阿铁夫妻二人乘坐竹筐免遭灾难。水退之后，竹筐漂到澜沧江边，他们在这里住下，生四男四女，配成四对，从此人类得到繁殖。

他们以打猎为生，为追赶野兽，逐渐迁至怒江沿岸，与当地黄蜂氏族居住在了一起，互通婚姻。从此阿铁家族内部不再允许兄妹通婚。当地麃子氏族在阿铁来后，即迁到俅江（即独龙族地区），成了后来的独龙族。

# Ancestor Ah Tie

Ah Tie and his wife Eva lived in Li River. In front of their house was a big tree with black fruit, which was said that it was planted by the ghost and the fruit could not be eaten. The couple did not believe it and ate the fruit, so Eva died and the tree became a man, who married his daughter to Ah Tie and gave them a bamboo basket as a gift.

Shortly after, the flood broke out, Ah Tie and his wife escaped from the flood for boarding on the bamboo basket. When the water subsided, the bamboo basket drifted to the Lancang River, where they settled down and gave birth to four men and four women, matching four couples. From then on, the human beings began to reproduce their offspring.

They made a living by hunting, and in order to chase the wild animals, they gradually moved to the bank of Nu River, living with the local wasp clan and intermarried with the local people. Since then, the Ah Tie family no longer allowed brothers and sisters to get married. The local muntjac clan moved to the Qiu River (or the Dulong area) after the arrival of the Ah Tie family and became the later Dulong Ethnic Group.

# 第四章　基诺族

## 玛黑、玛妞和葫芦里的人

玛黑和玛妞是一对兄妹，他们和爸爸妈妈一起居住在高高的山上，过着平静、幸福的日子。可是在他们刚刚成人的时候，世上忽然发了大水，整个人类面临着灭亡的威胁。在水还没淹到山顶的时候，玛黑和玛妞的父母为他们想了一条逃生之计：造一只大木鼓把他俩装在里面，这样水就淹不着他们了。于是爸爸妈妈赶快就去砍树造鼓。可是走到第一棵树面前，刚砍了第一斧，那树马上叫起来："哎喽！太疼了呀！"走到第二棵树面前，刚砍了第一斧，那棵树又叫起来："哎喽！太疼了呀！"……一直砍了九十九棵树，棵棵都叫疼。最后，他们来到寨子中间，那里生长着一棵苦果树。玛黑玛妞的父母就哀求说："苦果树呵苦果树，大水就要淹上来了，请你救救我们的孩子，让我们把你砍来做个鼓吧！苦果树点点头答应了。于是，玛黑玛妞的父母就把树掏空，做成了一个大木鼓。

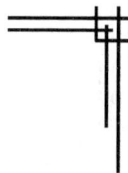

# Chapter Four  Jino Ethnic Group

## Mahei, Maniu and the People in the Gourd

Mahei and Maniu, a brother and his younger sister, lived a happy and peaceful life with their parents on the top of a high mountain. But just when they grew up, a sudden flood broke out and threatened the entire human race. Their parents came up with a plan to escape before the water covered the top of the mountain, that is, to make a big wooden drum and hide the brother and his sister in it so as to keep them away from the water. Their parents hurriedly tried to cut down a tree to make the drum. But when they went to cut the first tree for the first axe, the tree shouted, "Oh! It's too painful!" When they went to cut the second tree for the first axe, the tree shouted, "Oh! It's too painful!" They went to ninety nine trees and the trees responded the same. At last, they went to the center of the stockade, where stood a big bitter fruit tree. The parents pleaded, "Dear bitter fruit tree, please allow us to cut you down and make a drum and to save our children because the flood is coming." The bitter fruit tree nodded, and the parents cut the tree and hollowed it to make a big wooden drum.

玛黑玛妞的父母在木鼓里放了够吃九天九夜的粮食和一只小鸡，又交给玛黑玛妞一把小刀和一块蜂蜡，对他俩说："现在，你们要离开父母去逃生了。记住：水不干就不要出来。如果你们要看水势，可以用刀把鼓划个小洞往外看，看后就赶快用蜂蜡把洞堵上。什么时候可以出来，小鸡会叫你们的。"玛黑和玛妞就这样辞别了父母，开始在洪水中漂荡。

他们漂啊漂，漂了三天三夜，小鸡还不叫。玛黑忍不住了，就用小刀在鼓上挖了一个小洞往外看。呵！外面的景象多么惨哪：洪水在不断上涨，水面上漂着死人的尸体。玛黑吓坏了，赶快用蜂蜡把洞口堵上。他们又继续漂啊漂，漂了六天六夜，小鸡还是不叫。玛妞忍不住了，她用小刀在鼓上挖了个小洞往外看。呵！外面的世界变成白茫茫的一片，连人影也看不到了！她吓坏了，赶紧用蜂蜡把洞堵上。他们又继续漂啊漂，一共漂了九天九夜。小鸡终于开口了："啾啾啾，吱吱吱！水干了，可以出去了！"兄妹俩高兴得一头钻出了木鼓。

可是，眼前的情景使他们几乎哭了出来：四周静悄悄的，没有一丝人声，也没有一粒种子，迎接他们的是一座被水冲得光秃秃的山和山背后即将沉落的夕阳。他俩带着小鸡一面哭，一面找，希望能找到一个人。可是找遍整座大山，只找到了一粒葫芦籽。兄妹俩就把葫芦籽种下了。

The parents stored in the wooden drum enough food for nine days and nights and a chick, gave them a knife and a piece of beeswax, and said to them, "Now you two have to leave us to escape from the flood. Remember, Don't come out until the flood subsides. If you want to know the condition of the flood, you can dig a hole in the drum, look outside through it, and then plug it with the beeswax quickly. The chick will remind you when you can go out of the drum." Mahei and Maniu left their parents, hid in the drum, and began to drift in the flood.

They drifted and drifted for three days and nights, and the chick didn't crow. Mahei couldn't help digging a small hole in the drum and looking out of it. What a miserable scene it was! The water was increasing continuously, and the dead bodies were floating on the surface. Mahei was shocked and plugged the small hole with the beeswax quickly. They continued drifting for six days and nights, and the chick still kept silence. This time, Maniu couldn't help digging a small hole in the drum and looking out of it. Oh! The outside world turned into a vast land of whiteness, without a single man. She was shocked and plugged the small hole with the beeswax quickly. They continued drifting until the ninth day and night, the chick crew, " chirp, chirp, chirp, the water has dried up, and you can go out!" The brother and his sister went out of the wooden drum happily.

However, the sight in front of them made them almost cry: it was deadly quiet and there was no voice, nor was a seed. The only things they could see were a bare hill flushed by the flood and the sinking sunset behind it. Taking the chick with them, the brother and his sister cried and looked for something, hoping to find a human being. But they searched for the whole mountain only to find a gourd seed, and they sowed it.

　　种下葫芦籽以后，玛黑和玛妞说："妹妹，现在世上只剩下我们兄妹俩了，我们结成夫妻吧！"玛妞害羞极了："这怎么行呢？你是哥哥，我是妹妹，兄妹怎么能成亲呵！"玛黑使劲劝她，她就是不听。最后，玛黑想出一个主意，他对玛妞说："这样吧，对面山上有一位白发智者，你去问他，他会告诉你，我们能否成婚。"玛妞答应了。

　　通往对面的山有两条路，一条直路，一条弯路。玛黑指给玛妞走弯路，自己则走直路先到了那里，扮成一个白发老人守候在路旁。一会儿，玛妞也到了。她看到果然有个"白发智者"在那里，就跑过去跪在"老人"面前问："智慧的长者呵，现在世上只剩下我和哥哥两人了，请告诉我：我们可以结成夫妻吗？""白发智者"马上回答："按说兄妹是不能成婚的。但是人类不能绝代呵，所以你们可以结婚。"这样，玛黑玛妞兄妹俩就结成夫妻了。

After sowing the gourd seed, Mahei said to Maniu, "Dear sister, let's get married since there are only two of us left in the world." Maniu was very shy and answered, "How can it be? You are my brother, and I'm your sister. How can brother and sister be married?" Mahei tried to persuade her and she didn't listen to him. At last, an idea came to Mahei, and he said to Maniu, "Well, there is a white-hair wise man on the opposite mountain who will tell you whether we can marry when you go to ask him." Maniu agreed.

Two paths led to the opposite mountain, a straight one and a curved one. Mahei showed Maniu the curved one, and he himself chose the straight, dressed up as the white hair old man waiting on the roadside. In a moment, Maniu arrived too. She saw the old man and ran over and knelt in front of him and asked, "Your wise elder, could you tell me whether we can get married or not, now that my brother and I are the only two in the world?" The white hair wise man answered quickly, "It is said that brother and sister cannot be married. But the human being may be extinct, and you'd better get married." In this way, Mahei and Maniu got married.

那颗葫芦籽很快就发了芽，并且长得很快、很旺，藤子爬过了九条江、九座山，但是只结了孤零零的一个葫芦。到了玛黑玛妞结婚的那天，葫芦完全成熟了，有一座房子那么大，金黄金黄的，美丽极了。

早晨，玛妞去背水，路过葫芦旁，隐约听到里头有人说话，她以为自己听错了，没有在意；中午，玛妞去摘菜，又听到葫芦里头好像有人说话，她还是不相信自己的耳朵；下午玛黑和玛妞一齐收工回来，路过葫芦旁，这回两人都清清楚楚地听见里面有人在说话了。他俩大吃一惊，想了想，便在葫芦旁烧了一堆火，把烧火棍放在火中烤红，想在葫芦上烙个洞，让里面的人出来。可是烙上边，里面有人惊叫："会烙着我！"烙下边，里面也有人惊叫："会烙着我！"烙左边，里面也有人惊叫："会烙着我！"烙右边，里面也有人惊叫："会烙着我！"

玛黑玛妞急得团团转。正在这时，葫芦里忽然传出一个老婆婆苍老而和蔼的声音："你们从我这儿烙吧，我不怕烙，不然的话大家都出不去。但是，我死了以后，在天和地没有消灭之前，请你们不要忘记我阿匹娪①。"玛黑和玛妞难过地哭了。但是为了让葫芦里的人出来，他俩只好横横心，用烧火棍朝阿匹娪那个方向烙去。葫芦冒出一股青烟，阿匹娪死了，但葫芦上通了一个洞，刚刚够一个人出来。

---

① 阿匹娪：基诺语，婆婆。

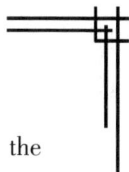

The gourd seed sprouted quickly and flourished, and the vine climbed over nine rivers and nine mountains, but only one gourd was born. On the wedding day of Mahei and Maniu, the gourd was fully mature, as big as a house in beautifully golden.

In the morning, Maniu went to carry water, passed by the gourd and heard someone speaking. She didn't care for she thought she must have misheard something. At noon, Maniu went to pick vegetables, and heard as if someone spoke in the gourd. She still didn't believe her ears. When she and Mahei finished their work and went back home in the afternoon, they passed by the gourd, and heard clearly that someone was speaking in it. They were very shocked and thought for a while, and then they lit a fire beside the gourd and roasted an iron stick in the fire, trying to iron a hole in the gourd and let the people out. However, just as they put the iron stick on the top of the gourd, they heard someone shouting, "It will burn me!" Putting the iron stick on the left side, they heard someone shouting, "It will burn me!" Putting the iron stick on the right side, they also heard someone shouting, "It will burn me!" Putting the iron stick on the bottom of the gourd, they also heard someone shouting, "It will burn me!"

Mahei and Maniu were so agitated that they were like an ant on a hot pan. Just then, they heard an affable voice of an old lady in the gourd, "Iron the hole here and I'm not afraid of it. Or nobody could get out of here. But after my death, please don't forget me, Apiyu①, unless the heaven and the earth were wiped out." Mahei and Maniu cried sadly, but they had to harden their heart and iron the gourd so as to free the people from it. Apiyu died with a cloud of blue smoke from the gourd, leaving a hole just big enough for one person to come out.

---

① Apiyu means an old lady in the Jino dialect.

　　第一个跳出来的是布朗族。他跳出来时碰着葫芦旁火堆里的焦树干，把脸染黑了，从此布朗族就长得很黑。布朗族不会说话，玛黑和玛妞说："去听听水声吧。"布朗人就去模仿水声说话，因此布朗话"咕噜咕噜"的，就像流水的声音一样。

　　第二个跳出来的是基诺族。他碰着的是栗树干，栗树干是不白不黑的，所以基诺族长得不白不黑。基诺话就是玛黑玛妞讲的话，所以基诺族不用再去学别的语言了。

　　第三个跳出来的是傣族。傣族跳出来碰着芭蕉杆，芭蕉杆是白的，所以傣族就长得白白的。傣族也不会讲话，但是他很聪明，他学着讲布朗话和基诺话，然后自己又进行了改进，所以傣话更好听些。

　　玛黑玛妞看到他们都会讲话了，就教他们数数字："从前有九座山，每座山上有九棵树，每棵树上有九条枝，每条枝上有九个鸟窝，每个鸟窝里有九个鸟蛋；九座山上又有九个塘，每个塘中有九条牛，每条牛有十六个蹄瓣……"

The first one who jumped out of the gourd was the Blang people. He touched a burnt trunk beside the gourd when he jumped out and darkened his face, so the Blang people grew black. He could not speak, and Mahei and Maniu told him to listen to the sound of water, so he went to imitate the sound of water. Therefore the "murmur" in Blang language sounds like the sound of flowing water.

The second one was the Jino people. He touched the trunk of chestnut, which was neither black nor white, so the Jino people were neither white nor black. Jino language was just what Mahei and Maniu spoke, so it was not necessary for them to learn a new language.

The third one was the Dai people. He touched the trunk of the Chinese banana, which was white, and the Dai people were white. The Dai people couldn't speak either, but he was very smart and learned to speak Blang language and Jino language, and then improved them, so the Dai language was better understood.

When they could speak their own languages, Mahei and Maniu began to teach them how to count number, "Long long ago, there were nine mountains, and in each mountain there were nine trees, and each tree had nine branches, and in each branch there were nine nests of birds, and in each nest of birds, there were nine eggs; in the nine mountains there were nine ponds, and in each pond there were nine cows, and each cow had sixteen hoofs..."

现在大地上又有了人，人也会数数字了，但是他们该怎样生活，每个人又干些什么呢？玛黑玛妞领着他们去请教天上的神。神说："这样吧：基诺族做官，布朗族种山地，傣族种坝子地。"布朗族和傣族都很高兴，只有基诺族不愿意。说："要我们做官，除非是先请我们吃九碗长脚蚊子的脑子和双头鸡的磕膝头！"所以后来基诺族就没有做官。接下来是分工具，布朗族拿了锄头，基诺族拿了背箩，傣族拿了扁担。最后开始分文字了。神把基诺族的文字写在牛皮上，给傣族的文字写在芭蕉叶上，给布朗族的文字写在麦面粑粑上。回去的时候，有九条江拦住了大家的路，等到渡过江后，大家才发现文字都被打湿了。于是就摊开来晒。晒了一下午还没干，布朗族饿了，就把粑粑吃了，所以今天布朗族就没有自己的文字。傣族的芭蕉叶被鸡扒烂了，非常伤心，这时正好飞来一只绿斑鸠，在芭蕉叶上拉了一泡屎，傣族马上高兴起来，照着绿斑鸠的屎来造字。于是现在傣族的字就像绿斑鸠的屎一样又细又弯。基诺族看到布朗族的文字晒不干被吃了，傣族的晒在地上又被鸡扒烂了，灵机一动，就把牛皮拿到火塘边去烘，认为这样又快又安全。没一会儿，牛

Now that there were human beings on the earth who could count numbers, how could they make a living? And what could they do? Mahei and Maniu took them to ask the God of Heaven for help. The God said, "Well, the Jino people will be officials, the Blang people will till the mountainous land, and the Dai people will till the dam land." The Blang people and Dai people were very glad while the Jino people was not. He said, "We won't be officials until we are treated with nine bowls of brains of long-leg mosquito and knees of the two-head chicken." So the Jino people had not been officials later. The following was to distribute the tools. The Blang people took the hoe, the Jino people took the packbaskets, and the Dai people took the shoulder pole. The last was to distribute the characters. The God wrote the Jino characters on the cowhide, the Dai characters on the Chinese banana leaves, and the Blang characters on the cakes made of wheat flour. On their way back home, they found their characters were all wet after they crossed the nine rivers which blocked their way home. They had to dry the characters in the sun. For a whole afternoon, the cakes were not dried, and the Blang people ate the cakes because of hunger, so nowadays the Blang people have no characters. The Dai people was very sad when the Chinese banana leaves were scratched by a chicken. Just at that time, a green turtledove was flying over it, leaving the excrement on it. The Dai people became happy and coined their characters according to the shape of the excrement. So today's Dai characters are as slim and bent as the green turtledoves excrement. Seeing the Blangs characters being eaten and the Dais characters being destroyed by the chicken, the Jino people came up with an idea, he took the

皮就被烤得膨胀起来，发出很香的味道。他越闻越想吃，实在忍不住了，就自言自语道："唔，不要紧的，吃在嘴里，记在心上。"说完就把牛皮吃了。于是，基诺族也失去了文字。后来，人们为了纪念葫芦里的老婆婆阿匹娱，每次开口唱歌的时候，第一句总要先唱阿匹的名字："娱（哎）……"

讲述者：白腊赛，白腊东

翻译者：白忠明，策白

整理者：赵鲁云


# 阿嬷尧白

女始祖尧白造了天又造了地以后，就召集各民族来分天分地。基诺族没有去参加，尧白先派了汉族、傣族去请，没有请来。她又亲自去请，还是没有请来，尧白一生气就走了。走到半路，到了孔明山。她想基诺族不参加分天分地，以后生活会发生困难，便站在孔明山上，抓了一把茶籽撒在曼卡寨和龙帕寨的土地上，这里从此便成了盛产茶叶的地方。

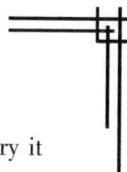

cowhide to the edge of the fireplace and baked it, hoping to dry it safe and fast. After a while, the cowhide was baked swollen and produced a fine flavor. The more he smelt it, the more he wanted to have it, and finally he couldn't help it and said to himself, "Well, it doesn't matter. I have it in my mouth and it will be kept in my heart." And then he ate the cowhide. So the Jino people lost their characters too. Later, whenever the Jino people begin to sing a song, the beginning of the first sentence must start with the name of Apiyu, "YU (AI)...", so as to commemorate the old lady in the gourd.

Narrator: Bai Lasai, Bai Ladong

Translator: Bai Zhongming, Cebai

Organizer: Zhao Luyun

# The Female Ancestor, Yaobai

After the creation of the Heaven and the Earth, the female ancestor, Yaobai, summoned the nationalities to distribute the Heaven and the Earth, but the Jino people did not join. Yaobai sent the Han people and then the Dai people to invite them, but they didn't come. Yaobai herself went to invite them, but still it did not work. Yaobai was very angry and went away. On her way to Kongming Mountain, she thought that the life of Jino people would be hard for they didn't take part in the distribution of the world, so she stood on the Kongming Mountain and scattered a handful of tea seeds on the land of Mankazhai and Longpazhai, where, from then on, abounded with tea.

　　尧白请人为基诺族造字，造好以后叫基诺族人去领。尧白把文字教给他们，他们记不住，就把文字写在牛皮上，回来时路上要过一道河，牛皮被水浸湿了，便拿到火上烘，结果牛皮烘糊，字迹便看不清楚了。他们想：吃在肚里，便能记在心上，便把牛皮吃了，所以基诺族没有文字。

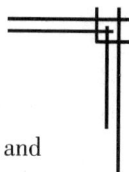

Yaobai had the characters created for the Jino people, and asked them to take it home. Yaobai taught them how to read and write the characters, but they could not remember and had to write down the characters on the cowhide. However, the cowhide got wet when the Jino people crossed a river on their way home. They tried to dry the cowhide on the fire but only to burn it and make it illegible. They thought that the characters could be kept in mind if the cowhide was eaten in stomach, and then they ate it. From then on, the Jino people had no characters any more.

# 第五章　普米族

## 采金光

　　远古的时候，天上没有太阳的光，没有月亮的光，也没有星星的光；地上没有树，没有花，也没有草生长。黑黢黢的天地死气沉沉，整个世间一片漆黑。时间在黑暗中一点一点地过去，岁月在无声中一天一天地过去，不知过了多少岁月。

　　有一年，遥远的东方突然出现微弱的闪光。那光芒瞬息一亮，眨眼又灭，原来那是东方汪洋大海边的一棵海螺树在开花。这神奇的海螺树一万年开一次花，开花时闪一下光，花谢光灭，如此轮回地复转着。

　　不知过了多少万年，海螺花又开了，花一开，光点像星星那么大，一闪一闪的。这时，离海边很远的地方住着一户人家，他们有四个弟兄和一个妹妹。那时候的人还不知道穿衣服，四兄弟和一个妹妹全都赤身裸体，在黑暗中闭眼度日。海螺花开，闪亮的金光使五兄妹异常欢喜，他们远远地望着，说不出那光明从何方照来。聪明的妹妹说：“我知道那金光是从东边来的，我要把它采来，照亮这黑暗的大地。”

# Chapter Five　Pumi Ethnic Group

## Gathering Golden Light

In ancient times, there was no sunlight, no moonlight, and nor was the light of stars. There were no trees, no flowers, and no grass growing on the ground. It was lifeless, and the whole world was as dark as night. Time and tide went by in the darkness and silence, and nobody knew how many years had passed.

One year, a faint flash of light sparked in the Far East, which blinked and extinguished quickly. It turned out to be the blooming of a conch tree in the east ocean. The magical conch tree would bloom with a flash of light and wither with the extinguishment of it every ten thousand years, which would take turns forever.

Thousands and thousands of years passed, and the conch tree bloomed again, which was as small as the shining stars. At that time, a family of four brothers and their younger sister, who were all naked and with their eyes closed, lived in the darkness far away from the seaside. They were very happy to know from the glittering golden light that the conch tree bloomed, but they didn't know where the light came from. The wise sister said, "I know the golden light is from the East, and I will take it to light up the dark earth."

四兄弟中的老四接着说："我愿意跟妹妹一起去，如果采着金光，也要给世间照明。"

大哥却冷冷地说："金光是神光，谁也别想采到。"

二哥说："那金光是阴光，谁采了谁就活不成！"

只有老三支持弟弟和妹妹的举动，说："你们勇敢地去采吧。要是真的采到金光，就让它永远在天上照明，我们三兄弟在地上辛勤劳动，世世代代伺候你们。"

兄妹二人得到三哥的鼓励，决心去采那一闪一闪的金光。

他们在黑暗中爬行，在黑暗中寻找，不知忍受了多少艰难困苦，经历了多少痛苦的时辰，终于爬到一座大山之顶。兄妹俩还想继续摸索着向前爬行，可是到处悬崖绝壁，无法再前进了。两兄妹正在绝望的时候，一个满头白发的老奶奶出现在面前，她问道："你们兄妹两个来这里做什么？"

聪明的妹妹回答说："奶奶，我们兄妹二人，要采寻那一闪一亮金光照明大地，爬了多少时间才来到这里。"

白发奶奶听后说："要采金光照亮大地，可要日日月月、永生永世呀，你们受得了吗？"

妹妹说："奶奶呀，我们兄妹二人为采金光，吃了无数的苦，受了不少的罪，只要能采着金光，我们什么都能接受。"

哥哥也紧跟着说："只要能采着金光，我们死也不怕。"

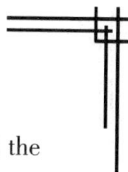

The youngest brother said, "I'd like to go with you, and the world would be lightened if we can gather the golden light."

But the eldest brother said drily, "The golden light is divine, and no one could pick it up."

The second eldest brother added, "The golden light is the shade, and no one could live with it!"

Only the third eldest brother supported his brother and sister and said, "You just go and get it and let it shine forever in the sky. We three brothers will work hard on the ground and serve you from generation to generation if you make it."

Encouraged by the third eldest brother, the youngest brother and sister set out to gather the glittering golden light.

The brother and his sister crawled and searched in the darkness, and finally arrived on the top of a big mountain after enduring endless hardships and going through painful hours. They wanted to go further, but were blocked by cliffs, and there was no way to go. When they were in despair, a granny with white hair appeared and asked, "What are you two going to do here?"

The clever sister replied, "Granny, we are brother and sister, and we have crawled a long time here to gather the glittering golden light to illuminate the earth."

After hearing this, the granny said, "The sun and the moon will shine on the earth forever if you want it. Can you bear it?"

The sister answered, "Yes, Granny, we two have overcome countless hardships and suffered a lot for gathering the golden light. And we could suffer anything for it as long as we can get it."

The brother also said, "We'd like to die for it as long as we get it."

　　白发奶奶听了很高兴，她满意地说："如今天地一片漆黑，我正在寻找能给天下照明的人。你们兄妹二人愿意承担，万物都要感谢你们。从现在起，哥哥白天给大地照明，妹妹夜晚给大地照明……"

　　白发奶奶还没说完，妹妹忙说："奶奶呀，我夜晚出去害怕。"

　　奶奶说："那你白天出去吧。"

　　"白天出去我害羞哇。"妹妹又回答。

　　奶奶说："我给你一包绣花针，谁敢看你，你就用针刺他的眼睛。"

　　说罢，白发奶奶给妹妹一把针，给哥哥一朵银白色的花。从此以后，妹妹当了金光闪闪的太阳，白天出来照明；直到现在，谁要直接看她，她就撒出那包绣花针，刺人家的眼睛。哥哥当了银光闪闪的月亮，到晚上才出来照明。

　　天上有了太阳和月亮，地上也就有了白天和夜晚。慢慢地有了树，有了花，有了草，有了动物。地上三个哥哥害怕在天上的妹妹和弟弟看见自己不穿衣服，他们就追猎捕兽，用兽皮做裤子穿。在打猎中，看见金色的鸟儿搭窝，三个哥哥也学着鸟儿，用树枝搭房子。有了房子居住，他们便砍林开荒，开始种庄稼了。

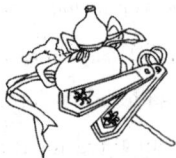

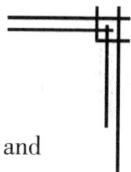

The white hair granny was very delighted to hear that and said, "I'm just looking for people who can give the world light since it is dark everywhere. The whole world would thank you if you two would like to take the responsibility. From today on, the brother lightens the earth in the daytime, and the sister lightens the earth at night.

Before the granny finished her words, the sister said, "Granny, I'm afraid of going out at night."

The granny said, "Well, you go out in the daytime."

"I'm shy in the daytime." The sister said.

The granny said, "I'll give you a package of embroidery needles. You'll prick his eyes if anyone dares to look at you."

Then, the white hair granny gave a package of embroidery needles to her, and a silver flower to her brother. From then on, the sister became the shinning sun, lighting the earth in the daytime. Until now, she would scatter the embroidery needle to prick anyone's eyes who wants to look at her directly, while the brother became the shinning moon, lighting the earth at night.

With the sun and the moon in the sky, there were days and night on the earth. Gradually, there were trees, flowers, grass and animals. The three brothers on the ground were afraid that their brother and sister in the sky could see them naked, tried to hunt animals and wore trousers made of the animal's skin. In hunting, they imitated the golden birds nest and learned to build houses with branches. Since they had houses to live in, they began to cut down the trees, till the virgin land, and grow crops.

# 洪水朝天

三个兄弟一连三天砍林开荒，可是头天砍下树木、开出荒地，第二天又还原了。第二天砍下树木、开出荒地，第三天又还原了。三个兄弟商量说："我们白天辛辛苦苦干活，晚上是谁捣鬼呢？让我们躲起来看看。"

于是，他们又砍了树林、开出荒地。第四天晚上，大哥拿着长矛，二哥拿着大刀，三哥拿着木棒，躲在老林里守候着。半夜三更的时候，跳出一只大青蛙。那大青蛙在砍下的树林旁边跳几跳，倒下的树木"刷"一下立起来，全都复原了；它在开出的荒地上抓几抓，荒地也复原了。这时，三个兄弟看得清楚。大哥端起长矛冲出来，大声吼着："刺死它！"

二哥举起大刀跳出来，呼喊着："砍死它！"

三哥丢了木棒，连忙跑出来拦住两个哥哥说："杀不得，杀不得。它深更半夜干这种事，一定有来历。让我问一问。"

# The Great Flood

The three brothers cut down the trees and tilled the virgin land for three days in a row, but the trees and land they worked with on the first day returned to their original form on the second. And it was the same case on the second and third days. The three brothers thought that, "We work so hard in the daytime, and who played tricks on us at night? Let's hide and find it out."

So they cut down the trees and tilled the virgin land on the fourth day. At night, they hid in the forest and waited with a spear in the eldest brother's hand, a big knife in the second brother's, and a wooden stick in the third brother's. At midnight, a big frog jumped out and leaped a few jumps beside the trees that were cut down, then, the fallen trees stood up suddenly, and all were in its original condition; and when the frog grabbed a few scratching in the virgin land, it recovered too. The three brothers saw it clearly, and the eldest brother rushed out with his spear and shouted, "Stab it to death!"

The second brother jumped out with his big knife and shouted, "Hack it to death!"

The third brother threw away his stick and hurried to stop his two brothers and said, "Stop, stop! There must be some special reasons since it did such a thing as this at midnight. Let me ask him why."

说话间，那大青蛙往地上一蹲，变成一个白胡子老头。三哥走上前去问道："老人家，我们三兄弟什么时候得罪你，让你生这么大的气？"

老头说："我看你心地善良，是个老实人，就实话告诉你吧：三天以后，洪水要朝天啦，你们砍林开荒全白做！"

三兄弟一听，都吓呆了，连忙问："老人家，那我们怎么逃脱呢？"

白胡子老头说："地上万物都无法逃脱，只有高大无朋的'巴杂甲初崩'① 大树能够独存。老大用绳子把自己拴在'巴杂甲初崩'大树底下，老二用绳子把自己拴在'巴杂甲初崩'大树中间，老三用细针粗线缝个黑牛皮口袋，口袋里装上狗、猫、公鸡和三个石头、二十七个粑粑，然后爬上高高的'巴杂甲初崩'大树顶端，钻进皮口袋里，躲在树梢的'晓鸡穷'② 大窝里，听见石头落地的声音就可以走出来了。"

三个兄弟按照白胡子老头的吩咐，做完了一切准备。

---

① 巴杂甲初崩：普米族传说中的树神，长在大地正中，与天地同生。

② 晓鸡穷：神鸟，兼有凤凰和大鹏的特征。

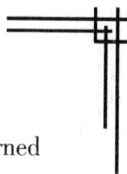

Just then, the big frog squatted on the ground and turned into a white-bearded old man. The third brother went up to him and asked, "Could you tell us what we had done that made you so angry and do like this, Grand old man?"

The old man said, "I know that you are kind and honest, and tell you the truth: three days later, the great flood is coming, and it is of no use cutting down the trees and tilling the virgin land."

The three brothers were shocked, and asked, "How can we escape from the flood, Grand old man?"

The white-bearded old man said, "Nothing on the earth can escape from it except the tallest tree named Bazajiachubeng①. The oldest brother could tie himself to the bottom of the tree with a rope, the second could tie himself to the trunk of the tree with a rope, and the third brother could climb up to the top of the tree with a cowhide pocket sewed with fine needle and thick thread, and filled with a dog, a cat, a rooster, three stones, and twenty-seven rice cakes. To climb into the cowhide pocket and hide in Xiaojiqiong's② nest on the top of the tree, you could not go out of it until you hear the sound of the falling stones.

Following his words, the three brothers finished all the preparatory work.

---

① Bazajiachubeng is a holy tree in the legend of Pumi ethnic group, which grows in the center of the Earth, and was born with the Heaven and the Earth.

② Xiaojiqiong is a holy bird with the characteristics of phoenix and roc.

过了三天，凶猛的洪水黑天黑地冲来了。老三躲在高高"晓鸡穷"窝里问："大哥，洪水到什么地方了？"

大哥的声音从很远的树底下传来："洪水从四面八方涌来，到脚底下了。"

过了一个时辰，老三又问："大哥，洪水到什么地方了？"

大哥惊慌的声音从很远的树底传来："洪水涌到脖子了！"

再过一个时辰，老三又问，大哥没有声音回答；他已经被洪水淹死了。

第二天，老三又问二哥："二哥，洪水涨到什么地方了？"

二哥从大树中间回答说："洪水到脚底下了。"

过了一个时辰，老三又问："二哥，洪水涨到什么地方了！"

二哥惊恐地回答说："洪水涨齐脖子了啊！"

二哥刚说完，只听得一阵巨浪轰响，二哥也被洪水淹没了。

洪水涨呀涨，巨浪翻又翻，眼看就要涨到"巴杂甲初崩"大树尖尖了。汹涌的巨浪向"晓鸡穷"窝底撞击着，发出万雷震吼的响声。

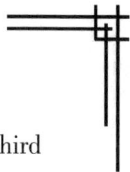

Three days later, the great flood came fiercely. The third brother asked from the nest on the top of the tree, "Eldest brother, where is the flood?"

The voice of the eldest brother came from the bottom of the tree, "The flood is coming everywhere, and now it comes to my feet."

One hour later, the third brother asked again, "Eldest brother, where is the flood now?"

The panic voice of the eldest brother came from the bottom of the tree, "It is coming to my neck!"

Another hour later, the third brother asked the question again, but there was no answer, for the eldest brother was drowned.

On the second day, the third brother asked the second one, "My brother, where did the flood go?"

The second brother answered from the trunk of the tree, "The flood is coming to my feet."

After an hour, the third brother asked, "My brother, where did the flood go?"

The second brother replied in horror, "it is coming to my neck."

Hardly had the second brother finished his words when a huge wave came, and he was drowned by the flood too.

The flood went up and up, and the waves turned over and over again, and it almost rose to the top of the tall tree. The rough waves dashed on the bottom of the nest, and the sound roared in the sky.

老三躲在牛皮口袋里静静地听着。过了好些时辰，波浪逐渐消歇，他便取出黑石头丢下去，只听见"咚"的一声水响，洪水还没退走呢。又过了很长一段时间，老三丢下黄石头，远远地仍听见石头落水的声音，洪水还没退完。再过了很长时间，老三丢下白石头，这时，从很远的地方传来石头碰石头的响声，接着又传来石头落水的声音，它告诉老三，洪水快退完了。于是，老三把公鸡丢下去，公鸡落地马上伸长脖子"喔喔喔"地叫起来，洪水很快退走。接着，老三把狗丢下去，狗一落地就"岗岗公公"叫起来，被洪水泡软的大地，随着狗的叫声，马上出现坑坑洼洼的高山峡谷。最后，老三把猫儿丢下去了，猫儿一落地就"咪妙——咪妙——"地叫，那些还没有来得及变成高山峡谷的大地，随着猫儿的叫声，又全变成平平展展的土地。如今地上有高山峡谷和平川坝子，就是这样来的。老三丢下鸡、狗、猫后，从皮口袋里钻出来，睁眼望去，大地已经没有洪水了。他想回到地上，可是"巴杂甲初崩"大树那样高，他怎么下去呢？这时，窝里的"晓鸡穷"展翅欲飞，老三心里一亮，突然有了主意，他发现窝里有"晓鸡穷"吃剩下的马鹿骨头，便拿起两根腿骨，骑上巨大的"晓鸡穷"，用力敲打它的脊背。"晓鸡穷"被敲打得疼了，便展开遮天翅膀飞出窝去。那"晓鸡穷"展翅奋飞，越飞越高，越飞越远，老三只得不停地敲打着奋飞的翅膀。不知飞了多长时间，"晓鸡穷"慢慢落下来，老三这才回到大地上。

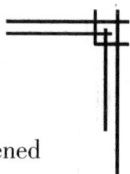

Hiding in the cowhide pocket, the third brother listened quietly. After some time, the surging waves gradually died away. The third brother took out a black stone and threw it out. With a sound of "Duang" in the water, he knew the flood had not yet withdrawn. After a long time, the third brother dropped the yellow stone and heard the sound of the stone falling far away. After another long time, the third brother dropped the white stone. And this time, he heard the sound of a stone hitting another, and then the sound of the stone falling into the water, which indicated that the flood had almost gone. Hence, the third brother threw the rooster out of the nest, which crowed with its neck stretching out as soon as it landed on the ground, and the flood subsided quickly. And then, the third brother threw the dog out of the nest, and it barked as soon as it landed on the ground, which was already softened by the flood. With the sound of the dogs barks, the high mountains and deep canyons came into being. At last, the third brother threw the cat out of the nest, and it mewed as soon as it landed on the ground. With the meows of the cat, the land that had not yet become mountains and canyons then turned flat. The mountains, the canyons, the plains and the dams on the earth came into being. After throwing the rooster, the dog and the cat out of the nest, the third brother climbed out of the cowhide pocket, and saw no flood on the ground as far as he could see. He wanted to go back to the ground, but how could he go down since the tree was so tall? Just then, the Xiaojiqiong tried to fly away from the nest. Seeing this, the third brother suddenly had an idea. He found some bones of the red deer eaten by the Xiaojiqiong, picked up two of them, rode on the huge Xiaojiqiong and beat its back heavily. The Xiaojiqiong was beaten and felt painful, so it stretched its wings and flied out of the nest. It flied higher and farther, and the third brother had to beat its wings without a stop. Nobody knew how long they flew, and finally, it slowed down and the third brother came back to the ground.

# 青蛙舅舅

洪水翻天后的大地，什么也没有。孤单单的老三四面望望，真伤心！他一个人在地上走呀走，一连几天，饭吃不着，肚子饿得很。

有一天，他走进阴森的峡谷里，来到一座大岩石下面的岩洞口，看见两个生不麻①对坐着递东西吃。生不麻都是独脚人样，上眼皮大得出奇，不仅遮住眼睛，还垂到地上盖着脚。老三饥饿难忍，便站在生不麻中间，把它们递送的东西接过来吃。过了一阵，两个生不麻一齐说："我怎么没吃到你递来的东西？"

刚说完，又一齐回答："都递过来啦，你不是拿去了吗？"

男生不麻皱皱鼻子说："不对，我嗅到了人味，一定有生人来这里。"

女生不麻说："大地上洪水翻天，人都淹死完了，哪还有人！"

说罢，伸出双手，从脚背上捧起眼皮一看，老三正狼吞虎咽地吃着东西呢。生不麻张开大嘴，一口就把老三吞进肚里。

---

① 生不麻：指妖怪。

96

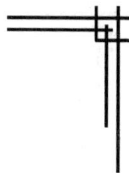

# Uncle Frog

Nothing was left after the great flood, and the lonely brother was very sad to look around him. He walked alone for several days, and felt very hungry for eating nothing.

One day, he went into a gloomy canyon, and arrived at the entrance of a cave below a big rock, where he saw two Shengbuma① (monsters) facing to each other and eating something. The monsters were like one-foot human beings, with large upper eyelids covering their eyes and hanging down to their feet. The third brother was so hungry that he stood in the middle of the two monsters and took the food they handed to each other. After a while, the two monsters said at the same time, "Why could I not get what you give me?"

And then, they answered at the same time, "I've given it to you. Haven't you taken it?"

The male monster wrinkled up his nose and said, "There must be something wrong. There must be a human being here for I can smell it."

The female monster said, "The human beings were drowned in the great flood. How can there be a human?"

Then, the female monster stretched out her hands to lift up her eyelids from her feet and saw the third brother devouring like a wolf. She opened her big mouth and swallowed him into the belly.

---

① Shengbuma: a monster in the Pumi dialect.

这时，正给生不麻推磨的青蛙看见了一切，它立即停下磨来，伤心地沉默着。两个生不麻听不到推磨的声音，便吼叫起来："什么时候了，还不赶快推磨，误了我们吃饭，你背罪不起！"

青蛙悲哀地回答说："我有伤心的事呀，无心给你们推磨了。"

两个生不麻很奇怪，平时蹦蹦跳跳的青蛙，怎么有伤心事呢？便问："勤快的青蛙，你有什么伤心事，说给我们听听。"

青蛙说："我的外甥来看我，面没见着，就被你们吞吃了，你们不吐出我的外甥，我再也不给你们干活。"

生不麻心想：好久没吃到人肉，刚吃下又吐出来怎么行，便说："你不干就走吧，还有蛇、乌鸦和喜鹊三个仆人呢。"

青蛙走了。生不麻叫蛇去推磨，蛇缠在磨把上，只会缠，不能使磨盘转动。生不麻又喊乌鸦去推，乌鸦用嘴壳衔着磨把，只会衔，也不能使磨盘转动。最后，它去请喜鹊推，喜鹊站在磨盘上"喳喳喳"地叫，只会叫，也无法使磨盘转动。蛇、乌鸦和喜鹊三个仆人都不会推磨，生不麻没东西吃了，想了想只得再去请青蛙。青蛙说："你把我外甥吐出来，我才推。"生不麻没办法，便说："你灌我三桶灶灰汤，用磨盘砸我的背，我就能吐出来。"

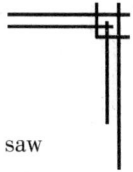

At this time, the frog who was grinding for the monsters saw it and stopped immediately, silent and sad. The two monsters heard no sound of grinding and shouted, "Watch your time! Why don't you grind? You can't afford to delay our meals."

The frog answered sadly, "I am so sad that I can't grind for you."

The two monsters were very curious and wondering why the happy frog could be so sad. Then they asked, "You hard-working frog, tell us what makes you so sad?"

The frog answered, "My nephew came to see me, but before I could see him, you have eaten him. I won't work for you unless you spit him out."

The monster thought that how I can have eaten the human flesh and spat it out since I haven't had it for a long time. Then she said, "You can go if you don't want to do it. I still have three servants: a snake, a crow and a magpie."

The frog had gone. The monsters required the snake to push the millstone. The snake twisted itself around the millstone handle, but the millstone didn't move. The monsters then asked the crow to push the millstone. The crow held the millstone handle in its mouth, but the millstone didn't move. At last, they invited the magpie to push the millstone. The magpie stood on the millstone and chirped, but the millstone didn't move. The snake, the crow and the magpie were unable to push the millstone, so the monsters had nothing to eat, and had to ask the frog for help. The frog said, "I won't grind until you spit out my nephew." The monsters had no way to go and said that, "I can spit him out only when you fill me with three barrels of ash soup and beat my back with the millstone."

青蛙照着办了，老三果然被生不麻吐出来。可一看，耳朵却不在。青蛙说："你不吐出耳朵，我还是不推。"

生不麻又再让青蛙灌三桶灶灰汤，在背上猛砸磨盘，这样，老三的耳朵才被吐出来，可已经不是原来的样子。生不麻用手捏捏扯扯以后，随便黏在老三的头两侧。如今我们人的耳朵成这个形状，就是那样来的。

老三死里复生，吃了大亏。青蛙把他送出岩洞，悄悄指点说："你不要再往深山峡谷里走啦，那是妖魔鬼怪住的地方，它们会吃掉你。你要往高山冒烟的地方走，那里才是神仙居住的地方，他们会帮助你。"

老三很感激青蛙，说："世上最大不过舅舅，永远不得罪舅舅。"老三的后代从此也记住了青蛙的恩情。所以，普米人至今还叫青蛙"阿克巴底"①，见着青蛙要让路，遇着青蛙要把它请到上面，这个老规矩从那时一直传到现在。

---

① 阿克巴底：普米语，青蛙舅舅。

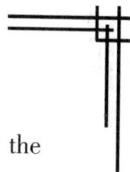

The frog did so, and the third brother was spat out by the monsters, but without ears. The frog said, "I won't grind until you spit out his ears."

The monsters asked the frog to do the same again, and then the ears were spat out, but the shape of which was not what they used to be. The monsters then pinched the ears and stuck them to the two sides of the third brother's head. That is why nowadays the ears of human being are like that.

The third brother suffered a lot and had a narrow escape. The frog sent him out of the cave and whispered to him that, "Don't go along the canyons, where the devils live, and they will eat you. Go to the mountains shrouded in mist, where the Gods live, and they will help you."

The third brother was very grateful to the frog, and he said, "The uncle is the greatest man in the world, and he can never be offended." From then on, the descendants of the third brother kept the words in their mind. Therefore, the frog is called Ahkebadi① by the Pumi people now. The tradition of giving way to the frog when they see it has been followed from that time to the present.

---

① Ahkebadi means uncle Frog in the Pumi dialect.

# 和仙女成亲

老三按照青蛙的话，向着高山走呀走，走到一座大山顶上。远远地有一缕青烟缭绕，他便径直向那青烟走去；走近了，却是一座房子。老三轻轻地推了门，里面没有人，只见桌上摆着三碗清水。老三口渴了，他就每碗喝了一口；走了这么多路，老三也累了，他就蜷在火铺下面休息。原来，那房子是天神木多丁巴的三个姑娘住的。天神木多丁巴看见地上洪水翻天后，人类被淹死完了，只有妖魔鬼怪活下来，便派三个姑娘来到大地，斩妖灭魔。三个仙女白天出去征讨妖魔，黄昏又回来休息。桌上的三碗清水，便是三姊妹临走前凉下的神水。

黄昏时候，三个仙女回来了。她们一进门就齐声说："我碗里的水被谁喝了一口？"

大姐说："有生人气味，一定是人进屋里来过。"

二姐说："洪水翻天后，大地上人都绝灭了，怎么会有人呢？"

# Marry A Fairy

Following the frog's instructions, the third brother walked for a long time to the top of a high mountain. Far away from it, he saw a wisp of smoke, and he went straight towards it until he saw a house. The third brother pushed the door open, but nobody was in, except for three bowls of water on the table. He was so thirsty that he drank a little of each bowl. He was also very tired for walking a long way, so he huddled up under the fire bed to rest. The house turned out to be the place where the three daughters of the God Muduodingba lived. The God saw that all the human beings were drowned in the great flood, but the demons and ghosts survived, so he sent her three daughters to the earth to kill them. During the day time, the three fairies went out to look for the demons and ghosts, and came back home to rest at dusk. The three bowls of water on the table were the cool divine water when they left home.

At dusk, the three fairies came back. As soon as they entered the house, they asked at the same time, "Who has drunk the water in my bowl?"

The eldest fairy said, "There must be someone coming in the house, for I can smell the stranger."

The second fairy said, "How can anyone be here since all the human beings were extinct after the great flood?"

三妹说："是呀，人种都绝灭了，哪会有人呢？"

三个仙姑娘你一言，我一语，个个都觉得奇怪。躲在火铺下面的老三听了，忍不住笑出声来。仙女们一听是人的声音，便齐声叫道："你是谁？快出来！"

在火铺下面的老三说："姑娘呵，我身上一丝不挂，没穿衣服没穿裤子呀，叫我怎么出来？"

大姐听完，丢下一匹麻布，用口一吹，麻布变成衣服了；二姐丢下一匹麻布，用口一吹，变成包头帕了；三妹丢下麻布，用口一吹，变成鞋子和绑腿了。然后，三个仙女齐声说："快穿上衣服出来吧！"

老三在火铺下穿好了一切，随后走出来。三姊妹一看，原来是个英俊高大的小伙子！她们很高兴，都说："我们以为大地上人都灭绝了，想不到你还活着，那就跟我们住下吧。"

于是，老三跟仙女们一起生活。

三个仙女每天练习射箭，老三闲着没事做。有一天，仙女们问老三："你会射箭吗？"

老三说："以前射过，可是手太笨。"

仙女们说："伸出手来让我们看看。"

The youngest fairy said, "It's right! How can we see a human since they were extinct?"

The three fairies felt very strange when they were talking about it. Overhearing the conversation, the third brother couldn't help laughing. The fairies heard the voice of a human being and shouted together, "Who are you? Come out quickly!"

Under the fire bed the third brother said, "Girls, how can I come out since I'm naked with no clothes and pants."

Hearing this, the eldest fairy threw him a piece of linen, which was turned into a coat with a blow from her mouth; the second fairy threw him another piece of linen, which was turned into a head scarf with a blow from her mouth; the youngest fairy threw him another piece of linen, which was turned into a pair of shoes and leggings with a blow from her mouth. And then, the three fairies shouted together, "Put on the clothes and come out!"

The third brother put on the clothes under the fire bed, and walked out of it. The three fairies saw a tall and handsome young man and said happily, "We haven't expected to see you alive for we thought that all the human beings on the earth were extinct. Stay with us since you are here."

Thus, the third brother lived with the three fairies.

Every day, the three fairies were busy with archery practice while the third brother had nothing to do. One day, the fairies asked him, "Can you shoot an arrow?"

The third brother answered, "I once shot, but I was very clumsy."

The fairies said, "Stretch out your hands and let us have a look."

老三伸出手，五个指头齐齐整整一般长，大拇指与其他四个指头黏在一起。仙女们看了后说："让我们给你修整修整。"

于是，大姐拿了把砍刀，把老三的手指砍成长短不一；二姐拿了把柴刀，把老三的大拇指与其他四指分开。人类的手变成现在这样子，就是当时仙女们修整的。

修好了手，三姊妹给老三一张弓，一壶箭，让他先射一箭看看。老三拿了弓箭，一只斑鸠正从空中飞过。他搭上箭，不慌不忙瞄准斑鸠射去。斑鸠应声落下。三姊妹争着去捡，最后，还是三妹捡着，一看，老三的箭正正地把斑鸠的下嘴壳和上嘴壳连着穿通了。从此，老三和三姊妹一起天天练习射箭。老三进步很快，箭术越练越精。为了再试老三的箭术，三姊妹拿来一根绣花针插在门坎上，叫老三一箭穿针眼。老三搭上箭，瞄准针眼射去。第一箭偏了，射断了针眼，第二箭不偏不斜，箭头正正地穿过针眼飞出去。仙女们高兴地说："你的箭术很高。从今以后，你可以在地上和那些妖魔鬼怪打仗去。"

He showed them his hands. The five fingers were of the same length, with the thumb stuck to the other four fingers. The fairies took a look and said, "Let's shape the hands for you."

So the eldest fairy took out a hacking knife, chopping his fingers in different length. The second fairy took out a chopper, separating his thumb from the other four fingers. Now, the human hands are like this just because the fairies had pruned them.

After shaping the hands, the three fairies gave the third brother a bow and a pot of arrows, and asked him to have a try. The third brother took out the bow and an arrow, aiming at a turtle dove which was flying in the air. He took the arrow and shot the turtle dove calmly. The turtle dove fell down, and the three fairies were eager to pick it up. At last, the youngest fairy took it and found that the arrow crossed the lower and upper parts of its bill completely. Hence, the third brother and the three fairies practiced archery every day. The third brother made very rapid progress, and the more he practiced, the better his archery became. In order to test his level, the three fairies pinned an embroidery needle to the threshold, and asked the third brother to shoot an arrow through the eye of the needle. The third brother put an arrow to his bow, aiming at the eye of the needle. The first arrow missed the target and broke the eye of the needle. The second one shot through the eye of the needle directly. The fairies were very happy and said, "You are very good at archery. From now on, your archery is good enough to fight against the demons and ghosts on the earth."

于是，老三和三个仙女经常出去与妖魔征战。

有一次，三个仙女告诉老三：不远的西方有两个大海。一个海水像牛奶一样雪白，一个海水像锅烟一样漆黑。白色的海子是吉祥的象征，黑色的海子是邪恶的象征。吉祥与邪恶经常战斗。谁要是消灭了邪恶，天下生灵就安全了，世间就会感激他。老三听后问道："要怎样才能消灭那漆黑的邪恶呢?"

三个仙女说："你坐在两个大海交界处，白色海浪翻腾时，你心里默念着'泽泽羊克依'①。黑色海浪翻卷时，你就准备好弓箭，那巨大的黑色漩涡中会涌出一个骑着黑马的大汉，大汉胸前有个土蜂大的光点在飞快旋转，你只要射中那旋转的土蜂光点，你就能够消灭邪恶。"

老三听后，决心消灭邪恶。他带上弓箭，往西方走了很久，来到黑白海子交界处。他按照仙女们的指点，坐在两个大海交界的中间，准备好弓箭等待着。不一会儿，黑色的海水动荡起来，接着掀起翻天黑浪。随着浪卷涛涌，一个骑着黑马的大汉出现在黑海中心。老三拉满弓，箭头准准地瞄着黑大汉胸前那飞快旋转的土蜂光点，然后一松手，只听得"当"的一声巨响，黑大汉立即从马上跌落下去，黑色海水也飞快下落，四周的山谷发出动地震天的哀叫。白色海浪这时翻腾不息，老三不停地念着"泽泽羊克依"。

① 泽泽羊克依：普米语，吉祥如意。

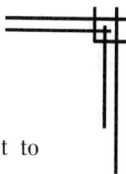

So the third brother and the three fairies often went out to fight against the demons and ghosts.

Once, the three fairies told the third brother, "Not far from here in the west, there are two seas, one as white as milk and the other as black as the bottom of a pot. The white sea is the sign of auspiciousness, and the black one is the sign of wickedness. They often fight with each other. The whole world will be grateful to anyone who can destroy the wickedness and keep the creatures on the earth safe." The third brother heard it and asked, "How can the wickedness be destroyed?"

The three fairies said, "You can sit at the junction of the two seas, and recite in your heart Zezeyangkeyi① when the white waves are rolling, and prepare your arrow when the black waves were rolling. A tall man will ride a black horse coming from the center of the black whirlpool, and a big light spot, as big as a scoliid, will rotate swiftly in front of his chest. If you can shot the whirling light spot, you will destroy the wickedness."

The third brother heard that and decided to destroy the wickedness. He was armed with his bow and arrows, walked towards the west, and got to the junction of the black and white seas. Following the fairies instructions, he sat there and waited with his bow and arrows. After a while, the black sea became turbulent, and the black waves were rolling up to the sky. With the rolling waves, a tall man riding a black horse appeared in the center of the black sea. The third brother drew the bow to its full length, aimed at the light spot in front of the man's chest, and loosened his hand. With a big sound, the black man fell down the horse immediately, the black water subsided quickly, and the surrounding valleys trembled with the mournful cries. At this time, the white waves rolled up and down, and the third brother recited the Zezeyangkeyi again and again.

---

①  Zezeyangkeyi means good luck in Pumi dialect.

老三消灭了邪恶，背着弓箭往回走。三个仙女早已来到半路迎接。大姐说："我们过去天天和邪恶的魔鬼打仗，总是打不过，现在你消灭了它，天下的生灵安全了，我们的愿望实现了：为了感激你，我们愿意做你的妻子。你站在高高的山丫口上，我们跑过来，你喜欢谁，只要碰一下就行。"

老三爬上山丫口去，他站在那里望着。不一会儿，一只老虎直奔山丫口，老三见老虎来了，吓得往旁边一闪，不敢动。接着，一只豹子又飞奔过来，老三一看是豹子，也不敢动。最后，一条大蟒爬过山丫口来了。老三想，再不碰，就没有机缘了，他慌慌忙忙用手里的弓碰了碰蟒尾，大蟒立即变成三姑娘。三妹对老三说："我大姐一颗麦子够做九个粑粑，我二姐一颗麦子能够做七个粑粑，你都不要；我一颗麦子只能做三个粑粑，你却要了。你为啥不要那聪明能干的大姐和二姐，偏偏选我呢？"

老三高兴地拉着三妹说："你也聪明能干。一颗麦子能做三个粑粑，你一个，我一个，还剩下一个，够吃了。"

于是，人间的老三与天上的仙女三姑娘成了一家。

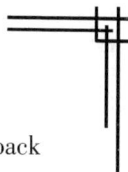

After destroying the wickedness, the third brother went back with his bow and arrows on his back. The three fairies had come to greet him on his way home. The eldest fairy said, "We used to fight against the devils every day but failed. Now that you made it, the creatures on the earth are safe, and our wishes come true. Thanks to your help, we are happy to be your wife. You stand on the top of the pass to the mountain, and we will run to you one by one, and you just touch the one you like."

The third brother climbed to the top of the pass to the mountain, standing there and watching. After a while, a tiger ran to him straightly. He was frightened to jump aside, and didn't dare to move. Then, a leopard ran to him straightly. He saw it and didn't move either. Finally, a python crawled across the pass. The third brother thought that there would be no chance if he missed this time. He hurriedly touched the python with his bow on its tail, and it turned into the third fairy at once. She said to him, "My eldest sister can make nine barley cakes out of a grain of barley, and my second sister can make seven, but you haven't chosen them. I can make only three, but you have chosen me to be your wife. My sisters are more capable than me, and can you tell me why you chose me?"

The third brother held the third fairy's hands and said, "You are as capable as them. It is enough to make three barley cakes out of a grain of barley, one for you, one for me and with one left."

Thus, the third brother from the earth and the third fairy from the heaven got married.

# 百鸟求种

老三和三姑娘成家后，三姑娘从父亲家里带来麦子、荞子等种子，他们一起生活，一起劳动，后来生了一个姑娘，取名索拉耳吉。索拉耳吉十三岁，要行成年礼啦，按规矩要去娘家报喜。可娘家在天上，凡人不能去，只有三姑娘才能去。老三依依不舍。临走时，三姑娘对老三说："我去了，你没有伴，我给你一个陪伴的人吧。"

她于是抓了一把灶灰捏几下，吹口仙气，变出一个姑娘来。那灰姑娘陪伴着老三，尽心尽力伺候他。日子久了，灰姑娘也生出了儿女。据说，我们现在的人抓抓身子，会在身上抓出灰灰，就是这样来的。

天上一天，地上三年。三姑娘在天上舅舅家玩一天，大姐家玩一天，又陪二姐玩一天，在娘家只住了一天，这样地上就过了十二年。老三与灰姑娘一起生活，渐渐把三姑娘忘了。到十二年那天，三姑娘要回来了，去接她的只有女儿索拉耳吉。那一天，索拉耳吉走了很远的路，走到高高的山顶时，看见白云滚滚，天光地明，三姑娘从娘家带着牛奶、吉祥的海螺花和种子瓜果等走回来。半途中，她看见自己的女儿来迎接，便拿出桃梨水果给女儿吃，可索拉耳吉没有吃，她把水果装在怀里。三姑娘问："你为啥不吃呢?"

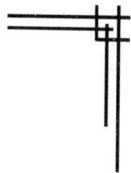

# Hundred of Birds Asking for Seeds

The third fairy took many seeds, such as barley seeds and buckwheat seeds, from her father's home when she married the third brother. They lived together and worked together. Later, they had a baby girl named Suolaerji. As a tradition, an adulthood ceremony would be held for her and reported to her grandparents when she was 13 years old. But her grandparent's home was in the heaven, and nobody could go except for the third fairy. Before leaving, the third fairy said to the third brother who was very reluctant to let her go, "I'll go back to my parents home, and I'll make a companion for you since you are alone at home."

So she took a handful of stove ash and blew it into a lady. The ash lady accompanied the third brother and waited on him with all her heart. After a long time, the ash lady also gave birth to children. It is said that is the reason why we can see the ash falling when we scratch our body.

A day in the heaven equaled three years on the earth. The third fairy stayed for one day in her uncles, for another in her eldest sisters, for another in her second sister's, and for only one day in her parents' home. So twelve years passed on the earth. The third brother lived with the ash lady and forgot the third fairy gradually. Twelve years later, when the third fairy came back, the only one to greet her was her daughter Suolaerji. On that day, Suolaerji walked a long way to the top of the mountain, and saw the white clouds and the sunshine in the sky, and her mother, who took milk, auspicious conch flowers, seeds and fruit with her, walked back. On her way home, the third fairy saw her daughter coming to greet her. She gave the peach and pear to her daughter, and Suolaerji did not eat but keep them in her arms. The third fairy asked, "Why didn't you have it?"

索拉耳吉说："我要带回去给家里的灰弟灰妹吃。"

三姑娘马上停下脚步。她不走了，她明白：自己的丈夫已经跟灶灰姑娘成了一家。于是她对人间充满怨恨，决定回到天上去。折回之前，她要把自己带来的粮食全部带走。这时跟在她周围的百鸟全都请求说："三姑娘，请你留点五谷粮食给我们吃吧，我们要生活哇。"

在百鸟请求下，三姑娘每样粮食留了一点。苞谷原先每个节都长一包，现在苞谷只结一两包。小麦等作物原先从底到顶都长籽粒，现在只剩下头顶上的一小点，留给百鸟吃。瓜瓜和蔓菁三姑娘拿不走，她就诅咒说："你们背起来像石头一样，吃起来像水一样。"

现在的瓜瓜蔓菁背起来很重，吃进肚里不经饿，就是这样来的。

# 狗找来了谷种

三姑娘一气之下，收完了所有的粮食。地上的人没有吃的了，只有跟雀子争粮吃。生活一天不如一天。

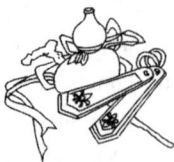

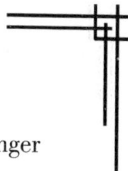

Suolaerji answered, "I'll take it back home to my younger brothers and sisters."

The third fairy stopped at once and understood: her husband and the ash lady had got married. So she began to resent the world and decided to go back to the heaven. Before she went back, she wanted to take back all the food she brought with her. At that time, all the birds around her pleaded, "Please leave us some grains and crops, and we have to make a living."

At the request of the hundred of birds, the third fairy left a little of each grain and crop. The maize originally grew a cob on each joint, but now there is only one or two on the top. Such crop as wheat used to grow long grains from the bottom to the top, but now only a few grains on the top are left for the birds. As to the melons and the turnip, the third fairy could not take away with her, so she cursed, "You would be as heavy as stones to carry on backs, and as tasteless as water to have."

Nowadays, it is very heavy to carry melons and turnips, and people may feel hungry easily shortly after they have had them.

## The Dog Had Found the Grain Seeds

In a burst of anger, the third fairy had harvested all the crops, so the people on the earth had nothing to eat but to compete with the flocks for food, and their living conditions devastated day by day.

有一年，老三过不下去，就烧了清香，向天神求种子，可仙女们不给。住在天上的太阳妹妹知道了，便主动向天神和仙女求情，最后，求到一小点青稞种和一条狗。老三想再要点谷种，便请太阳妹妹再去说情。太阳妹妹第二次去说情，就惹怒了天神，天神放出天狗咬太阳妹妹。老三帮不了妹妹的忙，便回到家里赶紧敲锣打鼓放鞭炮，撵天狗。现在太阳落难时，地上的人要敲锣打鼓放鞭炮，老规矩就是这样来的。老三的弟弟月亮也被看管起来，每个月有好几个夜晚不能出来。

老三没办法在天上要到谷种，只得在地上去寻找。他带着狗四处走啊走，走了一月又一月，走了一年又一年，忍饥挨饿，跋山涉水，都没找到。不知是哪一年，老三和狗来到东方的汪洋大海边，在那里，他听说：大海的对岸，全都居住着神仙，那里有谷子。老三望着一片汪洋，心里想着怎么过去。他想呀想，没有办法，只好对狗说："大海那边有谷子，可我过不去。要是你能过去就好了。"

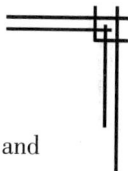

One year, the third brother could not make a living, and burned incense to prey to the God of Heaven for seeds, but the fairies didn't agree to give him the seeds. The sun, the younger sister living in the sky, knew it and asked willingly the God and the fairies for help. At last, some highland barley seeds and a dog were given to the third brother. But he wanted to get some grain seeds, and asked the sun to intercede for him again, which made the God very angry, and let out the heavenly hound to bite her. The third brother had no way to help the sun, and ran back home quickly to beat the gongs and drums and set off firecrackers to frighten away the heavenly hound. Now when the sun is in trouble, the people on the earth would beat the gangs and drums, and let off firecrackers, which has become an old tradition. The moon, the sun's younger brother, was also under control, and could not come out for several nights every month.

The third brother could not get the grain seeds from the heaven, and had to look for them on the earth. He took the dog with him and walked for month after month, year after year, enduring hunger and traveling across mountains and rivers, but failed. One year, as nobody knew which year it was, the third brother and the dog went to the great ocean near the East, where he heard that, at the other side of the ocean, there lived some gods who had grain seeds. Seeing the vast ocean, the third brother thought over and over again and could not find out a way to cross it. Then he had to say to the dog, "There are grain seeds on the other side of the ocean, but I can't get there. If only you could cross it."

那条狗摇着尾巴，竟然神奇地说出话来："我能够游过去，你要我做什么？"

老三很高兴，忙说："你游过汪洋大海，上了岸，看见有人晒谷子，就在谷堆上滚几滚，把谷种带点回来。"

狗听了老三的吩咐，便跳下海向对岸游。狗游上岸后，身上的毛全湿了。它看见有人晒谷子，便跑到谷堆上打了几个滚，于是全身都粘满谷子，然后它就游回来。等在岸边的老三，把狗抱在怀里收谷种，可身上粘的谷子都被海水冲掉了，只有脊背毛里还留着一小把。老三高兴极了。他带着那一小把谷子回到家，赶忙撒下去，终于有了收获。他没忘记狗的恩情，每逢收新谷以后，都要先给狗喂米饭，这个风俗就从那时兴起，直到现在都是这样：吃大米饭，先要喂给狗。

老三有了谷种，学会了种谷子，从此生活越来越富裕，日子越过越好，子孙也越来越兴旺。

整理者：贺兴泽，和学良，何顺明，王震亚

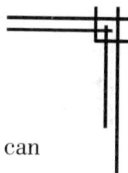

The dog wagged its tail and as if by magic it said, "I can swim across it, and what can I do for you?"

The third brother was very happy to hear that and said, "You swim across the ocean and go ashore. When you see someone drying grains in the sun, roll on the grain piles and take the grain seeds back."

Following the third brother's instructions, the dog jumped into the ocean and swam to the opposite. When the dog went ashore in wet hair, it saw a grain pile in the sun and ran to roll on it to get its body covered with grain seeds. But when it swam back, the third brother, who waited on shore, held the dog in his arms to collect the grain seeds, only to find that there were a handful of seeds left in the hair of the back, and most were washed by the ocean water. The third brother was still very happy and took the seeds back home, sowed them and finally harvested. He didn't forget the dog's favor, and in every harvesting season, he would feed the dog with rice first, which became a custom from then on. Until now, the dog would be fed with rice when the grain is harvested.

With the grain seeds, the third brother learned to grow crops. From then on, his living became better and better, and he had more and more descendants.

Collector: He Xingze, He Xueliang, He Shunming, Wang Zhenya

# 第六章　拉祜族

## 人类的起源

据说远古时代，世间还没有人烟。后来，从葫芦里出来一男一女，哥哥名叫扎底，妹妹名叫娜底。两人周游大地，却不见一个人影。他俩告诉天上的神仙说："地面上冷冷清清，空无一人。"神仙就叫他俩结婚，繁殖人类。兄妹两人感到很害羞，没有答应。

可是兄妹俩因常居住在一起，妹妹就怀了孕。一天，妹妹在南亚河边生下了一个小孩，却让河水冲走了。神仙发现他俩的脸色不对，便追踪至南亚河边，把淹死了的孩子捡回，用刀割成若干块。先用白布包了一块，就变成了拉祜族；其次用绸布包了一块，变成了汉族；再次用滑绸布包了一块，则变成了傣族；第四用黑布包了一块，就变成了哈尼族；第五红布包了一块，则变成了布朗族；第六用绿布包了一块，便变成了阿克（哈尼族支系）；第七用灰布包了一块，则变成了彝族。

# Chapter Six   Lahu Ethnic Group

## The Origin of Human Being

It is said that in ancient times, there were no human beings on the earth. Later, a brother and his younger sister came out of a gourd, with his name Zhadi and her name Nadi. They two traveled around the earth, but could see nobody. They told the God in the heaven, "The world was too desolate and empty." The God asked them to get marry so as to reproduce the human being, but they were too shy to agree.

However, the brother and his sister lived together and finally the sister became pregnant. One day, the sister gave birth to a child on the bank of the South Asian River, but the water washed the baby away, which made the God feel strange. The God followed them to the river bank, took back the drowned child, and sliced it into pieces with a knife. And then the God wrapped a piece in a white cloth, which became the Lahu people; the second piece in a silk cloth becoming the Han people; the third in a slippery cloth becoming the Dai people; the fourth in a black cloth becoming the Hani people; the fifth in a red cloth becoming the Blang people; the sixth in green cloth becoming the Ake people (a branch of Hani people); and the seventh in grey cloth becoming the Yi people.

（根据龚佩华、王树五《勐海县巴卡囡、贺开两寨拉祜族社会历史调查》中有关拉祜创世神话部分整理。）

整理者：杨毓骧

# 扎罗和娜罗

古时候，没有天地日月星辰，不分白天黑夜，世间黑茫茫一片。宇宙像悬空的蛛网，天神厄莎和他的助手就像蜘蛛居住在蛛网中间。

厄莎同两个助手扎罗、娜罗商量，应该造天造地才好。厄莎便叫扎罗去造天，叫娜罗去造地，他们造了七天七夜，天地就造成了。可是扎罗贪玩，把天造小了；娜罗勤快，把地造得很大，天小地大合不拢。厄莎用藤子做地筋，才把地收拢。从此大地上出现了高山、深沟、大河和洼地。天地造好后，地上红彤彤一片，什么也没有。厄莎种下一粒芭蕉籽，"用绿缎子做芭蕉叶，用绸子做芭蕉杆，用金子银子做芭蕉根，芭蕉树活起来了"。

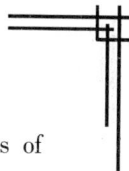

（Rewritten according to the part about creation myths of Lahu Ethnic Group in *The Investigation of the Social History of Lahu Ethnic Group in Bakanan stockade and Hekai stockade of Menghai County*, written by Gong Peihua and Wang Shuwu）

Collector: Yang Yuxiang

# Zhaluo and Naluo

In ancient times, there were no sun, no moon and no stars, nor were there day and night. The whole world was like a dangling web, and the God Esha and his assistants were living in the center of it like spiders.

Esha discussed with his two assistants, Zhaluo and Naluo, to create a heaven and an earth. He asked Zhaluo to make the heaven, and Naluo the earth, which cost them seven days to create. However, Zhaluo made a very small heaven because of his playfulness, while Naluo made a big earth because of her hardwork, so the heaven and the earth could not match. Esha tried to narrow the earth with a tendon made of vine, so there came mountains, canyons, rivers and lowlands. With the creation of the heaven and the earth, the world was red and empty. Esha sowed a Chinese banana seed, "with its leaves made of green satin, its trunk made of silk, and its root made of gold and silver, and the Chinese banana tree became alive".

可是世界上没有水，厄莎又搓下脚汗手汗，做出青蛙和螃蟹，青蛙螃蟹去找到了水；厄莎按照手上的花纹，"开出九十九个出水口，开了九十九条大江河"，大地上便有水了。厄莎又种出参天大树，枝叶和果实纷纷掉落，变成了地上的花鸟木石，水中的鱼虾，空中的飞禽和山上的野兽。万物有了，可是没有人，厄莎经过艰辛劳动种出葫芦，被老鼠啃通，便有了扎笛、娜笛两兄妹。"扎笛、娜笛呀，长得像月亮一样白，长得像太阳一样亮，吃的是最甜的蜜，喝的是最清的水，用的是最好的东西。"扎笛、娜笛长大了，可是不知道成婚，厄莎给他们讲述结婚的道理："太阳月亮手牵手走，天合着地皮，白天晚上不分开。地上的东西，样样配成对，扎笛、娜笛也该配成双，像花木雀儿形影不离。"扎笛、娜笛回答厄莎："我们同由一处来，只能做兄妹，不能成夫妻。""扎笛跑到阿基山，娜笛跑到阿约山，山山相隔看不见。厄莎神法大，把两座高山并一起。""扎笛跑到月亮里躲，娜笛跑到太阳里藏"，厄莎使用各种办法使他们成婚，才繁衍出了九双人来。"天上飞鸟在叫，地上野兽在吼。它们盯着扎笛娜笛，一心想吃人肉。"厄莎知道了，就设法叫飞禽走兽自投罗网，保护九双孩子长成人，并繁衍出后代。

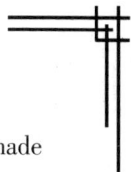

However, there was no water in the world, so Esha made frogs and crabs out of the sweat from her feet and hand to find water. And then, she dug ninety-nine water outlets and ninety-nine rivers according to the lines of the palm, therefore, there was water on the earth. Esha also planted towering trees, and the leaves and fruits fell down and changed into flowers, birds, woods and stones on the ground, fishes and shrimps in the water, flying fowls in the sky, and wild beasts in the mountains. Everything was there but without a human being. Esha worked very hard and produced a gourd, which was gnawed by rats and produced Zhadi and Nadi, a brother and his younger sister. Zhadi and Nadi were as white as the moon and as bright as the sun. They ate the sweetest honey, drank the clearest water, and used the best things. When they grew up, they didn't know that they should get married. Esha told them the reasons of marriage, "The sun and the moon walk hand in hand, the heaven and the earth stay together, the day and the night are not separated, and all the things are paired off. Zhadi and Nadi should be a pair, like flowers and sparrows". But they replied to Esha, "We were born from the same parents, and can't be husband and wife but brother and sister". Then Zhadi ran to the Aji Mountain while Nadi ran to the Ayue Mountain. The two mountains were far away from each other, but Esha applied her magic to draw them together. Then Zhadi ran to hide in the moon while Nadi ran to hide in the sun. Esha tried every means to make them get married and reproduce nine pairs of human beings. The crying fowls in the sky and the roaring beasts on the ground gazed at Zhadi and Nadi, eager to eat the human flesh. Esha knew it and tried to make the fowls and

厄莎又教他们打猎，用扫把草叶割兽皮，用石斧竹刀割肉，然后根据吃猎物的不同方法和叫法分出了九种民族。最后厄莎又教人们盖房子，寻谷种种地，欢欢乐乐地过新年。

# 雅卜与乃卜

远古的时候，刺腊拉棘树倒下之后，树身变成了龙，树根变成了蟒蛇，叶子变成大动物。龙和蟒蛇在大地上活动着，"公龙滚九下，变成九个坝子；母龙滚九下，变成九块地；蟒蛇翻九下，变成九条大河"。在一座峰峦重叠的山峰上，有着兄妹二人，哥哥叫雅卜，妹妹叫乃卜，同住在一起过着采集狩猎的生活："雅卜乃卜去采菜，早上找到阿沃山，晚上找到阿戈山。在一棵大橙树下，有九窝蜜蜂，酿出蜜来甜又甜。阿哥来掏蜂蜜吃，阿妹来掏蜂蜜吃……"他们就这样成天转呀转的，后来在罗果罗买山上定居，盖起了茅屋。有一天他们出去打猎："哥哥和妹妹，分头去打猎。妹妹打到一只马鹿，拿回来分成九份，分给九种民族吃，哥哥也分得吃。哥哥打到一只豪猪，不让人看见；妹妹只见猪毛有手肘长，不知身子有多大，妹妹从此生了气。"哥哥和妹妹分开了。妹妹在茅屋前边种出一蓬苦凉菜，一年四季绿油油，摘了又发，吃也吃不完。而哥哥每天爬山去打猎，找菌子，风

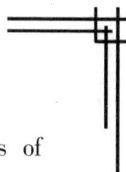

beasts fall into the snare, so as to protect the nine pairs of children when they grew up and reproduced offspring. Esha also taught them to hunt, to slice the beast skins with the leaves of kochia scoparia, to cut the meat with a stone axe or a bamboo knife, and divided them into nine nationalities according to the different methods of eating the prey. Finally, Esha also taught them to build houses, look for the seeds, till the land, and celebrate the New Year happily.

## Yabu and Naibu

In ancient times, when the spiny tree fell down, the trunk became a dragon, the roots became a python, and the leaves became large animals. The dragon and the python were very active on the earth. "The male dragon turned nine somersaults, which became nine dams; the female dragon turned nine somersaults, which became nine blocks; the python turned nine somersaults, which became nine big rivers." On the peak of a mountain with ridges lived a brother named Yabu and his younger sister Naibu, who stayed together and made a living of collecting fruits and hunting animals: "Yabu and Naibu went to pick vegetables in Awo Mountain in the morning and in Aga Mountain in the evening. Under a big orange tree, there were nine hives of bees, which could make sweet honey. The brother took out the honey to eat, and the sister took out the honey to eat..." They moved around the mountains like this day by day, and finally settled down in Luoguoluomai Mountain, and built a hut to live in. One day, they went out to hunt, "The brother and the sister went hunting

吹雨打太阳晒，日子真难熬。当他们看到地上的蚂蚁是那样成群结队地寻找食物多自在时，便感到"还是共同劳动好"，于是又请老鼠来说和："阿哥请来小老鼠，请它去见阿妹；阿妹请来小老鼠，叫他去找阿哥。小老鼠呵鼻子尖，小老鼠呵把口开：'阿哥阿妹来请我，你俩以后不要再分开！'阿妹阿哥合拢来啦，男人女人也不分开啦。"从此兄妹成了夫妻，一齐劳动，繁衍出了后代。

生产劳动没有合适的工具，二人去寻找铁匠，"用麂子角来做钳子，用麂子头来做砧子，用麂子身做风箱，用麂子屎当烧炭"，打出了锄头、犁头和犁耙等农具，在三座山梁三条箐上种了谷子，全都得到大丰收。"寨子定下啦，生产兴旺啦，就是没有当家人。选出阿朵做头人，选出阿戛当头人，阿朵阿戛来管理寨子。"于是子子孙孙繁衍不息。

separately. The sister killed a red deer, took it back home, divided it into nine parts, and distributed them to nine nationalities. The brother also got his share. But when the brother killed a porcupine, he kept it to himself. As the sister found that the hair of the porcupine was as long as an elbow, she was angry for she didn't know how long the porcupine was." Then the brother and sister broke up. The sister grew a row of Solallum nigrum in front of her hut, which were ever green all the year round, and couldn't be eaten out, while the brother lived a very hard life, for he had to go hunting and look for mushrooms every day, no matter it was windy or rainy or sunny. When they saw the ants on the ground were free to look for food together, they felt that "it is better to work together". Then a mouse was invited to mediate, "The brother asked the mouse to visit his sister, and the sister invited the mouse to visit her brother. The little mouse with a pointed nose said, the brother and the sister asked me to tell each other that they would never separate from each other! The brother and sister lived together, and the man and woman would never separate from each other either." From then on, the brother and his sister became husband and wife, and they worked together and reproduced offspring.

Being short of tools of production, they went to ask a blacksmith for help. "The pliers were made of the horn of a muntjac, the anvil was made of the head of a muntjac, the bellow was made of the body of a muntjac, and its excrement was used to burn as charcoal." When the hoe, the plow and the harrow were made, the grains grew on three mountain ridges and in three bamboo forests, and got good harvest. "The stockade has been settled, and the production has been thriving, but there is no family leader. Then Aduo and Aga have been elected to manage the stockade." Thus, the descendants thrived.

# 第七章　傈僳族

## 创世神话

传说在很久很久以前，没有天也没有地。世界是一团混混沌沌的气体，就像甑子里的蒸汽一样漂浮不定。

天神看着这单调混沌的世界，决定派男女二神去开天辟地。

造地的女神左思右想，想出来用梭子织地的好办法，但造天的男神自己却拿不出主意。他看女神织的地经纬分明，平坦整齐，而且还有一个湖泊和一片片树木，也照着女神织大地的办法去织天。但是，梭子到了男神的手中，却不听使唤。他本来想在天上织一些美丽的图案，却织出了一些谁也无法看清的东西，只见天上到处是一团一团的，这就是我们今天看到的云和雾。

# Chapter Seven　Lisu Ethnic Group

## Myth of Creation

It was said that long time ago there was no heaven and earth, and the whole world was a chaotic gas, floating like the steam in the steamer.

Seeing the monotonous and chaotic world, the God of Heaven decided to send a god and a goddess to shape the world.

The goddess, who was sent to shape the earth, came to a good idea: to shape the earth with a shuttle. But the god, who was sent to shape the heaven, had no idea at all. The goddess shaped an earth with clear longitude and latitude, flat and tidy, and with an ocean and forests. The god wanted to shape the heaven in the same way as the goddess did. However, the shuttle in his hands didn't listen to him, nor could he weave beautiful designs in the sky as he had thought, but just some unrecognizable scribbles, which became the masses of clouds and fogs we can see nowadays.

女神聪明勤劳，总是不停地织。日子一天天过去了，有一天，天神把男女二神叫到一块儿，准备把天地合拢。可是，任凭天神使多大的力气，也无法把天地合在一块儿。原来，造天的男神经常偷懒，常常放下手中的活计四处游玩，而且贪吃贪睡，把织天的事丢到一边，这样，他造出来的天就比地短了好长一段。

天神十分着急：如果让男神重新织一块天，那要等多长时间啊！他围着地看来看去，终于想出了一个办法。他一把抓住大地的筋脉猛力一拉，大地真的缩小啦，变成了皱巴巴的一块，高的地方形成了高山峻岭，低的地方形成了河流、峡谷。这样，天和地总算勉强凑在一起了。

虽然有了天地，但天神感到这空空天地之间还少了点什么。于是，天神就试着用泥捏了一个男人。一开始这个男人只是一个泥人，天神看他很好看，就把他放在手上仔细玩赏，心想要是能让他活过来就更好了，就对着泥人吹了一口气，泥人竟真的活起来了。天神多得意啊，但他转念一想，世界上只有一个人，那不是太孤独了吗？我再为他做一个伙伴吧。于是天神用剩下的泥做了一个女人。这个女人任凭天神吹多少口气，她都纹丝不动，天神想可能是做女人时用的泥太少了，就从男人身上取下一根肋骨放在女人身上，果然这个女人也渐渐活了起来。从此，天神让他们繁衍后代，世界上才渐渐有了人类。由于男人身上比女人少了一根肋骨，所以女人总是比男人聪明些。

The goddess was smart and hard-working, and she kept weaving day by day. One day, the God of Heaven asked the god and the goddess to come and see him put the heaven and the earth together. However, no matter how hard he tried, he could not manage it. It turned out that the god was so lazy that he often put aside his assignment and sauntered along, and he was always greedy and sleepy, ignoring his task of weaving the heaven. Therefore, the size of the heaven he made was much smaller than that of the earth.

The God of Heaven was very anxious, for he had to wait for a long time if he asked the god to reweave the heaven. He walked around the earth again and again, and then came to an idea. He held the tendon of the earth and grabbed it quickly, so the earth became smaller and crumpled, the high lands becoming mountains and the low lands becoming the rivers and canyons. In this way, the heaven and the earth were finally put together.

Now that there were the heaven and the earth, the God of Heaven still felt that something was in need between the heaven and the earth. So he tried to form a man out of mud. At first, the man was just a mud man, who was so good-looking that the God could not help putting the mud man in his hand and watched and appreciated it carefully. Thinking that if only the mud man could be made alive, he blew a breath to it, and the mud man really came alive. The God of Heaven was very proud of himself, but as he thought that wasn't it too lonely if there was only one person in the world? He decided to make a partner for the man. He then made a woman with the rest of the mud. But no matter how hard he tried to blow the breath to the woman, she never moved. The God of Heaven believed that the mud of which she was made was too little to make her alive, so he took a rib from the man and put it in the woman, and the woman began to move. Since then, the God of Heaven asked them to reproduce, and the human beings began to live on the earth. Because women have one more rib than men, they are always smarter than men.

天神为了让人们生活得愉快，就让地上长出了一种奇特的树，这种树顶尖上长着高粱或稻谷，下面长着芋头，中间还挂着苞谷，因此，人们不愁吃不愁穿。那时的稻谷是不带壳的，就跟现在的米一样，只是比较粗糙，人们总是要舂了才吃。天神看到后有些生气，心想："你们爱舂就舂个够吧，干脆让谷子穿上衣裳。"从此，谷子就有了一层金黄的谷壳，舂米这个习惯也就一直延续到今天。

那时，地上的野草也像鸡、猪一样会到处乱跑，到地里捣乱，人们只能把它赶跑。人们为了撵草，常累得精疲力尽，于是想出一个办法：不再把草撵走了事，而是把草弄死。这又一次触怒了天神，天神撒下了一把草籽，从此，草在地上深深地扎了根，虽然它不能到处乱跑了，但人们却不得不经常锄草。

那时，风调雨顺，万物都茂盛地生长着，苞谷、谷子、芋头几乎同时成熟，许多都因来不及收回就烂在地里。天神一怒，把树上的粮食从上到下全部收走。这一来大地闹起了饥荒，狗饿得瘫在地上，夜夜不停地对着天哀号。狗的叫声终于感动了天神，天神撒了一把粮食下来，人们急忙把它们留作种子，重新栽种。天神为了惩罚人类，当谷子、芋头、苞谷长出来时再也不是在一棵树上了。因为是狗要回了种子，所以谷穗的样子很像狗尾巴。人们为了感谢狗，每当吃新米饭的时候总要先盛一碗给狗吃。

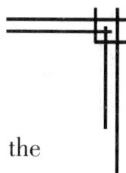

In order to make the human beings live a happy life, the God of Heaven planted a strange tree on the earth, with sorghum or grain on the top of it, taro below and maize in the middle, so people would not worry about food and clothes. At that time, the grain was not in the husk, just like today's rice, but a little rough and had to be pounded for food. The God of Heaven was very angry to see it, and thought that, "Since you like to pound the grain, just do it all the time and I'll cover it with husk." Since then, the grain was covered with a golden husk, and the habit of pounding the grain was kept to the present.

At that time, the weeds on the earth could run around like chickens and pigs, making trouble in the fields, and the human beings had to drive them away, which usually made them exhausted. Therefore, they came up with an idea to get rid of them instead of driving them away, which once again irritated the God of Heaven. He sowed a handful of weed seeds to take root on the ground, so the weeds couldn't run around but people had to mow very often.

At that time, the weather was favorable and everything was prosperous. The maize, grain and taro were mature at the same time, so a lot that could not be harvested in time rotted in the field. The God of Heaven was angry and took all the food away from the trees, which resulted in famine on the earth. The dogs was so hungry that they barked day and night, and finally moved the God of Heaven. The God scattered a handful of grain down to the earth, and people hurriedly saved them as seeds and planted them again. As the punishment to the human on the earth, the God didn't allow the grain, maize and taro to grow on one tree. Because the dog helped to have the seeds back, the grain looked like the dog's tail. And in order to thank dogs, the human being would feed them with a bowl of rice when new grains were harvested.

在那时，天与地之间的距离很近，天上和地下的人可以互相往来，人们很容易就可以到天上。地上的人到天上的多了，宁静的天界嘈杂起来，正常的秩序被打乱了，并且人们吃起饭来不知饱足，于是天神把凡人统统赶回地面，而且派了一个差官来告诉人们："用金碗、银筷，三天吃一顿饭。"这个差官粗心大意，误传为："用土碗、篾筷，每天吃三顿饭。"从那以后，一日三餐的习惯就一直延续下来。由于人们吃得多了，厕的粪便也就多起来，臭气一直熏到天上，天神就把天升高。从此，天地之间的距离越来越大，人就不能随意到达天界，天上人间成了两个世界。那个差官违背了天神的旨意，天神把他贬为牛屎拱公，罚他一辈子吃屎。因此，现在人们一碰到牛屎拱公，它就会说："我错、我错……"

人类在大地上繁衍着。由于人越来越多，心眼儿也就越来越多，不但人心不齐，而且还不敬天神。该纳的贡品也不纳了，有的人甚至还咒骂天神。因此，天神决定发洪水毁灭人类，重新造人。

At that time, the heaven and the earth were close to each other, which allowed the people in two places to come and go freely, and especially it was easy for the human beings on the earth to go to the heaven. Thus, more and more people went to the heaven, which made the quiet heaven noisy and disordered. Furthermore, they ate too much and didn't know when to stop eating. The God of Heaven drove them back to the earth, and sent an official to tell the human beings, "Eat with a gold bowl and silver chopsticks, and have one meal in three days." But the official was very careless, and mistook it for "Eat with a clay bowl and bamboo chopsticks, and have three meals in one day". From then on, the habit of "three meals a day" continued. But the more people ate, the more excrement they had, and the stink even could be smelt in the heaven. So the God of Heaven had to raise the heaven, which, from then on, made the distance between the heaven and the earth longer and longer. Since the people on the earth could not go to the heaven freely, the heaven and the earth became two different worlds. The official who disobeyed the God's will had been banished to become a bull and eat excrement all its life. Nowadays, whenever people see a bull, it would say, "It's my fault, it's my fault..."

The human beings thrived on the earth. But the more people there were, the more different minds there would be. They were not only of different minds, but also showed no respect to the God of Heaven. They didn't pay the due tributes to the God, and some of them even cursed the God. Therefore, the God decided to destroy the human world with flood and recreate the human beings.

于是，大地上爆发了洪水，淹没了一切。只有两兄妹心地善良，天神指点他们躲进一个葫芦里，在水上漂荡了三个月。后来洪水渐渐退了，兄妹二人便成了世界上仅有的幸存者。他们又开始了辛勤的劳动，一切都从头开始。为了繁衍人类，他们就顺从天意成了婚。以后，他们生下了九男九女，人类渐渐多起来。

但是，一件奇怪的事发生了：地上的石头会一天天长大。人们只要吃进一粒沙子，沙子就会越长越大，把人胀死。因此，七个太阳决定拢在一起，燃起了熊熊烈火，烧地三尺，把石头烧死。眼看人类又要葬身火海，天神又把男女二神找来，吩咐他们留下一男一女两个太阳，把其余的五个太阳全部捉回天官。留下的两个太阳很少见面，因为男太阳胆子特别大，他总是白天睡大觉，晚上才出来走动，久而久之，人们就不再叫他太阳，而叫他月亮了。相反女太阳胆子特别小，夜里从来不敢出门，只有白天才敢出来走动走动，只要天一黑，她就赶快回家。因为太阳姑娘长得美丽极了，她一出来，人们就要停下活计看她，所以太阳姑娘害羞极了，连白天也不敢出门了。天神给了她一把金针，告诉她："你出门的时候，如果人们再看你，就把金针撒出去，这样人们就不敢看你了。"太阳姑娘照着天神的话去做，果然没有人再敢对着太阳看了。

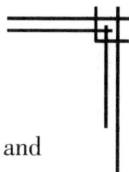

And then, the great flood broke out on the earth and drowned everything, with only a brother and his younger sister left because of their kindness. The God of heaven instructed them to hide in a gourd and float on the water for three months. Later, the flood subsided gradually and the brother and his sister were the only survivors on the earth. They began to work hard again and everything had to start over. In order to reproduce the human beings, they followed the God's will and got married. Later, they gave birth to nine men and nine women, and more and more people appeared on the earth.

But a strange thing happened: the stones on the earth grew day by day. As long as a grain of sand was eaten, it would grew bigger and bigger until the people burst. Seven suns decided to gather together and ignite a fire to burn the earth until the stones were burned to death. Seeing that the human beings would be buried in fire, the God of Heaven ordered the god and the goddess to leave a male sun and a female sun on the earth and take other five suns back to the heaven. The two suns seldom met because the male one was very bold and always slept in the daytime and came out at night. Gradually, he was called the moon instead of the sun. On the contrary, the female sun was very timid and dare not go out at night. She usually came out and walked around in the daytime, and went back home quickly when it was dark. The female sun was so beautiful that whenever she was out, people would like to stop working and look at her. She was so shy that later she dare not go out in the daytime. The God of Heaven then gave her a handful of needles and told her, "When you go out, throw out the gold needles if people look at you, then they dare not do it again." The female sun did as the God said, and nobody dared look at her again.

自从五个太阳被捉走以后，地上的火才渐渐熄灭，人类也才被保存下来。这时，兄妹二人的子女都已长大，他们两两成婚，又各自生了九个孩子，九九八十一，再加上各自的父母，就成了百家姓。人上一百，很难住在一起，九兄弟只好分家。这九兄弟，也就是我们所说的九民族：老大是傈僳族，老二是景颇族，老三是汉族……傣族是最小的一个兄弟。傣族最小，比较软弱，不能上山，分得一根扁担，所以今天的傣族善于挑担，并且居住在坝子里。傈僳族分得一支弩，景颇族分到一把长刀，因此他们都比较强悍，都居住在山上。汉族分到一些书和笔，所以他们长于书写计算。以后，九兄弟就各自回家了。但他们仍有一个共同的习惯，就是经过一年的辛勤劳动，都要进行庆祝活动，景颇族跳"木脑"，傣族赕佛念经，傈僳族是唱歌跳舞，汉族是过春节。

流传地区：云南德宏州陇川县邦外公社
口述者：李有华（傈僳族，男，52岁）
整理者：黄云松，任玉华，陈梅

Since the five suns were taken away, the fire on the earth gradually extinguished and the human beings were preserved. At this time, the children of the brother and his sister had grown up, and they got married in pairs, and gave birth to nine children respectively, that is, eighty-one children all together. These children, plus their parents, formed the 100 surnames of the Book of Family Names. It was difficult for one hundred people to live together, so the nine brothers' families had to live separately. The nine families became the nine nationalities: the first one became Lisu Ethnic Group, the second Jingpo, the third Han and Dai Ethnic Group was the youngest one. Since Dai Ethnic Group was young, weak and unable to climb mountains, they were given a shoulder pole, so nowadays Dai people are good at carrying heavy loads and living in the dams. Lisu people were given a crossbow and Jingpo a long knife, for they were comparatively strong and lived on the mountains. Han people got some books and pens, so they were good at writing and counting. Later, the nine brothers went back to their own homes, but they all had the same habit of holding celebrations after a year of hard work: Jingpo people danced during the Munao festival, Dai people worshiped Buddha and chanted scriptures, Lisu people sang songs and danced, and Han people celebrated the Spring Festival.

Spreading area: Bangwai Commune, Longchuan County, Dehong State

Dictator: Li Youhua (Lisu, male, 52 years old)

Collector: Huang Yunsong, Ren Yuhua, Chen Mei

# 天地和人的来历

## 木布帕捏地球

传说在遥远的古代，只有天，没有地，天没有柱子，四边没有东西托着，天就像一块云彩，晃晃悠悠地浮动着。

那时候，天上有个勤劳能干的天神，名字叫木布帕。他力气大，一个人能抬几架大山重的东西。他走得快，一天能绕天转一圈。他看到天没有东西托着，随时都有掉下来的危险，决心捏个地球来支撑天，使天不摇不晃、稳稳当当，于是辞别了父母妻儿，背上天泥来捏地球。

天神木布帕穿云破雾，来到蓝天底下捏地球。他从早干到太阳落，从晚干到晨星消失，汗流浃背，昼夜不停地捏着地球。他捏出一块平地，就种上一片花草树木，同时捏好飞禽走兽。这样，凡在他捏成的平原里，到处是鲜花盛开，蜂儿嗡嗡；在他种出的森林中，到处是虎吼猿啼，百鸟争鸣，生机勃勃，十分热闹。正当天神木布帕辛勤地捏着地球的时候，突然，降灾降难的魔王尼瓦帝来到他面前。尼瓦帝企图动摇木布帕捏造地球的雄心壮志，便定下了一条毒计。他装出一副神色慌张、悯天怜地的样子，气喘吁吁地对木布帕说："木布帕啊，木布帕！当初你就不该来管这闲事，我想不告诉你嘛我心里难受，告诉你吧，又怕你痛心，干脆说了吧：你的独生子死了。"木布帕听到这突如其来的噩耗，胸膛突突直跳，心儿像针戳一样疼痛。但他很快就平静下来，朝天看了一眼，然后对尼瓦帝说："儿子死了,以后还可以生,

# The Origin of the Heaven, the Earth and the Human Being

## The God Mubupa Moulded the Earth

It was said that in ancient times, the earth did not exist but there was the heaven, which had no poles to support and was like a cloud dangling and floating in the air.

At that time, there was an industrious and capable god named Mubupa in the heaven. He was strong enough to lift things as heavy as several mountains, and he could go fast enough to walk around the heaven once a day. When he saw that the heaven was in danger of falling down at any time, he decided to mould an earth to support it so as to make the heaven stable and safe and secure. Then, he said goodbye to his parents, his wife and his children, and moulded the earth with the mud taking from the heaven.

The God Mubupa went through the clouds and fog and came to mould the earth under the blue sky. He worked from the morning to the evening, from the sunset to the sunrise, sweaty and nonstop. He moulded a piece of flatland and then planted flowers and trees, and birds and beasts were made at the same time. In this way, in the plains he moulded there were beautiful blooming flowers and humming bees; in the forests he planted there were roaring tigers, whistling apes and chirping birds, vigorous and lively. Just as the God Mubupa was busy with his work, Niwadi,

143

这捏地球的活儿不能停下来。"说完头也不抬地继续捏地球。尼瓦帝看到木布帕没有掉进他挖下的陷阱，也没有踩着他插下的竹扦，只好灰溜溜地走了。没过多久，他又装着心情沉重的样子，来到木布帕跟前说："木布帕啊！事情不好了，你的妻子突然得病死去了！上一回你的独生子死了，你也不回去看看，你的妻子哭得死去活来，说你生的铁石心肠。现在妻子又死了，你们做一场夫妻，岂有不去看一眼之理？"木布帕听到妻子去世的消息，就像万把尖刀插入胸膛，悲痛万分。但他想：这捏地球的活儿没有完，怎么能半途而废呢？他忍着悲痛，含着泪水朝天上望了望，表示对妻子的哀悼，然后对尼瓦帝说："鸡食里不会有盐巴，人间没有后悔药。我既离妻别儿来造地球，灾难临门也不会回头！"说完又继续捏。尼瓦帝又只好垂头丧气地走了。

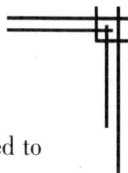

the demon of disaster, suddenly came to see him. Niwadi wanted to shake his ambition of moulding the earth and came up with an evil plan. He pretended to be panic and pitiful, and panted to Mubupa, "Well, you shouldn't be here to mould the earth. I would be very sorry if I hadn't told you this; and to tell you this, I'm afraid you would be painful. To be frank, your only son is dead." Hearing the unexpected bad news, Mubupa's heart beat quickly and was as painful as were stung by needles. But soon he calmed down, looking up at the heaven and said, "My son is dead, and another son may be born in the future, but my work cannot be stopped." And then, without raising his head, he continued. Seeing that his trick didn't work, Niwadi had to go away in disgrace. It was not long before he came back, looking as if he were very gloomy, and said to Mubupa, "Mubupa, What a calamity! Your wife fell ill suddenly and died. Last time, you didn't go home when your only son died, and your wife cried her heart out, complaining that you were hard-hearted. Now your wife is dead, as her husband, why don't you go back and see her for the last time?" Hearing the bad news of his wife's death, Mubupa was very grieved, as if tens of thousands of sharp knives had been plunged into the chest. But he thought: How could it be done halfway that he hadn't finished the work of moulding the earth? With his grief in heart and tears in eyes, he looked up at the heaven, which expressed his mourning to his wife, and said to Niwadi, "There is no repent in the world as there is no salt in the chicken's food. Since I chose to leave my wife and children and came here to mould the earth, I won't give up no matter what the calamity is." He then continued his work, and again Niwadi had to go away dejectedly.

　　就这样，天神木布帕为了很快捏完地球，头也不抬一下，腰也不直一回，汗水湿透了他的衣裳，铁鞋磨破了他的双脚。他一把汗、一把泥地捏着。眼看地球快要捏完了，就在这个时候，魔王尼瓦帝又施展毒计了。他愁眉苦脸地跑到木布帕跟前，说："不好了，不好了！你的父母双双去世了，这回你再不回去，就不合情理了。父母断气之时你不在场，等于白养你一场！父母死后你不亲手捧把土埋葬，那就对不起父母哪！"说完，扭头就走了。

　　木布帕自小很敬爱父母，听说父母双亡，就像霹雳打在他的头上，几乎昏倒在地。他想："儿子死了可以生，妻子死了还可以再娶，一个人一生只有一个父亲和母亲，作为儿子岂有不亲手埋葬之理？"想到这里，他把没有捏完的泥土捏成坨坨，然后向已造好的平地扔去。这些泥坨坨有的打进地里，成了峡谷深涧；有的落在地面上，成了高山奇峰。因为天神木布帕捏完地球就匆匆赶回天上去了，所以传说直到现在地球还缺着一小块边呢！因此，河水直往那缺凹的边上流淌。

　　地球虽然不满边，但是从此地球支架着天，天笼罩着地，天为雄，地为雌，天地配成一对夫妻。

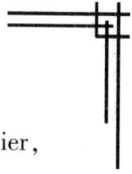

In this way, the God Mubupa tried to finish his work earlier, and he didn't raise his head or straighten his waist. The sweat soaked through his clothes and his feet were badly wounded in the iron shoes. He moulded the earth with every bit of mud and every drop of sweat. Just as the earth was going to be finished, the demon Niwadi came to play his trick again. He ran to Mubupa with a gloomy look and told him, "What a calamity! What a calamity! Your parents have died, and it is unconscionable not to go back home this time. If you can't be with your parents when they die, you have been brought up in vain; and if you can't bury them by yourself when they die, you would let them down completely." Niwadi finished his words and left quickly.

Mubupa loved his parents very much since he was very young, and it was just like a thunderbolt hitting on his head when he heard the news. He was so sad that he almost fell down onto the ground. Then he thought, "I can have another one after my son died, I can remarry after my wife died, but I can have only one father and mother in my life, and how can't I bury them with my own hand?" While thinking, he made the rest of the mud into some lumps, and threw them into the flatland he had already moulded. Some muddy lumps were thrown into the ground and became the canyons and deep valleys, and some were on the ground and became high mountains and peaks. Mubupa hurried back to the heaven, leaving the earth unfinished, so it is said that until now the earth is still in short of a small edge. As a result, the rivers flow straight to the concave edge.

Although the earth was not moulded to a complete one, it still could support the heaven, and was shrouded in the heaven. The heaven and the earth, one being male and the other female, were made into a couple.

147

## 猕猴变人

天神木布帕造出地球不久，又用泥土捏了一对猕猴，猕猴慢慢长大，变成人形，从此地球上开始有了人。过了很多年，地上的人逐渐多起来了。

有一天，猴人背着吃奶的小儿子外出采集，火辣辣的太阳晒得孩子啼哭不止。猴人停下手来，给孩子喂饱了奶，哄孩子睡着后，把孩子放在树荫下乘凉，然后自己忙着干活。这时，突然飞来一只鹦鹉啄松子吃，松球被啄落下来，正好打在小孩子的太阳穴上，孩子立即断了气。猴人号啕大哭，哭得天昏地暗，山崩地裂。她悲伤地哭了一阵子后，明白是天意也就想通了，于是对天念咒语道："树不倒呀，没有地方再生；人不死呵，地上容纳不下。"从此地上的人开始有生有死。

## 洪水泛滥

因为猕猴念咒，万物应该有生有死，所以，蓝天开始索人魂，大地开始要人骨，洪荒年代开始了。那时，在一个有十来户的村寨里，有两个从小失去父母的兄妹，无依无靠，住在村子旁边一个蒿枝窝棚里，过着野猪野牛一样的生活。

## The Macaque Became the Human Being

Not long after the God Mubupa created the earth, he made a pair of macaques with the mud. Gradually, the macaques grew up and looked like human beings. From then on, there were human beings on the earth. After many years, more and more human beings lived on the earth.

One day, the macaque-man went out to gather fruits with the baby son on the back. The baby cried badly in the scorching sun, so the macaque-man stopped to nurse the baby to sleep, put the baby in the shade of a tree, and then went on her busy work. Just then, a parrot suddenly flew over and pecked at the pine nut for food. A pine cone was pecked and fell off the tree and hit the baby on his temple, and the baby died immediately. The macaque-man burst into tears and cried her heart out. After crying bitterly for a while, she understood that it was the will of the Heaven, and then she uttered an incantation to the sky, "There would be no place to hold the reborn if the tree doesn't fall; there would be no place to hold the reborn if the living never die." Since then, the human beings on the earth began to live and die.

## The Great Flood

Because of the macaque's incantation "everything should live and die", the heaven began to ask for people's soul, and the earth began to ask for people's bones. And the age of great flood began. At that time, in a village of about ten families, there were a brother and his younger sister, whose parents died when they were very young. Helplessly, they stayed in a shack made of branches near the village, and lived a very miserable life, like wild boars and bisons.

149

有一天，兄妹俩把采回来的野菜下到土锅里，用蒿枝筷子搅拌一点荞面，准备度过一天的时候，突然，从天上飞来一对金光灿烂的金色鸟，落在蒿枝棚顶上说起人话来："可怜的孤儿呀！俗话说：烂柴烟子多，孤儿寡妇眼泪多。你们吃够了人间的苦水，尝够了人间的酸辣，但苦日子并没有过去，更大的苦难还在后头，滔滔洪水就要淹没大地。快快准备藏身的葫芦：听不见鸟叫你们别出来，等我们落在葫芦上边唤你兄妹时再出来。"说完鸟儿飞入云层不见了。

兄妹听到这可怕的消息，吃了一惊，你看看我，我瞧瞧你，吓得不知怎么做才好。他们定了定神，决定把这灭绝人类的消息告诉村里的人，让大家避过即将来临的灾难。兄妹俩，东家走来西家串，告诉这家，这家说：孤儿饿昏了说胡话；传给那一家，那一家说：孤儿没有爹妈教养，做梦也当真话讲。有的人家听了便哈哈大笑说：就算你们说的是真话，吐的是真言，我们住的是杉松楼板房，风吹它不摇，地动它不晃，是铁立的柱，铜围的墙，还怕什么洪水来淹？兄妹俩没法，只好回去自家找个大葫芦，锯开盖子准备洪水来时藏身避难。

One day, the brother and his sister cooked the plucked wild vegetables with a little buckwheat in the pot, and were ready to have it for the whole day. Suddenly, a pair of golden birds flew from the sky and alighted on the top of the shack and said in human being's voice, "Poor orphans! It is said that rotten wood burns more smoke, and that orphans and widowed mothers shed more tears. You have endured enough hardship and suffered enough pains on the earth, but the miserable life has never come to an end, and more difficulties are waiting for you. A great flood will drown the earth, and you go to look for a gourd to hide in. Don't go out until you hear the birds singing, and don't go out until we call you on the gourd." The golden birds then flew into the clouds and disappeared.

Hearing the terrible news, the brother and his sister was shocked and looked at each other and didn't know what to do. They then calmed down and decided to tell the villagers the news that the human world would be drowned, so they could escape from the coming disaster. They went to each house of the village, but the family said they spoke nonsense because of starvation when they told the news to a family. When they told the news to another family, the family said they were uncouth orphans and the words uttered in their dreams couldn't be trust. Some laughed and said, "Even if what you said is true, we won't be afraid of the flood because we live in the house made of cedar wood, which is like the house made of iron poles and bronze walls, and would not sway in the wind or shake in the earthquake." The brother and his sister had no choice but to go back home and find a big gourd, and prepared it for a hiding place in case of flood.

　　这一年啊，高高挂在天上的太阳好像往下掉了一截，显得离地面更近。大地晒得快要冒出火舌，地皮裂开一条条沟大的缝，沟里的水干了，茂密的森林成了光秃秃的枝枝桠桠。人们就像蒸在甑子里，嘴像干了的田，裂开一条条小缝，舌头像吃着毒药一样剥落了一层皮，个个瘦得像干竹笋。

　　这样过了九十九天、九十九夜，突然山风呼呼，电光闪闪，雷声隆隆，大雨下得麻杆一样密，江水喘着粗气，哗哗往上爬，毁了庄稼和房屋，冲着了人群和牛羊。兄妹俩躲在葫芦里，葫芦随洪浪到处乱漂，有时还听到葫芦碰着天底的咚咚响声。不知过了多少天，也不知过了多少夜。漂着漂着，浪声不响了。淌着淌着，葫芦不动了。兄妹俩不敢出声，不敢出来，只等金色鸟儿来报喜。等了一会儿，听到金色鸟儿唱着欢快的歌，张开口儿把兄妹呼唤："孤儿孤儿快出来，灾难已经过去了，不必怕来不消愁，大地宽阔任你走，天涯海角随你游。"兄妹俩打开葫芦盖，只见漂到一架山上。洪水退去了，大地平静了。兄妹俩又是喜来又是怕，喜的是躲过了一场大灾难，怕的是不见一点炊烟。

This year, the sun hanging high in the heaven seemed to fall a little and went closer to the earth. The scorching sun shone brightly on the earth, which was burned to split into big gaps. The water in the ditches had dried up, and the dense forest had become bare branches. People on the earth seemed to live in steamers, with dry mouths like fields full of slim cracks, and sloughed tongues like having drunk poison, all as thin as dried bamboo shoots.

After ninety-nine days and nights, the wind blazed, the lightning flashed, the thunders rumbled, and it rained as dense as the flax stalks. The river flooded and submerged the crops and houses, washing out the crowds and cattle and sheep. The brother and his sister hid in the gourd, floating around with the waves. Sometimes they could even hear the sound of the gourd hitting the bottom of the heaven. Nobody knew how many days and nights passed. While the guard was floating, the sounds of waves could not be heard, and later, the guard stopped drifting. The brother and his sister dared not speak or go out of the guard, waiting for the golden birds coming. After a while, a joyful song could be heard and the golden birds called the brother and sister, "Come out, kids! Don't be afraid and the disaster has passed. You could go everywhere and travel to the ends of the earth." They uncovered the gourd and found them on the top of a mountain. The flood subsided and the earth calmed down. They were glad to escape a great calamity, but afraid to see nothing left after the great flood.

## 射太阳月亮

洪水退落后，连绵起伏的群山又展现在眼前。可是天上出了九个太阳，七个月亮，白天晒得大地冒烟，夜晚寒风飕飕，兄妹俩的心头笼罩了一片阴影。正在他们为出现这不祥之兆感到恐惧的时候，两只可爱的金色鸟又唱着欢乐的歌儿飞来了，它们带来了金榔头、银火钳，告诉兄妹俩有一个深不见底的龙潭。潭里有个礁石，半截露在水面上，礁石下面就是龙宫。龙宫里住着一个头长九叉角，胡须有七拿长的老龙王。设法取到它的金弩银箭，便可征服烈日和寒月。金色鸟还指给他们龙潭的方向，教给他们治服龙王、取宝弩宝箭的办法。

于是，兄妹俩顺着金色鸟指引的方向去寻找龙潭，走了三天三夜，一个碧绿的龙潭出现在他们的眼前。他们很快找到了礁石，按照金色鸟的话，举起金榔头，"咚咚"地敲打起来，敲得礁石迸出一道道火光，敲得龙潭里的水激起一阵阵浪花，敲得龙宫晃晃悠悠，把闭目养神的龙王吓了一跳。龙王睁开双眼，捻着银灰色的胡须，哼着鼻子说："快去给我看看，是哪个大胆的人在那里胡搅蛮缠，赶快给我轰走。"小白鱼领旨走了，过了两袋烟的工夫也没有回来，而"咚咚"的敲打声还是响个不停。龙王又派了鲫壳鱼去看个究竟，鲫壳鱼也和小白鱼一样，一去不回。震耳欲聋的响声不

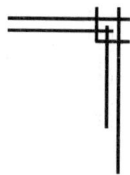

## Shooting the Suns and the Moons

The flood subsided and the rolling mountains appeared again. The brother and his sister were shrouded in the shadow of nine suns and seven moons in the heaven, which made the earth burned to smoke in the daytime and the wind very chilly at night. Just when they were afraid of the bad omen, the two lovely golden birds, singing the joyful songs, came and brought the golden hammers and silver tongs. The birds told them to find a dragon pool, where there was a rock, half of which was above the water, and the dragon's palace was just under the rock. In the dragon's palace lived a Dragon King, with nine horns on the head and seven-fen long beard. The scorching sun and the chilly moon could be controlled as soon as they got the Dragon King's golden crossbow and silver arrows. The golden birds also showed them the direction to the dragon poor, and taught them how to control the Dragon King and how to take away the crossbow and arrows.

Following the golden birds instructions, the brother and his sister began to look for the dragon pool. They walked for three days and nights until a green dragon pool appeared in front of them. They soon found the rock, and according to the golden birds' word, they raised the golden hammer and knocked the rock to burst out flashes of fire, which stirred a spray of waves, and shook the dragon pool. The Dragon King, who was dozing off with his eyes close, was shocked and opened his eyes. He twirled his silver gray beard and grunted, "Go and see who dares make trouble here and drive him away." A little white fish went with the Dragon King's word and didn't come back for a long time, but

仅没有消失，却一声比一声响得更厉害了。龙王只好派镰刀鱼出去看看到底出了什么事，可是这个最得力的助手也一去不复返。原来兄妹俩一见小白鱼、鲫壳鱼、镰刀鱼杀气腾腾地又吼又叫，就用银钳子把它们一个个夹住丢到沙滩上去了。结果龙王只好亲自出马，它一露出水面，看见两个青年男女在敲打着礁石，气得抖动着胡子怒吼道："你们这两个蠢人，生来是聋子，还是耳朵里生了蛆，灌了脓，听不见我的吩咐！"龙王不知利害，还想骂下去，但一件金光闪闪的东西往鼻子伸来，疼得它喊不出声，叫不出口。它在水里翻滚着，搅得水像锅里涨了的开水，激起一阵阵恶浪，水浪哗哗地拍打着岸边，弄得天昏地暗。兄妹俩丝毫没有松手，龙王支持不住，点头示意认输。兄妹俩对龙王说："我们不想伤害你的生命，只要你拿出你的弩和箭，我们就放你。"龙王只好规规矩矩地把金弩银箭献了出来。

兄妹俩拿着金光闪闪的龙弩、银光灿灿的龙箭，高高兴兴地爬到最高最高的山峰上，哥哥拉弦，妹妹搭箭，一连射落了八个太阳，只留下一个最亮的。射落了六个月亮，只留下一个最明的。从此，和风习习，枯木吐绿，大地恢复成原来的样子了。

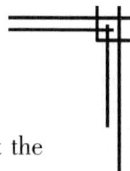

the sounds of knocking continued. The Dragon King then sent the carp shellfish to see what had happened, but it didn't come back either. The deafening noise didn't fade away but was louder than before. The Dragon King had to send the sickle fish, which was regarded as the most capable assistant, to see what had happened, but it didn't come back either. It turned out that they were thrown to the beach one by one by the silver tongs when the brother and his sister saw them roaring and shouting murderously. The Dragon King had to go out and see himself. As soon as he came out of the water, he was angry to see the brother and his sister knocking at the rock and roared with his beard trembling, "You two stupid human beings. Were you born to be deaf or were your ears filled with maggots or pus, so you couldn't hear me?" The Dragon King scolded the brother and his sister, but didn't realize the danger of being hit by a glittering object on his nose. He felt so painful that he couldn't shout or utter a word. He rolled in the water, making it wave like boiling water in the pot, which lapped against the river bank bitterly. The brother and his sister didn't stop until the Dragon King couldn't hold out and nodded his head to give in. They said to him, "We don't want to kill you, and we'll let you go as long as you give us your crossbow and arrows." The Dragon King had to do so honestly.

Taking the glittering crossbow and the silver arrows, the brother and his sister climbed up to the top of the highest mountain. The brother pulled the crossbow and the sister set the arrows, and they shot eight suns and six moons in succession, leaving only the brightest one. From then on, the breeze blew gently, the trees turned green, and the earth returned to what it used to be.

## 兄妹配偶

　　九个太阳射落了八个，七个月亮打掉了六个，地上无灾又无难。可是仍然听不到狗吠鸡鸣，看不见人烟，大地像死一般寂静。兄妹俩悲痛万分，决定分头去找人。兄妹俩要分手了，哥哥怕妹子一人山高路险无人相助。妹妹担心哥哥棘深林密，衣服破了无人补。哥哥叹气往北走，妹妹挥泪往南去。江北找人人不见，江南寻人人不遇，哥哥顺流回头找，妹妹逆流往回寻，兄妹又碰在一起。兄妹垂头丧气，闷闷不乐。正在这时，那对金色鸟儿又飞来了。它们告诉善良的兄妹，天下再也没有第三个人，劝兄妹结婚。但兄妹不肯，说一个娘肚里生的哥妹，吃的是一个娘的奶，喝的是一锅里的汤，兄妹配偶不成理，天降石斧会劈成两半，山滚巨石会砸成两截，兄妹不肯配成偶。金色鸟说这是天意，可用贝壳来卜卦："若是一个底面朝上，一个底面朝下，兄妹即可成夫妻。"哥哥不信，拿贝壳卜卦，妹在一旁仔细观望：果然一个底面朝上，一个底面朝下，卜了三次，三次都一样。于是，兄妹遵照天意结成夫妻。

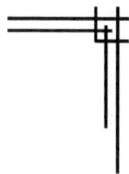

## The Brother and the Sister Got Married

Eight of the nine suns and six of the seven moons were shot, and there was no more disaster on the earth. But it was deadly still for no dog barked, no cock crowed and no human being could be seen. The brother and his sister were very sad and decided to look for human beings. They had to separate from each other. The brother was worried about the sister being alone and helpless on the way of high mountains and hard journey, and the sister was also worried that nobody could help the brother mend his clothes in the deep forests. The brother signed and walked north while the sister walked south with tears in her eyes. The brother could not find a man in the north and the sister couldn't do in the south. They had to go back and met each other again, depressed and sullen. Just then, the pair of golden birds flew back, told them that there were no other human beings on the earth, and persuaded them to get married. But the brother and sister didn't agree. They said they were brother and sister, sucking the same breast and drinking the same pot of soup. If they got married, the stone axe from the heaven should split them in half, and the huge rocks from the mountain should break them into two parts. They didn't agree to get married, but the golden birds said it was the god's will and it could be forecast by the shells, "The brother and sister could be husband and wife if one bottom faced upwards and the other faced downwards." The brother didn't believe it, so he took a shell and tried, with the sister standing by and watching. It turned out to be like what the golden birds said. The brother tested for three times and got the same results. Then the brother and his sister had to get married in accordance with the god's will.

兄妹成婚后，生了六男六女，弟兄姐妹逐渐长大成人，各自谋生。一对往北走，成了藏人，一对往南走，成了白族，一对往西走，成了克钦人，一对往东走，成了汉人，一对往怒江走，成了怒族人，一对留在父母身边，就是傈僳族。

整理者：刘辉豪，胡贡

# 岩石月亮

相传，很古很古的时候，洪水淹没了人间，地面消失了，人畜死光了，没有人声，没有鸟鸣，只有风卷狂涛的声音。碧罗山、高黎贡山，都只露出了峰顶，而且都变得像糯米饭团一样松软。天空和水面连成一片，云雾在水面上飘飘荡荡，世界变得一片凄凉。

于是，天神就发出一声长啸，他呼出的气化成一道闪电，他发出的声音化成霹雳，天空炸开了一条裂缝。天神从裂缝中投下了两个葫芦，一个葫芦落到了怒江江头，一个葫芦落在了怒江江尾。一个吃力地往上漂，一个飞快地往下滚，在"里底"这个地方相遇了。

After their marriage, the couple gave birth to six men and six women. The men and women made their own living when they grew up. A pair went northwards and became the Tibetans, a pair went southwards and became the Bai people, a pair went westwards and became the Keqin people, a pair went eastwards and became the Han people, a pair went towards the Nu River and became the Nu people, and the last pair lived with their parents and became the Lisu people.

Collector: Liu Huihao, Hu Gong

# Rock Moon

It was said that in ancient times, the flood drowned the human beings and the earth disappeared. The human beings and animals died completely. There was no human voice, no birds singing, but the noise of the rolling waves caused by the howling wind. The peaks of Biluo Mountain and Gaoligong Mountain emerged from the water and were as soft as the glutinous rice balls. The heaven and the surface of the water linked together, with the clouds and fogs floating on the water. The whole world became desolate.

So the God of Heaven uttered a long whistle. His breath became a flash of lightning and his sound became a thunderbolt, which made the heaven cracked. The God threw two gourds into the crack, and one fell on the head of the Nu River and the other on the tail of it. One drifted up hardly and the other rolled down quickly, and finally they met at the Lidi.

　　这时，天神又从天缝中投下一柄金刀，一柄银斧，金刀和银斧各自劈开了一个葫芦，从一个葫芦里出来一个男人，从另一个葫芦里出来一个女人。男人的名字叫西沙，女人的名字叫勒沙，他们两人都是长发披在后背，赤裸着全身。他们感到很害羞，各自在水边找呀找，找到了浸得又烂又软的棕片围在腰间。

　　他们两人踏上又松又软的峰顶，上转转，没有一个落脚的地方，下转转，没有一块歇宿的地方。他们疲倦极了，上下眼皮像两片含羞草的叶子，开了又合，合了又开，站在烂泥塘里怎么也睡不着觉。后来身体实在支持不住了，终于倒在泥塘中，烂泥冰冷刺骨，两个人依旧不能入睡。他们想呀想呀，勒沙终于想出了办法。她说："西沙阿哥呀！这样下去我俩都会活活困死，不如我躺在泥里，你睡在我身上吧！"

　　西沙再三推让，勒沙执拗不肯，她满眼泪水，恳求西沙睡个觉，保存生命，西沙为她真诚的泪水所感动，就依从了。

　　洪水中，有一个主宰名叫路帕，性情非常残暴。就是他，卷动了洪水，淹没了人间，他把淹死的人和畜逐一吞食，连小蚂蚁和小蜢虫都不放过。

　　路帕有个独生女儿，生得十分美丽，心地也十分善良，她每天在深水中游来游去，由于没有一个伙伴，感到十分寂寞。

　　这天，她游到了"拉沟"① 洪水边上，看见一对青年男女，看见他们艰难地生活着，便决定帮助他们。于是她慢悠悠地游上岸来。

--------

　　① 拉沟：地名。

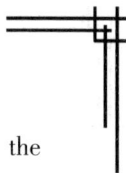

Then the God threw a golden knife and a silver axe from the crack to split a gourd respectively. From one gourd came a man named Xisha and from the other came a woman named Lesha. They both were naked with long hair on the back. They felt ashamed and looked for something along the river bank to put on. Finally they found some palm leaves, which were soaked to be rotten and soft, and tied them around their waist.

They stepped on the loose and soft peak of the mountain, but there was no place to have a rest or to have a sleep. They were extremely tired, with their eyelids open and close in turn, like two leaves of the mimosa. However, they couldn't sleep while standing in the mud. Finally they couldn't stand and fell in the cold mud. They still could not sleep and thought over and over again until Lesha came up with an idea, "Xisha, we both would die if we couldn't sleep, so I'd rather lie in the mud and you sleep on me!"

Xisha refused, but Lesha insisted, and, with tears in her eyes, pleaded with him to sleep and save his life. Xisha was moved by her honest tears and agreed.

In the flood, there was a master named Lupa, who was very cruel. It was he who started the flood and drowned the human world. He swallowed the drowned men and animals one by one, even if there were the small ants and grasshoppers, and nothing escaped.

Lupa had an only daughter, beautiful and kind-hearted. She swam in the deep water every day, but felt very lonely because she had no friend.

One day, when she swam to the edge of the Lagou[①], she saw a pair of young man and woman struggling in the mud, and decided to help them. She then swam ashore slowly.

---

① Lagou is a name of place.

西沙和勒沙，见到路帕女儿突然到来，吓了一跳，见她浑身长满了金红色的鳞，闪闪发光，腰身围着一圈一圈的水藻，大眼睛像星光一样明亮，方方的嘴唇血红血红，黑黑的牙齿像刚嚼过槟榔。嘿！真美极了。西沙和勒沙看呆了。

路帕姑娘说："你们不要害怕，我来帮助你们。"

说着，她又返回水里，摇起双臂，把水中漂荡的那些圆木一根又一根，推向岸边。她力大无比，把一根根粗圆木，用手托到岸上，并列成排，铺成地面，铺成屋基，然后又把一根根细圆木，搭成窝棚，又用棕榈叶遮盖屋顶。水面的风吹来，把铺地的圆木吹干了，把窝棚吹干了。他们就这样住进了新屋。

路帕姑娘再次游入水中，把大批大批的扁头鱼、尖嘴鱼驱赶到岸边，一条条扔上岸去。西沙和勒沙高兴极了，他们开始用鱼充饥。

路帕姑娘为他们准备了吃和住，准备返回水中。

勒沙说："鱼有吃完的日子，相爱之情不应有完结的日子，请你留下吧！"

他们苦苦相留，路帕姑娘就留下不走了，他们像兄妹一样，一同生活。后来，西沙和勒沙，也对路帕姑娘同时产生了爱慕之情。

Xisha and Lesha were shocked to see the sudden arrival of Lupa's daughter, who was in glittering golden red scales and circles of algae tied around her waist. Her big eyes were as bright as the stars, her square lips were as red as blood, and her teeth were black as if they had just chewed betel nuts. She was so beautiful that Xisha and Lesha looked in amazement.

Lupa's daughter said, "Don't be afraid and I'm coming to help you."

Then she returned to the water, and shook her arms to push the logs one by one to the shore. She was so powerful that she held up the thick logs and took to the shore, put them in rows to make the foundation of a cabin, and then built the cabin with the thin logs and covered the roof with palm leaves. The wind from the surface of the water dried the logs and the cabin, and then they moved in.

Lupa's daughter swam into the water again, driving schools of flat-head fish and pipe-fish out of the water and threw them to the shore. Xisha and Lesha was very happy and began to take fish as food.

Lupa's daughter had prepared the food and house for them and was ready to go back to the water.

Lesha said to her, "The fish could be eaten up, but the love could stay forever. Could you please stay with us?"

They tried their best to persuade Lupa's daughter to stay, and she agreed and stayed with them like brothers and sisters. Later, Xisha and Lesha both fell in love with Lupa's daughter.

不久，路帕姑娘怀了孕，再不能进入深水了。路帕得知女儿恋慕陆地，倾爱人间，他一怒之下，咆哮一声，水面激起很高的水柱。他一挥臂膀，激起巨浪，洪水又暴涨了，直涨到云端，淹没了所有山峰。西沙的窝棚已被洪水围困，急得他们三人一齐仰天大呼："密握粗含帕①呵！我们都是你的儿女，你快来搭救我们！"

天空响起雷鸣般的声音回答："我的儿女只有两个人，我不搭救恶人的后代。"

勒沙争辩说："恶人的后代，不都是恶人呵！"

天空又响起了雷鸣一样的回声："你们袒护恶人，也变成了恶人，你们每人必须做一件最大的好事，才能生存，我只能暂时搭救你们，我困了，要去睡了。"

天神的话音刚落，天空又裂开一道裂缝，掉下来一个木筏，像一片树叶一样，轻飘飘地落到他们面前，他们三个跳到木筏上，发现木筏上还拴着一张弩弓，三支竹羽箭。

他们开始在木筏上生活，木筏随着洪水涨落，随着浪涛摇摆。路帕再也奈何他们不得。

日子依旧很难过，人间是混混沌沌的人间，不分白天和夜晚。日子一天天过去，他们生了九个儿子，七个女儿。

---

① 密握粗含帕：对天神的称呼。

Soon, Lupa's daughter was pregnant and couldn't enter into the deep water. When Lupa learned that his daughter adored the land and loved the human world, he growled in anger, which caused a very high water spout on the surface. He swung his arms to stir huge waves and the flood increased to the cloud, drowning all the peaks of the mountains. Xisha's cabin was surrounded by the water, and they all shouted hastily, "Come and help us, my God of Heaven①, we all are your children."

A sound as loud as a sudden storm came from the heaven, "I've only two children, and I don't save the lives of the evil's descendants."

"The descendants of the evil are not necessarily evil." Lesha argued.

The same sound came, "You became the evil since you are partial to the evil. Only when every one of you does a good deed can you survive, and I can only save you temporarily. I'm tired and going to sleep."

With the God's words, the heaven split a crack, and a raft dropped like a leaf and landed in front of them lightly. They jumped onto the raft and found that there were a crossbow and three bamboo arrows on it.

They began to live on the raft, which rose and fell with the flood and swayed with the waves. And Lupa could do nothing to them.

Life was still very hard, and the human world was still chaotic without day and night. As time passed by, they gave birth to nine sons and seven daughters.

---

① Refers to "Miwocuhanpa" in the Lisu dieclect.

　　勒沙终日发愁，他们三个一件最大的好事还没做，生命只是有限的时光，怎能不发愁呢！

　　他们在木筏上漂呀漂，漂到一个叫"宣哇怕"的地方，看见一面岩壁挡住洪水。勒沙灵机一动，说：

　　"这儿不是有弩箭吗！把岩壁射个洞，水不是能泄走吗！"

　　"对呀！"

　　西沙拉起弩弓，装上竹箭，"啪"的一箭，射在水面上端，从峰顶滑过，把岩壁划了一道裂缝，洪水没有流走。

　　西沙又拉起弩弓，使劲地射出第二箭，"啪"的一声巨响，岩壁射穿了，洪水哗啦啦地直往外喷流。为使洪水快点泄出，西沙又射出第三箭。第三箭没有射穿上岩壁，仅在岩壁上射出一个岩石洞。第三箭虽然没有射穿岩壁，但箭射着岩石，岩石崩裂的巨响震开了浓云迷雾，天空爽朗了，人间转暖了，长期浸在水中的鸟蛋，又孵化出各种小鸟。

　　水逐渐下降，露出了山峰、山坡、山谷，露出了树木。小鸟又落在树枝上唱起了歌。

　　西沙做了第一件最大的好事。

　　九个儿子，七个女儿，都长大了，人间也苏醒了。可是，他们三个依旧发愁。因为，第二、第三件好事还没做。他们又苦苦地思，细细地想，勒沙终于想出了好主意，但她不说出来。

Lesha was worried all the time, for they hadn't done any good deed. Life was limited and how could they not worry about it?

They drifted on the raft until they arrived a place named Xuanwapa. Seeing a cliff blocking the flood, Lesha came up with an idea, "Isn't there a crossbow here? Couldn't the water discharge if we shoot at the cliff and make a hole on it?"

"That's a good idea!"

Xisha drew the crossbow and put the bamboo arrow on it. The arrow was shot above the water and slid over the peak, which cut a crack on the cliff, but the water didn't flow through it.

Xisha drew the crossbow again, and shot another arrow vigorously. With a loud sound "Bang", the cliff was shot through, and the water flew through it. In order to release the water quickly, the third arrow was shot and dug a hole on the cliff, which didn't go through the cliff, but the big sound of the rock burst cleared up the thick cloud and dense fog. The heaven became bright, the world became warm and the bird eggs, which were soaked in the flood for a long time, began to hatch a variety of little birds.

The water gradually declined and the peaks, hill slopes, the valleys and trees emerged. The birds came back to the tree branches and sang songs.

Xisha did the first good deed.

Nine sons and seven daughters had grown up, and the human world had revived. But they were still worried for the second and the third good deeds hadn't been done. They thought it over and over again, and Lesha finally got a good idea, but she couldn't speak it out.

这天，他们的木筏漂到三塔江地区，勒沙嘱咐说："西沙呵！阿妹呵！当你们看见有路有桥的时候，就让儿女们出去，让人类世代接续，这就是第二件最大的好事了。"

说完，勒沙一纵身跳入三塔江中，这时，江面上好像传出木鼓的声音，接着，翻起一层层浪花，像贝珠一样洁白。接着，又从浪花里冲出一道彩虹，一直伸向天空，又从天空垂向山外。

勒沙就这样化成一座彩虹桥，西沙和路帕姑娘流着眼泪，率领着九儿七女仅双手捏着自己的下颚①，跪倒在木筏上。

九儿七女拜别了他们的父母，踏上彩虹桥，分散走向四面八方。一对儿女走向汉人地区，成了汉人。一对儿女走向彝人地区，成了彝人。一对儿女走向傣人地区，成了傣人。一对儿女走向藏人地区，成了藏人。一对儿女走向景颇人地区，成了景颇人。一对儿女走向老缅地区，成了缅人。一对儿女又走向纳西地区，成了纳西人。

还有两个小儿子就留在身边。

---

① 傈僳族古代行大礼的一种姿势。

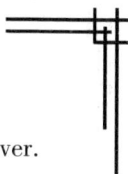

One day, their raft arrived at the area of the Santa River. Lesha told Xisha and Lupa's daughter, "Dear brother and sister, Let the children go out and reproduce their offspring when you could see roads and bridges, which would become the second good deed."

Then she jumped into the Santa River. At this time, there seemed to come the sound of wooden drums on the surface of the water, then layers of waves were stirred as white as the shell beads, and finally a rainbow dashed from the sprays, stretched to the sky, and reached to the other side of the mountain.

In this way, Lesha turned into a rainbow bridge. Full of tears, Xisha and Lupa's daughter, including their nine sons and seven daughters, knelt on the raft with their chins pinched in their hands.[1]

Nine sons and seven daughters left their parents, set their foot on the rainbow bridge and went to different places. A pair of them went to the place where the Han people lived, and joined them. A pair went to the Yi area and became the Yi people. A pair went to the Dai area and became the Dai people. A pair went to the Tibetan area and became the Tibetans. A pair went to the Jingpo area and became the Jingpo people. A pair went to the Mian area and became the Mian people. A pair went to the Naxi area, and became the Naxi people.

Two little sons stayed with their parents.

---

[1]　This is a gesture of giving a solution in ancient times in Lisu ethnic group.

世间留下的两个人，完成了两件最大的好事。勒沙是做出最大好事的人，所以世间的人都对她感念。每当彩虹出现的时候，全世间的人都以崇敬的心情向她张望。

西沙射穿的石壁，至今还留有一个圆圆的洞，洞边已长了几株小树，在夜晚从山下看去，跟月亮一模一样，人们就称它为"岩石月亮"。

翻译、整理者：曹德旺，周忠枢

# 神　匠

远古的时候，有一个聪明的神匠，能做种种木偶，惟妙惟肖，还能行动。那时宇宙间除了他和他的妻子及一个女儿外，并没有什么人，神匠以为这茫茫大地，如果没有人类繁殖起来，必成为一个荒凉的世界。

有一天，神匠和他的妻子商量说："我现在山中削木偶，能叫他行动、说话、饮食，还能生育，和自己形状一样，就是你母女二人也不能辨别出来，我将以这些木偶传播人种。"他妻子说："你真有如此神技吗？"神匠说："我自有神术，所削的木偶，和我的形象相同，叫你们母女来辨认，若是能找出我来，我就认输。"到第二天女儿往山中送饭，看见十三个人都特别像他父亲，竟不能辨别出来哪个是她真父亲，同时自己也辨别不出哪个是木偶，就把所带的食物，分给十三个人，回去后她把这种情形告诉她母亲。母亲说："你年纪小所以不能认出你父亲来，你父亲有一个特别记号，我能

Xisha and Lesha, who were left in the human world when it flooded, finished their two good deeds. Lesha did the best deed so the people in the world thanked her very much. Whenever the rainbow appeared in the sky, the whole world looked up at her in reverence.

The round hole on the cliff which Xisha shot was still there, and some small trees grew around it. Every night, seen from the foot of the mountain, the hole looked like a moon, so it was called "Rock Moon".

Collector and Interpreter: Cao Dewang, Zhou Zhongshu

## The Magical Craftsman

In ancient times, there was a smart craftsman who could make all kinds of vivid and movable puppets. At that time, there was no one in the universe except him, his wife and daughter. The craftsman believed that without human beings, the earth would be a desolate world.

One day, the craftsman told his wife, "I'm now making puppets in the mountain, which I can make them move, speak, drink and reproduce. The puppets look like myself, and you and our daughter can't distinguish them from me. And I'll make these puppets reproduce the human beings." His wife asked, "Do you really have the magic power?" The craftsman answered, " Of course I do. All the puppets that I will make have the same appearance as mine. You and our daughter come to find me out. If you can do it, I'll admit my defeat." The second day, the daughter

辨别出来。"第二天他妻子去送饭，十三个人都来拿吃的，他的妻子几乎不能分辨出来，因为神匠和十二座木偶，一模一样，一丝一毫都相同，他的妻子赶紧想出办法来，叫他们十三个人不要动，说："我带的饭，是给我丈夫的，不是给你们木偶的。"她一面用这句话掩饰，一面细察十三个人的面孔，看见有一个人，鼻子发出几点汗，知道是亲夫，于是上前接着说："你能欺骗女儿，可瞒不过老妻！"十二座木偶听后就退避到山林里，和猿猴交配，生出各种人类，现在傈僳族也是其中的一种，父是木偶，母是猿猴。

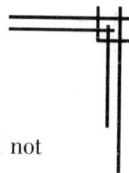

brought the meal to her father in the mountain, but she could not distinguish her father from the thirteen puppets who all looked like him, and she couldn't tell which ones were the puppets. She had to divide the food into thirteen portions. She went back home and told her mother all about it, and her mother said, "You are too young to tell who your father is, but I can recognize him for your father has a special feature." The next day, the wife brought the meal to her husband. The thirteen people came to take the food, and the wife almost could not distinguish them from each other because the craftsman and twelve puppets looked like the same, without any difference. His wife tried to find out her husband hurriedly, so she asked them not to move and said, "The food I brought here is for my husband, but not for you puppets." While speaking, she watched the thirteen people carefully. Seeing that one of the thirteen people sweated on the nose, she knew he must be her husband. So she went to him and said, "You can deceive your daughter, but you can't cheat your wife." Then the twelve puppets went into the forests and mated with the apes, reproducing a variety of human nationalities. The present Lisu people were one of them, whose forefather was a puppet and foremother was an ape.

# 第八章　毛南族

## 盘和古

　　盘和古本是两兄妹，他俩种葫芦，天天浇水放肥，葫芦结得像禾仓一样大。后来地上涨大水，盘和古就进到葫芦里，浮在水面上。水退后，世界上只剩他们两个。如何再造人和世界呢？兄妹商量，总认为不好成婚。后来他们约定，两人各扛一边石磨到山顶上，各自把石磨从山顶滚下来，如滚下的石磨上下合在一起，就证明有姻缘。说也奇怪，石磨滚到山下，当真合在一起。于是兄妹成婚，生了一个胞衣小孩。他俩把小孩剁成碎块，让乌鸦、老鹰啄去撒在四方，三天以后，到处都有人了。

# Chapter Eight　Maonan Ethnic Group

## Pan and Gu

Pan and Gu once were a brother and a sister. They planted a gourd, and watered and manured it every day, so the gourd grew as big as a barn. Later, it flooded on the earth, so Pan and Gu hid in the gourd which floated in the water. When the flood subsided, they were the only ones left in the world. How to reproduce the human being and recreate the human world? The brother and sister discussed with each other and thought that it was not good for them to get married. Later, they made an appointment that they each carried a part of the millstone to the top of the mountain, and let it roll down to the bottom, and they would get married if the upper and the lower part of the millstone coincided with each other. Oddly enough, the two parts really did when they rolled down to the bottom of the mountain. So the brother and sister got married, and gave birth to a child. They chopped the child into many fragments, and let the crows and eagles peck at them and scattered to different places. Three days later, there were human beings everywhere.

# 第九章　德昂族

## 人类的起源

在天地刚刚分开以后，大地上还没有一切生物，只有天王和地母。后来，他俩便结成夫妻，生了一个女孩。

一天，天王一人外出，走到一处漫无边际的密林中去打柴，忽然一阵狂风吹来，刮落了一百片树叶。天王自言自语说："一百片树叶，若果能变成人，我就有伙伴了。"他话刚说完，果然这一百片树叶就变成了一百个人，男女各五十人。这五十个男子的面貌与天王模样完全相似。地母叫女儿去给天王送饭，女儿始终认不出谁是她的父亲，只好折回家中向母亲禀明情况。地母告诉女儿说："你看见谁身上会出汗，谁就是你父亲。"女儿照母亲的吩咐，又到山上给父亲送饭，看到有一个人正在砍柴，身上出了很多汗，便认出这个人是他的父亲。

# Chapter Nine   De'ang Ethnic Group

## The Origin of the Human Being

After the separation of the heaven and the earth, there was no creature on the earth except the Heaven and the Earth. Later, they got married and gave birth to a baby girl.

One day, the Heaven went out to cut firewood in the boundless dense forest. Suddenly a strong wind came and blew a hundred pieces of leaves off the tree. The Heaven said to himself, "I would have partners if the one hundred pieces of leaves could be changed into human beings." With his words, the leaves changed into a hundred human beings, fifty men and fifty women. The fifty men were of the same appearance as the Heaven. The Earth asked the daughter to bring meals to the Heaven, but the daughter could not recognize her father, and had to go back home and tell her mother about it. The Earth told her that, "The one who sweats the most should be your father." Following her mother's words, the daughter went to the mountain again, and saw a man sweat all over his body while he was cutting the firewood, and she knew that he must be her father.

至此，在世界上便生活着一百零三人，他们就是现在德昂族的祖先。

当时，这一百个人，每人都有一个姓。他们把这棵被风吹落了树叶的大树，称为"生人树"，因为人是从这棵树的树叶变成的。既然有了人，就得有房子住，于是他们又把这棵生人树锯成了木板，盖起了房屋，住在附近的山坡上。从此，这一百个男女，便结成了五十对夫妇。

由于人口的增加，他们所种的粮食便不够吃，于是天王就到天庭向仙人要粮食种子。天王带回了玉米、稻谷、大豆、小麦、瓜、果、葫芦等种子，撒种在地上、山坡上和海边。他们把葫芦种子撒在海边上，它的秧生长在海中心，枝叶长出后，结了一个葫芦，浮在海中央，葫芦长得很大，如一座山，只听里面有人在闹。

一天，突然电闪雷鸣，天空下起了暴雨，炸雷劈开了这个大葫芦，里面却装着许多人，他们乘着葫芦划到海边，上岸后，这些人变成了汉、傣、回、傈僳、景颇、阿昌、白等民族的祖先。同时，还从葫芦里走出了许多动物和植物。

整理者：杨毓骧

So far, the 103 people living in the world were the ancestors of the De'ang people.

At that time, each one of the 100 people had a family name. The tree whose leaves were blown off was called "Tree of the human being", for the human beings were born from the leaves of the tree. Since there were human beings, there must be house to live in. So they cut the tree into pieces and built houses on the hill slopes nearby. Since then, the 100 men and women became 50 couples.

With the increase of the population, the crops they grew were not enough, so the Heaven went to ask the immortals for seeds. He took back the seeds of corn, grain, bean, maize, melon, fruit and gourd, which were sowed in the field, on the slopes and on the coast. The seeds of gourd was sowed on the coast, but sprouted in the center of the sea. When the stems leaves grew out, a gourd came out and floated in the sea. The gourd grew as big as a mountain, in which the human beings' noises could be heard clearly.

One day, it rained heavily with the sudden thunderstorms and lightning, and the gourd was split by a loud crash of thunder. In the gourd were a lot of people, who rowed the gourd to the seashore and went ashore. These people became the ancestors of the Han people, the Dai people, the Hui people, the Lisu people, the Jingpo people, the Ahchang people, the Bai people and so on. At the same time, a variety of animals and plants came out of the gourd.

Collector: Yang Yuxiang

# 祖先创世纪

## 祖先帕达然

很古很古的时候，大地上没有人。水和泥巴搅在一起，土和石头分不清楚。没有鱼虫虾蟹，没有豹子老虎，没有绿草青树，没有红花黄果，没有日月星辰，天空和大地一片混浊，只有雷吼风呼。

狂风吹啊吹，越吹越大，越吹越紧，不知吹了几万年，终于吹出了一团黑糊糊的东西。这团东西在天上转呀转，越转越黑，越转越紧，不知转了多少万年。有一天，风和雷碰到一起，风说："我的力气大无比。"雷说："我的力气谁也比不过。"它们一个不服气另一个，就打了起来。风拼命吹，要把雷赶走。雷拼命打，要把风打死。他们从天上打到地下，从东打到西，从北打到南。有时风把雷赶走，但是雷很狡猾，悄悄躲到最高处，等到风歇气时，他又突然冲下来。他们两个打打停停，停停打打，谁也不服输，不知打了几万年，一直到现在，雷声一响，风就大发脾气。

# Creation of the Ancestor

## Padaran

In ancient times, there was no human being on the earth. The water and the mud were mixed together and the soil could not be distinguished from the stones. There were no fish and worms and shrimps and crabs, nor were leopards and tigers. There were no green grass and trees, nor were red flowers and yellow fruits. There were no sun and moon and stars, but the roaring thunders and howling gales. It was so chaotic in the universe.

The winds blew stronger and stronger and nobody knew how many years passed until a black mess appeared. The mess turned around and around in the heaven for thousands of years, and became blacker and tighter. One day, the Wind and the Thunder met. The Wind said, "I'm the strongest." The Thunder said, "No one is stronger than me." Neither of them could convince the other, and finally they fought against each other. The Wind tried its best to blow the Thunder off while the Thunder tried its best to hit the Wind to death. They fought from the heaven to the earth, from the east to the west and from the north to the south. Sometimes the Wind drove the Thunder away, but the Thunder was very cunning and hid on the highest place quietly. When the Wind had a rest, the Thunder would suddenly rush down. They fought and stopped and fought for thousands of years, and no one would admit defeat. Until now, whenever the Thunder begins to roar, the Wind would begin to howl.

　　有一天，风正围着那团黑糊糊的东西转，越转越高兴。雷在天空看见了，恨得咬牙切齿，就吼叫着冲下来，争抢这团黑糊糊的东西。

　　抢呀抢，谁也不让谁。最后两个使出了全部力气，"哗啦"一声，黑糊糊的东西被撕成两半，从中间掉出了一个人。这个人慢慢张开了嘴巴，一口一口地吸气，吸一口就大一点。不知过了多少年，他长成了大人。但是，他什么也看不见，分不清东西南北。雷神就与老婆商量，为了让这个人看清世界，雷吼着，电婆"哗啦"一声，就把人的脸凿开两个洞，装上两小粒火，这就是眼睛；风神看见雷神给人做了好事，很不服气。他看到人会吸气，能看见东西，但是不会听，就在人的头两边撕开两道口子，吹开小洞，让人听到声音，这就是耳朵。接着，雷神又给人塑了鼻子，风神给人画了眉毛和头发。由于风神和雷神争着帮助人，人有了眼、耳、鼻、眉和头发，看得见，听得着，聪明无比，叫作"帕达然"。他就是最早的人，也是智慧的神。

One day, the Wind turned around the black mess happily. Seeing this, the Thunder gnashed his teeth in hatred, roared and rushed to snatch the black mess. Both tried to get it and neither would give in. Finally, they both tried their best only to tear it into two pieces, from which a human being came out. The human being opened his mouth slowly, took a breath over and over again. The more breath he took, the bigger he became. Many years passed, and he grew up, but he couldn't see anything, nor could he tell the directions. the Thunder then discussed with his wife to make the human being see the world clearly. With the Thunder's roar and the Lightning's flash, they dug two holes in the human's face and put on two spots of fire, which became the eyes. The Wind was very uncomfortable to see the Thunder did good deed for the human being. He found that the human being could breathe and see, but couldn't hear, so he tore a piece of crack on each side of the human being's head and blew two small holes to make him hear, which became the ears. Then the Thunder formed the human being's nose, and the Wind drew his eyebrow and hair. the Thunder and the Wind were competing for helping the human being, so he had eyes, ears, a nose, eyebrows and hair, and could see and hear. He was so smart that he was called Padaran, who was the first human being and the God of wisdom in the world.

帕达然天天靠吸气生活，一个人非常孤寂，就去请求风神和雷神归还衣胞，他还是要躲进衣胞里去。风神气得头发都立起来，雷神气得瞪圆了眼睛，把衣胞撕得粉碎抛给了帕达然。说也奇怪，碎衣胞竟变成了一棵棵小树，这就是茶树。所以，德昂族都说茶树和人的生命连在一起。不同的是，古时候的茶树是会说话的，现在的茶树只有到夜静更深的时候才互相说悄悄话。

帕达然有茶树做伴，十分高兴。他摘了一片茶挂在天上，变成了月亮；又采了一个茶果挂在天上，变成了太阳；他把茶花揉成碎片，洒在蓝幽幽的天上，变成了星星。从此，太阳、月亮、星星与茶树给帕达然做伴。

## 茶树小精灵

帕达然有茶树做伴，和太阳、月亮、星星一起，时而四处出游，时而互相嬉戏，快快活活地生活。

不知过了多少万年，帕达然始终兴致勃勃，可是茶树却厌倦了，跟着帕达然出游得越来越少，一起玩的时候，茶树老是提不起精神。有一天，帕达然问茶树："我们的天空到处明亮，走到什么地方都有彩霞踩在脚下，你们为什么愁眉不展？"茶树都低下了头，谁也不敢开腔。

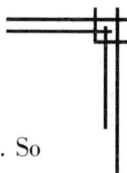

Padaran made a living by breathing, and felt very lonely. So he went to ask the Wind and the Thunder to return his placenta, which he would like to hide in. The Wind was so angry that all its hair were erected, and the Thunder was so angry that it stared at him with round eyes, and tore the placenta into pieces and threw it to Padaran. It was very strange that the pieces turned into small trees, which were nowadays' tea trees. Therefore, the De'ang people believe that the tea trees are connected with the human lives. But the tea tree in ancient times could speak while nowadays they would talk with each other only at dead of night.

Padaran was very happy to have the tea trees. He picked a tea leaf and hung it in the sky, which became the moon; he then picked a tea fruit and hung in the sky, which became the sun; and then he crumbled the tea flower into pieces and scattered them in the blue sky, which became the stars. From then on, the sun, the moon, the stars and the tea trees accompanied Padaran forever.

## A Tea Tree Angel

Padaran lived a very happy life with the tea trees, the sun, the moon and the stars. Sometimes they went out for traveling, and sometimes they played with each other.

Nobody knew how many years passed. Padaran was always in high spirits, but the tea trees were tired of it. They went out with Padaran less and less, and while playing with him, the tea trees were always in low spirits. One day, Padaran asked the tea trees, "Why are you so depressed since it is bright in the sky and there are rosy clouds under our feet wherever we go?" The tea trees lowered their heads and nobody dared open their mouth.

帕达然问了九遍，没有得到回答。他正转身要走时，突然一株最小的茶树开了腔："尊敬的帕达然啊，天空为什么五彩斑斓？大地为什么荒凉？您为什么只领我们在天上走？为什么不带我们到地上逛？"帕达然听了小茶树的话，大吃一惊。他细细地看了看小茶树，一字一句地说："这不是你们应该问的事，千万不要胡思乱想，一丝一毫的邪念也会带来万世难解的灾难。"

茶树都被吓住了。有的愁眉不展，有的发抖打颤，有的下跪磕头，有的直淌冷汗，只有小茶树纹丝不动地挺直腰杆。它镇静地说："尊敬的帕达然啊，天上和地下为什么两样？我们为什么不能到地下生长？"帕达然发怒了，声音震动了天庭："天下一片黑暗，到处都是灾难，谁要想让地上繁华，他就要吃尽万般苦楚，永远也不要想再回到天上。"

帕达然的话，像磐石压在每株茶树的心上，只有最小的茶树一点不慌："尊敬的帕达然啊，只要地上能够像天上一样繁华，我愿意去受万般灾难。"帕达然吃了一惊，想不到一株焦黄的小茶树竟有这么大的胆量，于是又进一步试探："小茶树啊，你要仔细思量，地下有一万零一条冰河，会把你冷死；地下有一万零一座火山，会把你烧死；地下有一万零一种妖魔，会把你杀死。天上清吉安康你不在，为什么一定要下去尝苦水？"小茶树听了帕达然的话，一点没有动摇。它拿定主意后又说："尊敬的帕达然，请你开恩，请你帮忙，让我下去试一试……"

Padaran asked nine times and didn't get an answer. Just as he turned around and wanted to go, the smallest tea tree opened its mouth, "Distinguished Padaran, why does the heaven look so colorful? Why is the earth so desolate? Why do you lead us travel only in the heaven? Why not take us to visit the earth?" Padaran was shocked to hear that. He looked at the smallest tea tree carefully and said word by word, "This is not what you should ask. Never think about it, and any evil thought would bring lasting disaster to the earth."

All tea trees were scared. Some frowned, some trembled, some knelt down and kowtowed, some sweated, and only the smallest one stood straight and asked calmly, "Distinguished Padaran, why are there differences between the heaven and the earth? Why couldn't we grow on the earth?" Padaran was so angry that his voice shook the heaven, "It is completely disastrous in the dark earth. He who wants to make it prosperous has to endure all the hardships and never wants to go back to the heaven."

Like a massive rock, Padaran's words made every tea tree oppressed except for the smallest one, and it said calmly, "Distinguished Padaran, I am willing to endure all kinds of hardships as long as the earth is as prosperous as the heaven." Padaran was surprised to hear that and he had never expected the smallest tea tree was so brave. He said to him inquiringly, "Think over it carefully, little tree! There are ten thousand and one glaciers on the earth, which would freeze you to death; there are ten thousand and one volcanoes on the earth, which would burn you to death; and there are one thousand and one kinds of demons on the earth, which would kill you. It is safe and sound to be in the heaven, but why do you want to taste the bitterness on the earth?" Hearing Padaran's words, the smallest tea tree didn't change its mind, but said firmly, "Distinguished Padaran, please let me have a try..."

小茶树的话还没有说完，狂风吹得天昏地暗，阵阵雷打电闪。狂风撕碎了小茶树的身子，雷电把乌云凿开一道葫芦形的口子。小茶树身上的一百零二片茶叶飘出天门，悠忽悠忽地下降。

雷鸣电闪，狂风嘶叫，茶叶被吹得在空中打转，越转越快，转了三万年，化出了一百零二个人，单数叶变成五十一个精悍的小伙子，双数叶化成五十一个美丽的姑娘。所以，直到现在德昂族还流传着一首古老的歌谣："茶叶是德昂的命脉，有德昂的地方就有茶山。茶叶和德昂一样代代相传，德昂人的身上飘着茶叶的芳香。"

## 昼与夜

一百零二个青年男女，被风沙簇拥着在天空飘荡，睁着眼睛什么也看不见，你碰我，我碰你，疼得没有办法。女的哭了，男的也哭了，他们的声音越哭越大，一直传到九天之上。正在嬉戏的日、月、星、辰听见了，赶紧跑来帮忙。太阳搬出金钵，月亮端出银盘，星星射出光芒，把大地照得明明亮亮。

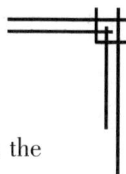

Hardly had the smallest tea tree finished its words when the wind blew violently and the thunderstorm flashed heavily. The strong wind tore the smallest tea tree into piece and the thunderstorm split a guard-like crack in the dark cloud. One hundred and two tea leaves flew out of the heaven door, falling slowly.

The tea leaves were blown to turn around in the air with the flashing thunderstorm and the roaring wind. They turned around more and more quickly for thirty thousand years, until one hundred and two human beings came into being. The odd number tea leaves became fifty-one strong boys, and the even number tea leaves became fifty-one beautiful girls. Till now, there is an old ballad in De'ang Ethnic Group, "Tea leaves are the lifelines of De'ang, and where there are De'ang people, there are mountains of tea trees. The tea leaves, like the De'ang people, pass down from generation to generation, and the De'ang people smell of the pleasant fragrance of the tea leaves.

## Day and Night

Surrounded by the wind and sand and drifting in the sky, one hundred and two young men and women could see nothing with their eyes open. They bumped into each other and felt so painful that the young women cried, and then the young men cried too. Their cries grew louder and louder until it could be heard up in the Ninth heaven. The sun, the moon, and the stars which were playing at that time heard and rushed to help. The sun took out the golden bowl, the moon took out the silver plate, and the stars shone out with great brilliancy, which made the earth very bright.

　　五十一对青年男女高兴得手舞足蹈，高兴得淌下了泪水。这些泪水落到地下汇成一股，划出一条小沟；一串眼泪汇成一条小河，一百零二串眼泪汇成了大江。泪水越来越多，聚成了大海。大海越涨越高，越来越大，使整个大地变成一片汪洋，到处白浪滔滔。

　　茶叶兄妹随着风走，因为水神作怪走到哪里都没有落脚的地方：兄妹们走到东边，水神张开大嘴要吃人；兄妹们走到西边，水神举起寒光闪闪的宝剑要杀人；兄妹们走到南边，水神伸出黑茸茸的大手要抓人；兄妹们走到北边，水神拍拍肚皮说："我要吃人。"

　　兄妹们没有办法，飘了几万年还在天上游荡。因为时间太长了，太阳疲劳得打起瞌睡，月亮疲劳得呼呼大睡，星星疲劳得闭上了眼睛。这一来，天空又是一片黑暗，一百零二个兄妹跌跌撞撞，眼看就要掉进海洋里，急得大声呼喊："尊敬的帕达然啊，尊敬的日月星辰兄长，我们又在遭难，请快来帮忙！"

　　呼喊声传遍四面八方，星星吓得直眨眼，月亮吓得打转转，太阳吓得红了脸。他们醒来了，天空、大地又是一片明亮。

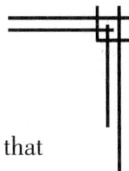

Fifty-one pairs of young men and women were so glad that they danced with joy and shed happy tears. The tears fell to the ground and merged into a small ditch. A bunch of tears formed a stream, and tears from one hundred and two converged and formed a big river. More and more tears converged together and formed a sea, which grew higher and higher and became larger and larger until the whole world became a vast ocean with surging waves everywhere.

The tea brothers and sisters followed the wind and couldn't find a place to rest because of the troubles made by the God of Water: when they went to the east, the God of Water opened its mouth and wanted to eat them; to the west, the God of Water held up his sword to kill them; to the south, the God of Water reached out his big black hand to catch them; and to the north, the God of Water patted his belly and said, "I want to eat you."

The brothers and sisters had no way to go but wander in the sky for tens of thousands of years. It was so long that the sun was tired and dozy, the moon was tired and sleepy, and the stars were tired and closed their eyes. Then the sky became dark again. The brothers and sisters stumbled, and just before they fell into the ocean, they shouted for help, "Distinguished Padaran, our respectful sun and moon and stars, we are in trouble again! Please come and help us quickly!"

The shouts spread to all directions, and the stars were frightened to wink, the moon to turn around and the sun to turn red. They all woke up and the sky and the earth became bright again.

又过了几万年，太阳、月亮和星星都实在疲劳了，想睡又怕茶叶兄弟会遭难。他们想啊想，还是小星星最聪明，他想出了一个主意：太阳的胆子大，独自照一半，月亮和星星合着照一半。从此以后，人们就把太阳照耀的时间叫白天，把星星和月亮照耀的时间叫晚上。

## 山川与河流

地上的洪水仍然泛滥，兄妹们还是落不到地上。他们没有办法，急得大声呼喊，他们的呼声惊醒了万能的帕达然。他伸了个懒腰，打了个呵欠，一股气冲下天庭，把大地震出若干条裂缝，水就顺着裂缝淌。帕达然又请来风神，带着天上积了几千万年的茶树叶下去帮忙。

狂风带着茶叶驱赶洪水。茶叶撵到的地方，洪水就逃跑，现出了大地。眼看洪水就要被灭掉，帕达然突然出现在空中，他说："天要分东西南北，地要有河谷山川，四时要分寒热暖凉，人也要有个洗澡的地方。"听了帕达然的话，茶叶停住了脚步，折回天上。

Tens of thousands of years passed, and the sun, the moon and the stars were really tired, and they wanted to sleep but they were afraid that the tea brothers and sisters would be in trouble again. They thought and thought until the clever stars came up with an idea: the brave sun would shine half of the time, and the moon and stars would shine the other half. From then on, the time the sun shone was called the "day" while the time the moon and the stars shone was called the "night".

## Mountains and Rivers

The tea brothers and sisters couldn't land on the earth because of the flood on the earth. They had no way but to shout in hurry. Their shouts woke up the almighty Padaran. He stretched out, yawned and rushed out of the heaven, which caused some cracks on the earth, so the water ran along the cracks. Padaran then invited the God of Wind to take the tea leaves accumulated for tens of millions of years to help.

The Wind took the tea leaves to drive off the flood. Where the flood was driven off by the tea leaves, the ground emerged. Just before the flood was about to subside completely, Padaran suddenly appeared in the sky and said, "There should be four directions in the heaven: the east, the west, the south and the west; there should be valleys and mountains on the earth; four seasons should be cold or hot or warm or cool, and people need a place to take bath." Hearing Padaran's words, the tea leaves stopped and went back to the heaven.

因为茶叶赶洪水赶了三万年，已经精疲力尽，步子越来越慢。有力气的慢慢赶路，没有力气的就躺下来歇息。说也奇怪，茶叶只要停住脚步躺下歇息的，再也站不起来，化作泥土铺在地上。没有力气的茶叶越来越多，大地越积越厚。原来，这是帕达然怕大地太冷，叫茶叶来保护。有的地方薄些，就是平展展的坝子；有的地方厚些，就是山丘；茶叶堆得最厚的地方，就是地上最高最大的山。一条条小河、大江是茶叶兄妹留下的眼泪流淌，大海是帕达然洗澡的地方，大大小小的湖泊是茶叶兄妹照脸的镜子。这就是平坝、高山和江河湖海的来历。

## 四色的土地

洪水退去，天空明朗，茶叶兄妹高高兴兴落到地上。

茶叶兄妹在地上正玩得高兴，突然白雾滚滚，填平了山洼，笼罩了坝子。茶叶兄妹什么也看不清楚。浓雾中夹着水珠，水珠滴在茶叶兄妹身上，长出一个疮，疮慢慢长大，痛得他们撕心裂肺。

The tea leaves had driven off the flood for thirty thousand years, so they were very exhausted. Some still had energy to walk slowly, and some had to lie down and had a rest. Strangely enough, those which stopped and lied down to rest had never stood up, and became soil on the ground. More and more tea leaves without strength rest on the ground and made the ground thicker and thicker. It turned out that Padaran asked the tea leaves to protect the earth from being too cold. Places with less tea leaves became the flat dams; those with thicker tea leaves became hills and those with the thickest ones became the highest mountains on the earth. The streams and rivers were the tears left by the tea brothers and sisters, the seas were Padaran's bathing places and the lakes in different sizes were the mirrors for the tea brothers and sisters. That is the origin of the dams, the mountains, the rivers, the lakes and the seas.

## Lands of Four Colors

The flood subsided and the sky was very clear. The tea brothers and sisters landed on the earth cheerfully.

The tea brothers and sisters were playing gladly on the earth when the rolling fog suddenly filled the lower land and covered the dams, which made them see nothing. Mixed in the thick fog, beads of water dropped on their bodies, and a boil grew. It became bigger and bigger and made them very painful.

茶叶兄妹痛得打滚，却见两个妖魔在那里猛笑。一个是雾妖，满身白毛，张着大嘴喷出一团团雾气；一个是毒妖，满身黄毛，张着大嘴喷出一股股毒气。雾妖说："大地是我们的世界，不准人来侵占。"毒妖说："想在地上生活的东西，我要叫他一个也不能活着。"听了他们的话，茶叶兄妹就分成两股，弟兄们在前面奋战，姐妹们在后面呐喊。可是，他们斗不过两个妖魔。眼看茶叶兄妹要一个个死去，最小的妹妹亚楞突然想到天上的亲人，就赶忙跑回天庭。

听亚楞说了情况，太阳、月亮和星星都很气愤，帕达然请风神带着太阳去帮助茶叶兄妹。

亚楞领着风神和太阳来到地下，风神张开嘴喷出狂风，把雾妖吹得无影无踪；太阳用金箭把毒妖射得疼痛难忍，只好与雾妖一齐逃跑。

茶叶兄妹过来感谢风神和太阳时，想不到又有两个妖魔赶来，一个红头发、红胡子、红身子，张着血盆大口，一边喷出一团团烈火，一边怪叫："我是火妖，要为雾、毒二位兄妹报仇！"一个遍体都是黑漆漆的，一边抛撒瘟疫一边狂叫："我是瘟妖，要来收拾你们！"

The tea brothers and sisters were rolling on the ground because of the pain while two demons were seen laughing there. One was the Demon of Fog, with white hair and a mass of mist spraying out of its big mouth; the other was the Demon of Poison, with yellow hair and a blast of poison gas spraying out of its big mouth. The Demon of Fog said, "The earth is mine, and nobody is allowed to stay here." The Demon of Poison said, "I will kill anyone who wants to live on the earth." Hearing the words, the tea brothers and sisters fell into two groups. The brothers' group fought in the front and the sisters' group followed and cheered for them. But they couldn't defeat the two demons. Seeing the tea brothers and sisters die one by one, the youngest sister Yaleng suddenly thought of the relatives in the heaven, and hurried back for help.

The sun, the moon and the stars were very angry at what Yaleng had said, and Padaran asked the God of Wind to take the sun to help the tea brothers and sisters.

Yaleng took the God of Wind and the sun back to the earth. The God of Wind opened its mouth and buffed a blast of wind and flew the Demon of Fog out of sight; the sun shot the Demon of Poison with its golden arrows, who couldn't bear the pain and ran away with the Demon of Fog.

Unexpectedly, another two demons came just as the tea brothers and sisters thanked the God of Wind and the sun. One was all in red, with red hair, red beard and red body. It sprayed a blaze of fire from its big bloody mouth and shouted, "I'm the Demon of Fire, and I'm coming to revenge for the Demon of Fog and the Demon of Poison." The other was all in black. It spread the plague and shouted, "I'm the Demon of Plague, and I'm coming to clear you all!" The God of Wind had no idea but to ask the sun to resist, and he hurried back to the heaven and invited the God of Thunder, the moon and the stars for help.

风神没有办法抵挡，只好让太阳去抵挡。风神急忙跑回天上，请来了雷神、月亮和星星。

雷神打起了闪，星星用刺芒戳，月亮用弯弓射，打得天昏地暗。双方打了三千年，谁也不能取胜。雷神又去请了雨神来。雨神下起瓢泼大雨，一下就把火妖打翻。火妖被打死了，瘟妖看看抵不住，正想逃跑，月亮的弓弩从他前身射进，星星的刺芒从他脊背插入。瘟妖倒在了地下。茶叶兄妹把四个妖魔的身子劈成四块，剁成肉泥，深深地埋在地下。埋着火的地方，土变成红色；埋着雾妖的地方，土变成白色；埋着毒妖的地方，土变黄色；埋着瘟妖的地方，土变成黑色。这就是土分红、白、黄，黑四种颜色的来历。

## 大地的衣裳

战胜四个妖魔以后，茶叶兄妹把风神等送回天上，就踩着云彩四处遨游，高兴时就唱歌跳舞，累了就在云上歇息。有一天，最小的弟弟达楞突然发问："天空的颜色会变幻七彩，可怜的大地却赤身露体，这究竟是什么道理？"他们都回答不出来，就回到天上问帕达然。帕达然说："只要你们舍得身子，大地就有衣裳。"

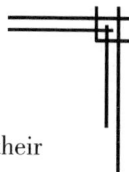

The God of Thunder flashed, the stars stabbed with their lights, and the moon shot with a bow. They fought bitterly against the demons for three thousand years, and it was hard to tell which one could win. The God of Thunder then went to ask the God of Rain for help. The God of Rain poured down and extinguished the fire completely. Seeing that the Demon of Fire was destroyed, the Demon of Plague tried to run away, but it was shot by the moon's crossbow from the front and stung by the stars' light from the back, and it fell down and died. The tea brothers and sisters split each of the four demons' body into four pieces, chopped into meat mud and buried in the deep ground. The ground where the Demon of Fire was buried became red, where the Demon of Fog was buried became white, where the Demon of Poison was buried became yellow, and where the Demon of Plague was buried became black. This is the reason why there are red soil, white soil, yellow soil and black soil on the earth.

## The Clothing of the Earth

The four demons were defeated, so the tea brothers and sisters escorted the God of Wind back to the heaven. They traveled around on the colorful clouds, singing and dancing when they were happy and resting on the clouds when they were tired. One day, the youngest brother Daleng suddenly asked, "The sky is colorful, but the poor earth is naked. What on earth are the reasons?" Nobody could answer the question, and they went back to the heaven to ask Padaran. Padaran answered, "As long as you are willing to give up your bodies, the earth will have clothes to wear."

茶叶兄妹告别了帕达然，来到空中，各自撕碎自己的皮肉撒在地上。茶叶的皮肉一着地就长出一片新绿，大的变成树，小的变成草，肉筋筋变成一条条青藤，从此以后大地郁郁葱葱。

大地有了草和树，茶叶兄妹的身子轻了，更加灵活，不论是飞到平坝还是高山，树木草藤都低头迎接，因为它们知道，茶叶兄妹是自己的生身父母。

鲜艳的百花开了就谢，一年只能开一回，不能传宗接代，只有素白的茶花开了就结果，茶果落地生出子孙。茶叶兄妹又请了太阳、月亮、风神和雨神来帮助，把茶果碾成粉末撒在百花上，凡是茶果粉撒着的花都结出果子来。世上从此有了各种果子，味道有酸有甜，只有茶果又苦又涩。所以，至今德昂族教训子女，都要叫他们像茶花一样纯洁，像茶果一样无私。有一句谚语说：吃着香甜的桃李菠萝，莫把结子的茶果遗忘。

## 飞禽与走兽

茶叶兄妹的快活日子过了九万年，突然一股黑风卷起，把兄妹吹散。姐妹被吹到天空，兄弟跌落在地上。

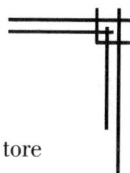

The tea brothers and sisters bid farewell to Padaran, tore their flesh into pieces in the sky and scattered them on the earth, which grew into a stretch of green on the ground. The big ones grew into big trees, the small ones grew into grass, and the tendons became green vines. From then on, the earth was always green.

With the grass and trees on the earth, the tea brothers and sisters became lighter and more flexible. Whenever the tea brothers and sisters flew to the dams or to the mountains, the grass and trees would lower their heads to greet them, because they knew that the tea brothers and sisters were their parents.

The bright-colored flowers bloomed and withered once a year, but they couldn't reproduce. Only the white tea flowers bloomed and yielded fruit, and reproduced their descendants. The tea brothers and sisters invited the sun, the moon, the God of Wind and the God of Rain to help grind the tea fruit and scattered the powder over the flowers. Those which were scattered the tea fruit powder all bore fruits. Since then, there were a variety of fruits with the taste of sourness or sweet, but the taste of the tea fruit was bitter and astringent. So the De'ang people taught their children to be as pure as the tea flowers, and as selfless as the tea fruit, just like the proverb saying, "Don't forget the tea fruit when fragrant and sweet peach and pineapple are eaten."

## Birds and Beasts

The tea brothers and sisters had lived happily for ninety thousand years. Suddenly, a black wind rolled the tea brothers and sisters apart from each other, blowing the sisters into the heaven, and bringing the brothers down to the earth.

天上的姐妹望着地下，地下的弟兄望着天上，一百零二对眼睛泪水汪汪，谁也舍不得离开谁，互相呆呆地痴望着。帕达然走出天门对茶叶兄妹说："天地相通有九十九条路，懒惰的人再过九万年也不能团圆。"

听了帕达然的话，姐妹使劲按云彩，弟兄拼命往上跳。不知过了多少年，还是隔云相望。

姐妹又把云彩搓成线，要把兄弟拉上去，搓了九百九十九丈，黑风"呼啦"一声，线断了。弟兄们搬土筑高台，台子堆得九百丈，还是接不到天上。弟兄们又跑到高高的山上，爬到最高的树上，朝天伸出龙竹，兄弟与姐妹的手还是隔着八百丈。

弟兄们耗尽了力气，只好在树林里歇息。小兄弟达楞最贪玩，扯得一根青藤扎成藤圈，丢到地上套住小草，向上抛去套住白云，他使劲往上丢，藤圈套着最小的妹妹亚楞来到身旁。

达楞的办法提醒了哥哥们。他们每个人都扯了一根青藤，扎成圆圈，五十个藤圈抛上天，二十五对姑娘被套下地。神奇的藤圈搭起了上天的路，拆散的骨肉又团圆，五十一对男女结成双。

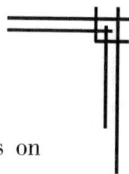

The sisters in the heaven looked down and the brothers on the earth looked up, with 102 pairs of tearful eyes looking at each other dully, and no one was willing to depart. Padaran went out of the heaven door and said to the tea brothers and sisters, "There are ninety-nine roads to connect the heaven and the earth, but lazy people will not reunite in ninety thousand years."

Hearing the words, the sisters tried their best to press the clouds towards the earth and the brothers tried their best to jump high to the heaven. Many years passed, they still looked at each other through the clouds.

The sisters then twisted the clouds into thread, trying to pull the brothers up to the sky. The thread was ninety-nine hundred feet long, and it broke when the black wind blew. The brothers built a high platform with the earth, which was nine thousand feet high but still far away from the heaven. The brothers then ran to the highest mountain, climbed up the tallest tree, and reached out the bamboo, only to find that there was a long distance between the sisters and them.

The brothers were exhausted and had to rest in the forest. The youngest brother Daleng was very playful, and he pulled a vine and twisted it into a circle, which could entangle the grass when thrown on the ground, or the white clouds when thrown to the sky. He then tried his best to throw it upwards, and it entangled the youngest sister Yaleng back to his side.

Daleng's vine circle was a reminder to his brothers. Each of them pulled a vine and made a circle. With fifty vine circles throwing upwards to the heaven, fifty sisters were trapped back to the earth. The magic vine circles set up the path to the heaven, and the reunion of the separating brothers and sisters formed fifty-one pairs.

　　茶叶兄妹结成五十一对后，慢慢地就觉得光有人太单调，于是他们用泥巴捏了许多东西，吐上一口唾沫丢进水里。有的变成摇头摆尾的鱼，有的变成甲壳坚硬的蚌，有的变成举大钳子的螃蟹……水里有了各种动物，流水有了伙伴。

　　茶叶兄妹来到山林，花草树木对着他们哭诉："白天冷冷清清。"岩石来哭诉："夜晚实在凄凉。"它们都要求有亲密的伙伴。于是，茶叶兄妹又用泥巴捏了许多东西，吐上一口唾沫撒出去。姐妹们捏的撒在山林，变成了各种鸟，既会唱歌又会跳舞；兄弟们捏的撒在山洞，变成了各种野兽，既有温驯的金鹿，也有勇敢的狮子。

　　从此以后，水里有鱼蚌虾蟹逐浪，山里有百兽跳舞，空中有百鸟欢唱。

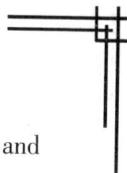

With the fifty-one pairs formed, some of the tea brothers and sisters felt it was too dull to live with only human beings on the earth. So they made many things out of mud, spat at each one a mouthful of spittle and threw them into water. Some turned into fish shaking their head and lashing their tail, some turned into clams with a hard shell, and some turned into crabs with a pair of big pincers... There were a variety of animals in the water, and the flowing water got partners.

The tea brothers and sisters went to the forest in the mountains. The flowers and trees complained tearfully, "It is too desolate in the daytime." The rocks also cried, "It is too lonely at night." They all asked for intimate partners. So the tea brothers and sisters made many things out of mud, spat at each one a mouthful of spittle and threw them out. The sisters threw them in the forest, which turned into a variety of birds that could sing and dance; the brothers threw them into the caves, which became a variety of wild beasts, including the tame golden deer and the brave lions.

Since then, there were fish and clams and crabs chasing the waves in the water, beasts dancing in the mountains and all kinds of birds singing in the sky.

## 亚楞与达楞

茶叶兄妹见大地上有了一切，十分高兴。为了玩得更痛快，有的姐妹嫌腰上的藤箍碍事，就把它解下来摆着。有一天，大家跳得满头大汗，五十个姐妹解下了腰上的藤箍，只有最小的禾妹亚楞忙着与最小的弟弟达楞谈情，没有解下腰箍。突然一阵清风吹来，五十个姐姐飘上了天空，只有亚楞留在地下。所以至今德昂族的姑娘腰上随时都系着腰箍，并流传着一句谚语："腰上没有藤圈的姑娘，心空靠不住。"

五十个姐妹上了天，五十个弟兄悲痛地死去，只剩下亚楞和达楞。掩埋了哥哥们的尸体，他们凄凄怆怆躲进岩洞度时光。太阳出了又落，月亮缺了又圆，亚楞和达楞生下了儿子和姑娘，一代又一代地生殖繁衍，人口一年比一年兴旺。小岩洞太挤，他们住进了大岩洞。过了一万年，天下的岩洞都被人住满了。

为了让子孙世代生存，亚楞和达楞仔细商量，他们按照石洞的样子搭竹架，按照牛肋巴的样子编竹笆，按照芭蕉叶的样子扎草把，盖起了竹楼。从此，人类有了自己的住房。

## Yaleng and Daleng

The tea brothers and sisters were very happy to see everything there on the earth. In order to have more fun, some sisters untied the vine circle on their waist and put it off for it got in their way to dance. One day, fifty sisters untied their vine circles when they were dancing to sweat heavily, except for the youngest sister Yaleng, who was busy with dating with the youngest brother Daleng. Suddenly, a breeze blew the fifty sisters to the sky, leaving Yaleng on the earth. So nowadays, the girls of De'ang Ethnic Group would tie waist circle at any time, and a prevailing proverb says, "The girl who doesn't tie the waist circle is empty and unreliable."

The fifty sisters went to the heaven, and the fifty brothers died in grief, leaving Yaleng and Daleng, who buried the brothers and hid in the cave heartbreakingly. The sun rose and set, and the moon waxed and waned, and Yaleng and Daleng gave birth to sons and daughters. Generation after generation, the human being became more and more prosperous, moving from the small caves into larger ones, until all the caves on the earth were filled with human beings after ten thousand years.

In order to survive on the earth forever, Yaleng and Daleng discussed carefully, and made a bamboo stand according to the shape of the cave, made a bamboo fence according to the bull's rib, made bundles according to the leaves of the Chinese banana, and then built bamboo houses. Since then, human beings had their own housing.

亚楞和达楞活了三万年。为了让子孙的日子过得好，他们分别走进大山和海里。达楞走到高山上，一次牵回了牛，一次牵回了猪，一次牵回了羊。他还要去牵老虎豹子时，已经精疲力尽，倒下去就再没爬起来，化作一座大山。人们都说，要是达楞再有一点力气，现在老虎豹子也不会在山林里乱跑了。

亚楞去到海洋，一次牵回了鱼，一次牵回了鹅，一次牵回了鸭。她还要去牵龙和乌龟，但是没有力气了。她倒在海里，变成了银晃晃的海浪。人们都说，要是亚楞再有一点力气，龙和乌龟也会被人养在家里。

## 乐器

达楞和亚楞的子孙，为了传颂祖先的恩德，他们觉得光靠嘴巴还不能表达心意，还要用更美更动听的声音。

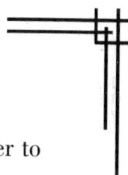

Yaleng and Daleng lived for thirty thousand years. In order to make their descendants live better, they went to the mountains and seas respectively. Daleng went to the mountains three times, taking back the cow, the pig and the sheep respectively. He was too exhausted, fell down to the ground and turned into a mountain and never stood again when he wanted to take back the tiger and the leopard. It was said that if he had been strong enough to take them back, the tiger and the leopard would not run around in the mountain forest.

Yaleng went to the sea three times, taking back the fish, the goose and the duck respectively. She tried to take back the dragon and the turtle, but she failed for she had no strength. She fell into the sea, and became the silver waves. It was said that if she had been strong enough to take the dragon and the turtle back, they would be kept at home.

## The Musical Instruments

For the sake of spreading their ancestors' virtue, the descendants of Daleng and Yaleng wanted to express their gratitude not only by their mouth, but also with a more beautiful and pleasant voice.

他们想了一万年，东边山上有个人把园子边的葫芦摘下来，掏空了心，凿了个洞，吹出了呼呼呼的声音，又插了几根竹筒，就发出了悦耳的声音，这就是今天的葫芦笙；西边山上有个人砍了两节金竹，凿了个眼，拼在一起，吹出了悠扬的声音，这就是"吐良"；南边山上有个姑娘在剥竹篾时，嘴上含了薄薄的一小片，吹出了清雅的声音，这就是口弦；北边山上有个老人，把攀枝花的树心掏空，蒙上羊皮，做成了鼓，因为是仿照大象脚做的，所以叫象脚鼓；住在坝子的小伙子把黄铜打扁，中间凸，可以提着打的叫做铓，中间凹，两只手抬着敲的叫做镲。各个山头的人都做出了乐器，大家吹吹打打，都是一个意思：要牢记祖先的恩情。

因为这些乐器都是为了纪念达楞和亚楞的，所以，每逢吹打乐器时，高山都要答应，大海都要回响。

过了九万年之后，达楞和亚楞的子孙分成了不同的民族。不同的民族心肠都一样善良。直到现在，各民族的好心人都相亲相帮。

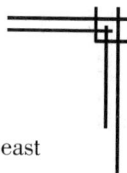

They had thought for ten thousand years. In the east mountain, a man picked a gourd in the vegetable plot, emptied it and chiseled a hole to blow the air, and then several bamboo tubes were equipped on the gourd to produce cheerful voice, which is called Hulusheng nowadays; In the west mountain, a man cut two pieces of golden bamboo. Each was chiseled a hole and two were joined together to produce melodious voice, which is called Tuliang nowadays. In the south mountain, a girl put a thin bamboo skin in the mouth when she peeled the bamboo and played in elegant voice, which is now called Harmonica. In the north mountain, an old man emptied a tree, covered it with the sheep skin and made a drum. It looked like an elephant's foot, so it was call Elephant-foot drum. A young man living in the dam flattened a piece of bronze with the center protruding, and hung it to play, which was called Mang; the flattened bronze with the center concave and played with two hands lifting was called Cymbals. People living in different places had made various musical instruments to beat or blow for the purpose of remembering their ancestors' virtue.

The musical instruments were made to memorize Daleng and Yaleng, so whenever they were played, the mountains and seas usually echoed.

After ninety thousand years, the descendants of Daleng and Yaleng were divided into different nationalities, but they were of the same kindness. Till now, the people in different nationalities love and help each other.

现在世界上的各个民族都喝茶，是对达楞和亚楞的怀念。喝着苦甜苦甜的茶水，是要人们不忘祖先创世的艰辛，也不要忘记未来的日子还会有艰难。

流传地区：云南省德宏州德昂族地区
整理者：陈志鹏

Nowadays, people in every nation of the world like drinking tea to cherish the memory of Daleng and Yaleng. The purpose of drinking the bitter and sweet tea is to let people not forget the hardship their ancestors endured in the creation of the world, and also to remind the people of the difficulties in the future.

Spreading area: Dehong State, De'ang Region
Collector: Chen Zhipeng

# 第十章　景颇族

## 开天辟地

远古时代，世界上是一片蒸腾的雾气，没有天，没有地，整个都是混混沌沌的，这个时期，景颇人叫作"几应扎"。不知过了多少年，雾气升腾，进入了景颇人称之为"比应吧"的时期。这时世界朦朦胧胧的，有了一些光亮，开始呈现出不太明显的轮廓，就好像现在天快亮时的样子。又过了很长很长的时间，就到了"简应扎"① 时期，也就是进入了"盘古"时期。"简应扎"是一个人，这时他正孕育在一个像鸡蛋一样的东西里面。北方大海的一个海岛——才召，就是这个人孕育的地方。

---

① 简：在景颇语中是看得懂的意思。应扎：是感觉到的意思。

# Chapter Ten　Jingpo Ethnic Group

## Creation of the World

In ancient times, the universe was in thick foggy and there were no the heaven and the earth but a chaotic mess. At that time, the Jingpo people were called Jiyingzha. Nobody knew how many years passed when the fog rose and it entered the period of what was called Biyingba by the Jingpo people. The world was dimly lit with some light, and it began to show an unclear outline as if it were almost dawn. A long, long time passed, and it was the period of Jian Yingzha[①], that is, the period of Pangu. Jian Yingzha was a human's name, who was conceived in a container looking like an egg. On an island named Caizhao in a northern sea, the human would be born.

---

① Jian means "to understand by seeing"; Yingzha means "to sense" in Jingpo dialect.

也不知过了多少年，简应扎在这个海岛上睁开了眼睛。他看到的只是一个天地不分的世界，随时都处在一种动荡之中，十分闷人。简应扎深深地喘了一口气，决定把天地分开，就从那像鸡蛋样的东西里升到了高高的天空。他使劲往下一踩，下面硬邦邦的就成了地；他又用双手往上一捧，就形成了天。就这样，天地造成了。但他怕天地会再次合拢来，就用手顶着天，用脚踩着地，一直支撑了三十六万年，天地才渐渐牢固了。这时，简应扎也支持不住了，他的手软了，后来就慢慢地死去。

虽然有了天地，但天地都是缺的，龙木格萨就派了两兄弟潘娃能桑①、简娃应扎②来到了世上。哥哥潘娃能桑补天，弟弟简娃应扎补地。天从东方补下来，地从西方补起来。这时东边的天上由混沌的气体变成了九个太阳，其中六个比较接近地面。太阳似火，晒裂了大地，弟弟撒在地下的树种都没有出。弟弟去找哥哥商量："哥哥，你的九个太阳把我的地都晒裂了，我无法补地。你得想个办法帮帮我。"哥哥想了很多办法，最后用白云彩捂住了最下面的六个太阳。剩下的三个，一个离地面很远，两个在中间，地还是无法补。弟弟又去找哥哥商量。

---

① 潘娃能桑：补天的人。
② 简娃应扎：补地的人。

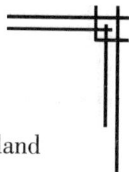

Many years later, Jian Yingzha opened his eyes on the island and saw a chaotic world in a state of turbulence. He took a deep breath and decided to separate the heaven from the earth. He stayed in the container which looked like an egg and rose to the sky. He stepped hard on the bottom, which became the hard earth; he then put his hands on the top to form the heaven. In this way, the heaven and the earth came into being. But he was afraid that the heaven and the earth would come together again, so he held the heaven with his hands and stepped on the earth for three hundred and sixty thousand years until the heaven and the earth became solid. At last, Jian Yingzha couldn't hold any longer, for his hands softened and he died later.

The heaven and the earth came into being, but they were deficient. So Longmugesa sent two brothers, the elder brother Panwa Nengsang① and the younger brother Jianwa Yingzha②, to the world. Panwa patched the heaven from the east and Jianwa patched the earth from the west. At this moment, the chaotic air in the east became nine suns, six of which were close to the earth and burn the earth into cracks. The younger brother had sown the seeds of trees but they did not sprout, so he went to discuss with his brother, "Elder brother, your nine suns had burnt the earth into cracks and I couldn't patch it. You'd better find a way to help me." The elder brother tried many ways and finally covered the six lowest suns with the white clouds, leaving one of the other three far away from the earth and two in the middle. But the earth still couldn't be patched. So the younger brother went to see his brother again.

---

① Panwa Nengsang is the man who patched the heaven in the Jingpo Ethnic Group.

② Jianwa Yingzha is the man who patched the earth in the Jingpo Ethnic Group.

弟弟对哥哥说："这两个太阳还是太辣了，你不帮我想办法，地上就什么也不长了。"哥哥觉得弟弟说得对，决定用黑云彩来捂这两个太阳。结果一个太阳被捂住了，另一个太阳跑掉了，从此就只剩下一个太阳高高地悬挂在天上，离地面已相当远了。跑掉的那个太阳是公的，变成了月亮，所以不暖和。剩下的太阳是个母的，它的光亮是由七千兆个火塘拼成的，这些光亮照耀着大地，给万物以光和热。

可是这样，又形成了两层天、一个地。弟弟简娃应扎说："不要有两层天，一天一地就行了。"哥哥潘娃能桑听从了弟弟的话，把一层天拿掉了，逃跑到中层天的月亮还留在那里，当作晚上的火把。接着两人又商量，认为天应比地大，决定再补天。这次还是用云彩来补。云彩有三种：灰色的、白色的、黑色的。前两种用来补天。黑色的云彩让它在天空流动，冬天流到海洋，秋天又上升，下到海洋就吸水到天空下雨。雨量以箩来计算，每年不能超过六箩，超过了就成灾。

The younger brother said, "The two suns are still too hot, and if you can't find a way to help me, nothing will grow on the earth." The elder brother agreed and decided to cover the two suns with black clouds. As a result, one of them was covered and the other ran away. From then on, only one sun remained high in the sky and far away from the earth. The sun that ran away was a male one and became a moon, so it was not warm. The sun staying in the sky was a female one, and its sunshine was made up of seven thousand trillion fire pools, which shone in the sky and gave light and heat to all things on the earth.

However, two layers of heaven and one earth were formed in this way. Jianwa said, "Two layers of heaven are too much, and just one heaven and one earth is enough." The elder brother thought it right and took a heaven away, leaving the moon in the middle as a torch at night. Then they considered that the heaven should be larger than the earth and decided to patch the heaven with the clouds again. Among the three colors of clouds, the grey, the white and the black, the first two colors of clouds could be used to patch the heaven, and the black were allowed to drift in the sky from the oceans in winter to the land in autumn, which absorbed the water from the oceans and then rained on the land. The rainfall was calculated by the basket, and it would flood if there were over six baskets a year.

这样天就补全了。但地的西边还缺着。兄弟二人请黑云彩带着水来补，所以西边海水多。天地补好了，兄弟二人就死了。哥哥死在谁也不知道的地方。弟弟死时，头朝着东方，脚伸向西方，头变成了巍峨的昆仑山。大肠变成奔腾咆哮的大河，小肠变成了缓缓流动的小河。头发、汗毛变成了森林、草木。牙齿和下巴变成了坚硬的岩石。右手变成绵绵不断的大娘山，左手变成了美丽的景栋山。眼睛变成天上闪烁的星星，肺变成了碧波万顷的湖泊。

森林、河流、星星、草木的出现，给世界增添了生气。但这时世上还没有人类，没有出没在森林中的动物。龙木格萨又派了一个老人，名叫智桐瓦的女神来到地上，让她创造人类，繁衍生命。智桐瓦来到地上，就用泥巴捏人。捏了一个又一个，渐渐地这些人都活了起来，在她周围蹦蹦跳跳的，跳着跳着就结成一对对地走光了。智桐瓦很奇怪，就到处去找。在无边的大森林里，智桐瓦好不容易找到了一对。等智桐瓦把他们带回来时，发现一个头发变长了。她很奇怪，想这可能是天神安排的，短头发是男的，长头发是女的。从此，人类就开始分性别了。

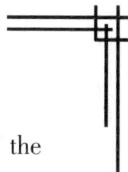

Finally, the heaven had been complete, but the west of the earth was still incomplete. The brothers asked the black clouds to take water to patch the earth, so there was more water in the west. Just after they finished their work, the two brothers died, and nobody knew where the elder brother died. As the younger brother died, his head looked to the east, turning into the lofty Kunlun Mountains, and his feet extended towards the west. His large intestine turned into a big roaring river while the small intestine turned into a flowing stream. His hair and fine hairs turned into the forest and the grass respectively, and his teeth and his chin turned into hard rocks. His right hand turned into the continuous Daniang Mountain, and his left hand turned into the beautiful Jingdong Mountain. His eyes turned into the shining stars and his lung turned into the boundless lakes with blue waves.

The emergence of the forests, rivers, stars, grass and trees added vitality to the world, but there were no human being on the earth and no animals in the forests. Longmugesa sent an old goddess named Zhitongwa to the earth and created human being and reproduce creatures. Zhitongwa came to the earth and made human beings out of mud one by one. Gradually they began to be alive, jumped and danced around her and went away pair by pair. Zhitongwa felt very strange and went to look for them everywhere. She had a hard time and found a pair in the boundless forest. When she took them back, she was very surprised to see that one of them had shorter hair than the other. She thought it must be decided by God to make the male human with short hair and the female with longer hair. From then on, there were male and female human beings on the earth.

智桐瓦年复一年地造人，造了许多人。当时这些人还不会劳动，肚子也不会饿。智桐瓦累了，就准备回天上去了。但龙木格萨不同意，他说："人类还在混混沌沌地过日子，你要继续帮助他们。"

智桐瓦又回到了地上，继续帮助人类。就在这时，大地上发生了一场战争，天上的黄龙和陆上的黑龙为了争东西打起仗来。打来打去，谁也不服谁。最后天上的黄龙就请了雷神来帮助。雷神把它炽热的火焰喷到地上，整个大地燃起了熊熊的大火。大火整整烧了七天七夜。智桐瓦急忙请水神来帮忙，这才扑灭了大火。这时，大地已被烧焦了，人也烧死了许多，只有一对兄妹被智桐瓦放在金鼓里，才没有被烧死。可是，水神洒下的水太多了，大地又变成了一片汪洋。金鼓浮了起来，载着一对兄妹漂走了。智桐瓦就到处去找。她先找到了东边的景江给坎①，又走了九十九天，翻了九十九座山，涉过了九十九条河，还是没有找到。她又往西边找了很久。这时水开始落了，山峰已经露出来了，路也找不着了。智桐瓦只好请天神帮忙，派了一群动物来领路，把智桐瓦领到了南边的大海，果然见金鼓就在那儿漂着。智桐瓦看见了，但没有办法拿到，就请鸭子来帮忙。鸭子游过去了，

---

① 景江给坎：意为雷音寺。

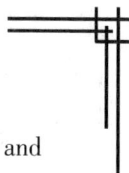

Zhitongwa made many human beings year after year, and they never felt hungry because they didn't work. But Zhitongwa felt tired and wanted to go back to the heaven. Longmugesa didn't agree and said, "The human beings are still living in chaos and you must go on helping them."

Zhitongwa stayed on the earth and helped the human beings live better. Just then, a war broke out on the earth. The yellow dragon in the heaven and the black dragon on the earth fought for something. They fought against each other and no one wanted to give in. At last, the yellow dragon invited the God of Thunder for help, who ignited a blaze of fire to the earth and it burned badly for about seven days and nights. Zhitongwa hurried to ask the God of Water to help put out the fire. But the earth had been scorched and many people were burned to death, with only a brother and his sister, who were hidden by Zhitongwa in a golden drum, alive. However, the God of Water sprayed too much water on the earth and it became a vast ocean. The golden drum floated and carried the brother and his sister away. Zhitongwa looked for them everywhere. She first went to Jingjiangjikan① in the east, and then walked for ninety-nine days, climbed ninety-nine mountains and forded ninety-nine rivers, but she failed to find them. She then went to the west and looked for them for a long time. At that moment, the water began to fall, the mountain peak had emerged and the road couldn't be found. Zhitongwa had to ask the God of Heaven for help, who sent a group of animals to lead her to the southern sea. Zhitongwa saw the golden drum floating there, but she couldn't get it and asked a duck for help. The duck swam to push the golden drum, but it didn't move. Zhitongwa then asked an eagle for help, and the golden drum was finally dragged to the river bank with the duck pushing and the eagle pulling. But the

---

① Jingjiangjikan means Leiyin Temple.

但推不动金鼓。智桐瓦又请大鹰来帮忙。它俩一个推，一个拉，终于把鼓拉到了岸边。两兄妹被封在鼓里，智桐瓦很焦急，就请啄木鸟来啄，但是啄不开；请老鼠来啃，可声音太响，怕吓坏两兄妹。最后智桐瓦请来了燕子，燕子的翅膀非常锋利，划开了金鼓（所以现在家燕的翅膀像刀一样）。两兄妹救出来了，大地上终于又有了人类。这时智桐瓦又想回天空了，龙木格萨还是不准，他说："两兄妹还没有传代，你得再帮助他们。"

智桐瓦又留下来，并教两兄妹结成夫妇，繁衍后代。可是妹妹害羞不同意，哥哥也不同意。智桐瓦说了几箩筐的话，他们都不听。智桐瓦没办法，就拿出了两支点燃的香来，让他们一人拿一支香，哥哥到东边山上，妹妹到西边山上，一起把山上的草点燃，火焰如果烧了接在一起，就要结成夫妇。两兄妹听后，照着做了。火一点燃后草马上就接在一起了，可是兄妹还是不愿意结为夫妇。智桐瓦又想了一个办法，把一块石头分为两半，要兄妹二人将它们一起滚下山洼，如果滚下去的石头合成一块，就结成夫妇。兄妹二人同意了。真巧，滚下去的石头又合成一块了，可他们还是不干。智桐瓦又领着兄妹俩来到了河边，折下一截树枝，又断成两节，让他们各拿一节，一起丢到河中。树枝一碰到河水，马上变成了两条鱼，一条公鱼，一条母鱼。兄妹二人看到了，只有听智桐瓦的话，结为夫妇。结婚的日子订在三天以后。

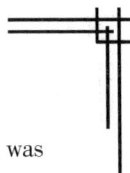

brother and his sister were sealed in the drum, and Zhitongwa was very anxious and asked a woodpecker for help, but it couldn't peck it out; she then asked a mouse to bite it, but was afraid that the brother and his sister might be frightened by the loud noise. At last, Zhitongwa invited a swallow to cut out the drum with its sharp wings (So nowadays the swallow's wings are like knives). Finally, the brother and his sister were saved and there were human beings on the earth again. Zhitongwa wanted to go back to the heaven again and Longmugesa didn't agree and said, "The brother and his sister had no offspring and you'd better help them."

Zhitongwa had to stay again and taught the brother and his sister to be husband and wife and reproduce offspring. However, the sister was too shy to agree and the brother didn't either. Zhitongwa said a lot but they didn't listen to her. Zhitongwa had no way but to take out two pieces of lighted incense and asked them each to take one. The brother took one to the eastern mountain, the sister took the other to the western mountain, and they were asked to light the grass on the mountains. They should get married if the flames went together. The brother and sister followed her words and the flames went together as soon as it was lighted. But the brother and sister still didn't want to marry. Zhitongwa thought of another way. She split a stone into two halves and asked the brother and sister to push their half one to the same valley, and they would get married if the two halves came together. The brother and sister agreed. It was really coincident that the two halves came together, but they again didn't want to marry. Zhitongwa then led them to the river, cut down a branch and broke it into two and asked each of them to take one and throw it into the river. As soon as the branch met the water, they turned into two fish, a male one and a female one. Seeing this, the brother and his sister had to listen to Zhitongwa and get married, and the ceremony was decided to be held three days later.

到了结婚那天，就要开始举行结婚仪式了，但没有主婚人、媒人以及帮忙的人，他们就请黄梨树叶来搭成了新房，公巴①来做媒人，请挺拔的马尾松来做主婚人。

办喜事前，又请了木梨岛鸟来舂米，请鸽子来煮饭，请老鸹来挑水，小麻雀端饭，野鸽子唱歌。请公巴务杜鸟来做酒药，吴日鸟来熬酒，最后请美丽的孔雀来跳舞。

结婚后，两人的生活很幸福。妹妹在三年后怀孕，生下了个狗皮口袋。这个狗皮口袋在家里又搁了整整三年，才崩开来，原来袋子里有九个小孩：五男四女。四男四女自然形成了对，生儿育女去了。剩下一个男的，没有伴，就到鬼家去做儿子，受尽了鬼的虐待，最后跑了出来，又累又饿，跌在一个坑里死了。

智桐瓦又想回天上去了，但龙木格萨还是不同意，要她帮助人类寻找五谷，养育牲畜。

---

① 公巴：一种草本植物。

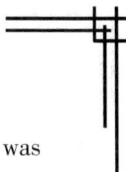

On the wedding day, when the wedding ceremony was ready, there were no officiator of marriage, no matchmaker and no helper. They then invited the yellow leaves of the pear tree to build a new house, Gongba①to be the matchmaker, and the upright Chinese red pine to be the officiator.

Before the wedding ceremony, they also invited a bird to pound rice, a pigeon to cook, a crow to carry water, a little sparrow to serve the dinner and a wild dove to sing. Wudu bird was invited to make the yeast, Wuri bird to make wine and a beautiful peacock to dance.

They lived a happy life after they got married. Three years later, the sister was pregnant and gave birth to a bag made of dog's skin, which remained intact before it burst open another three years later. Nine children came out of the bag, five men and four women. Then four men and four women got married and born children, with one man left without partner and going out to be a son in a ghost family. But he was badly abused by the ghost, so he ran out and died of tiredness and hunger in a pit.

Zhitongwa wanted to go back to the heaven again, but Longmugesa didn't agree, and asked her to help the human look for the five cereals and raise livestock.

---

① Gongba is a herb, a plant with a soft stem that dies down after flowering.

智桐瓦又帮人类去寻找五谷种子，找到以后，她先吃，然后选出不会中毒的种子撒在泥土里，让它们春天发芽、开花，秋天成熟。这些五谷有的种在天上，有的种在地下，年年丰收。有一天清晨，有几只野兽跑来偷吃谷子，人们设法逮住它们，这就是现在的牛、羊、狗、猪。从此人类就开始有了家畜。

那时，在天上偷吃了长生不老药的一些动物也被龙木格萨赶到了地下，森林中就出现了更多的动物，它们拉出来的屎中夹着从天上带下来的长生不老药的种子，长出来以后就成了现在的中草药。

智桐瓦终于没有回到天上，她死在了孕育着无穷生命的大地上。至今，景颇族的老人们仍然在深深地怀念着她。

口述者：云南省德宏州陇川县商业局雷老大

整理者：杨红昆，朱珊

# 人类始祖的传说

在天地形成不久的时候，世上没有人类，没有草木，没有飞禽走兽，也没有庄稼，只有几个神在游荡着。有一个名叫诺强的神和他的妻子住在北方的高地；另一个叫松昌的神和他的九个儿子住在南方。

Zhitongwa then help the human beings look for the seeds of five cereals. Every time she found one, she would eat it first, and chose the seeds that were not toxic to sow in the soil, so that they could sprout and blossom in spring and mature in autumn. Some of the five cereals grew in the heaven and some on the earth, and harvested every year. On one morning, the human beings managed to catch some wild animals which wanted to steal the grains, and now they are called cows, sheep, dogs and pigs. From then on, the human beings began to raise livestock on the earth.

At that time, some animals in the heaven which stole the elixir were driven out by Longmugesa to the earth, so more animals appeared in the forests. Their excrement contained the seeds of the elixir from the heaven, which grew to be the present Chinese herbal medicine.

Zhitongwa finally didn't return to the heaven, and she died on the earth with endless lives. So far, the old people in Jingpo Ethnic Group are still thinking of her deeply.

Dictator: Lei Laoda, Business Bureau, Longchuan County, Dehong State

Collector: Yang Hongkun, Zhu Shan

# Legends of the Ancestor of Human Beings

Not long after the universe came into being, there was no human being, nor were grass and trees, birds and animals and crops, except for some wandering gods. There was a god named Nuoqiang and his wife living on the highland of the north, and another god named Songchang and his nine sons living in the south.

　　有一天，松昌和诺强碰到一起了。他们都觉得世上太荒凉寂寞了，应该建造万物，让世上到处都充满生气。松昌满以为自己家人多力量大，自己的主意又多，一定可以比诺强建造得更好。他非常傲慢地提出："我们各自建造自己管的地方吧！但最后要比一比，看谁建造得最好！"诺强表示同意，就各自分手了。

　　诺强回到北方后，和他的妻子苏琼商量着手建造万物。他们一边商量一边做，因为家里人少力量弱，就日以继夜地赶着做。松昌回到南方住地后，就命令儿子们去做，而他自己只出主意，从来不要儿子们出主意。他凭自己人多力量大，做活时做做又闲闲，闲闲又做做。松昌天天想着：诺强没有主意，人又少，肯定建造不出什么来，这回肯定能赢他。

　　过了没多久，松昌和诺强来到原来相会的地方。松昌劈头就傲慢地说："你先到我那里去看看吧，我建造的地方可宽啦，我已经建造好了许多许多的树木和各种各样的草，造好了各种各样的飞禽走兽和虫子，造好了谷子和各种粮食，还建造了军营……"

　　"这些东西，我也造出来了。我还造了两个人：一个姐姐和一个弟弟。"诺强轻声地说着。

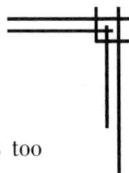

One day, they met and both thought that the world was too desolate and lonely, and that things should be created to make the world full of life. Songchang believed that he should do better than Nuoqiang because he had a big and powerful family and he had more ideas than Nuoqiang. So he said very arrogantly, "Let us create our own world and see who would do better!" Nuoqiang agreed and they went back home.

After returning to the north and discussing with his wife, Nuoqiang and his wife began to create everything. They were discussing with each other while working day and night, and trying to finish it early because they were short of hands. After returning to the south, Songchang ordered his sons to do it and never asked them to give advice, which he would do by himself. His sons worked sluggishly because they had more people than Nuoqiang. Everyday, Songchang thought that Nuoqiang couldn't create anything better than him for he was not shrewd and was short of hands, and that he would certainly defeat Nuoqiang.

Soon, Songchang and Nuoqiang went back to the place where they first met. Songchang said to Nuoqiang directly and arrogantly, "Come to my place and have a look at what I have done. I have planted a lot of trees and various kinds of grass, a variety of birds and animals and insects, grain and crops, barracks and so on."

"I have created all the things you have done, and I've made two human beings: an elder sister and her younger brother." Nuoqiang said quietly.

　　"你会有那么大的本事和力量？我才不相信呢。你会造出很齐全的树木和竹子吗？你会造出最好的白谷吗？你会造出各种各样有翅膀的飞禽吗？我知道了，你只造了一只野鸡，整天咯咯咯咯的，叫都叫不响。"松昌轻蔑地数落着。

　　"那就请你先来我的地方看看吧！"诺强说完转身走了。

　　松昌决定亲自去看看，当面数落他一回，出出这口气。他一回到家就对儿子们说："我要亲自到诺强的地方看看，狠狠地羞他一回。"九个儿子齐声说："阿爹，诺强的地方去不得，那个地方，又小又冷，你去了不冻死，也要饿死。"松昌回答说："不行，我已经决定了，你们不要阻拦我，他的地方又小又冷，我就把衣服穿得多多的，头上戴上厚厚的帽子，脚上穿上袜子，把米口袋装得满满的，再把我那把刀鞘上镶有豹子牙齿的刀带上，我就什么也不怕了。"临走前，他又向儿子们嘱咐道："如果过了九天九夜我还不回来，蜂子又来房头上转着飞的话，就说明我已经死了。那时，你们九兄弟都要来领尸，要对诺强说：'我们要喝山上的血，吃山田里的谷。'要消灭诺强，要毁灭他建造的一切东西。"一切安排妥当后，松昌就上路了。

"Have you such ability and power to do it? Can you make all the trees and bamboo? Can you make the best white grain? Can you make birds with various kinds of wings? I have known that you had just made a pheasant which clucks every day but with no sound." Songchang said scornfully.

"Well, just come and have a look at my creations first." Nuoqiang answered and went away.

Songchang decided to see it with his own eyes and scolded Nuoqiang face to face so as to vent his anger on him. He said to his sons as soon as he went back home, "I'll go and have a look at Nuoqiang's house in person, and give him a hard time." His sons answered in a chorus, "Daddy, you can't go there for it is small and cold, and you'll freeze to death or starve to death." Songchang said, "I've decided and don't stop me. Though it is small and cold, I won't be afraid if I wear enough clothes, with a thick hat on my head and socks on my feet. I'll make my pocket full of rice, and take my knife with me, whose sheath is mounted with leopard teeth." Before leaving, he told his sons again, "If I don't come back in nine days and nights, and the bees fly over the houses, it will indicate that I have been dead. At that time, all of you must go and take my body home, and tell Nuoqiang that you would drink the blood in the mountains and eat the grain in the valleys. You must destroy Nuoqiang and all that he had created." All things arranged, Songchang set out on his journey.

九天九夜过去了，不见父亲回来，九弟兄非常着急。有一天，蜂子突然来房顶上转着飞。九弟兄知道父亲已经死了。怎么办呢？九弟兄商量了半天，商量来商量去，认为最好还是先请熊三哥去叫诺强赔人命。第二天，九弟兄去找到了熊三哥，请他去诺强那里帮着讲赔人命的事，并许他事成后送给他一个最好的项圈。

熊三哥来到了诺强住的地方，诺强告诉他："松昌是自己死的，他身上穿的衣裳太单薄，肚子里又没有米，哪有不被冻死饿死的道理，我没有责任赔人命。"熊三哥转回来，把诺强的话告诉了九弟兄。可是九弟兄都不信，他们说："我们的父亲是穿了很厚的衣服去的，是带着很满的米袋去的，不会是冻死饿死。如果诺强再不承认，我们弟兄就要拉完他的牛马，拿完他塘子里的鱼，收完他山上的谷子。"他们再三请求熊三哥再去说一回。

熊三哥又来到了诺强住的地方，把九弟兄的话如实地转告给诺强。诺强反复说明了松昌冻死饿死的原因，最后愤愤地说："如果他们九弟兄不讲道理，一定要来抢的话，我就用黑暗笼罩他们，用洪水淹死他们。"

熊三哥走回来，向九弟兄转告了诺强的话。九弟兄听后，下决心打仗。他们造好九层船，一层装柴，一层装粮食……准备应付洪水。诺强也在积极准备对付这场战争。

Nine days and nights passed, and the nine brothers didn't see their father come back and became very anxious. One day, the nine brothers saw bees flying over the house and they knew that their father died. What should they do? The nine brothers discussed it for a long time, and thought that it would be better to invite Brother Xiong to help them ask Nuoqiang to pay for their father's death. On the second day, the nine brothers went to the Brother Xiong's and asked him for help, and promised to give him the best necklace after he made it.

Brother Xiong went to the Nuoqiang's, but Nuoqiang told him that, "Songchang died on himself. His clothes were too thin and his stomach was empty, so it was not surprising that he died from cold and hunger, and I'm not responsible for his death." Brother Xiong went back and told the nine brothers Nuoqiang's words, but they didn't believe it, and said, "Our father went there with thick clothes and a full bag of rice, and he couldn't die from cold or hunger. We'll cart off his cattle and horses, take his fish from the pond and harvest his grain in the mountain if he doesn't admit it." They repeatedly begged Brother Xiong to see Nuoqiang again.

Brother Xiong went again and told Nuoqiang the nine brothers' words truthfully. Nuoqiang also repeated the reasons of Songchang's death, and finally he said angrily, "If they don't believe me and want to rob my place, I'll cover them with darkness and drown them in the flood."

Brother Xiong went back and passed the message to the nine brothers. Hearing this, the nine brothers decide to fight against Nuoqiang. They made a nine-layer ship, one layer of woods, one layer of food... to be ready for the flood. At the same time, Nuoqiang was also actively preparing for the battle.

这一天，诺强想起了他们造出来的姐弟俩。他不想让他们在这场战争中被毁灭，应该保存下来，让他们繁衍人类。于是，他立即派出野猫，告诉姐弟俩躲避灾难的办法。

野猫找到了姐弟俩，说："松昌来到我们的北方被冻死了，现在他的九个儿子要来打仗，到时世上一片黑暗，洪水要淹没整个大地，大地上万物都要毁灭。诺强叫我来告诉你们，赶快准备下一个大木鼓，两头蒙上皮子，再准备下九个饭团、九只公鸡和九根针，洪水一发就躲进鼓里去，每天吃一个饭团，每天丢出一只公鸡和一根针，等到听见鸡叫和针响，你们就可以出来了。"

两姐弟送走了野猫后，就忙着按诺强吩咐的去办了。

不久，九弟兄和诺强打起仗来了。天果然黑了下来，洪水从北方铺天盖地涌过来。两姐弟赶紧躲进了木鼓，随水漂流。他们按照诺强的吩咐，第一天，吃一个饭团，丢出一只公鸡和一根针，没有听到鸡叫，也没有听到针响。第二天也这样做，第三天也这样做……一直到第八天，仍然听不到鸡叫和针响。最后只剩下一个饭团、一只公鸡和一根针了，怎么办呢？姐弟俩十分着急。

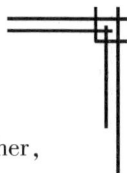

One day, Nuoqiang remembered the sister and her brother, who he didn't want to be destroyed in the battle and should be preserved to reproduce human beings. Then, he sent a wild cat to tell them the way to avoid the disaster.

The wild cat found the sister and her brother and said, "Songchang had been frozen to death here in the north, and now his nine sons want to fight. Then the earth would be dark and the flood would drown the whole world, and everything on it would be destroyed. Nuoqiang sent me to tell you to prepare a big wooden drum, which must be covered with skin, and nine rice balls, nine cocks and nine needles must also be ready. When the flood come, hide in the drum, eat a rice ball and throw a cock and a needle out of the drum every day. Don't go out of the drum until you can hear the cock crow and the needle falls on the ground.

The sister and her brother saw off the wild cat, and hurried to be busy with the preparation work.

It was not long before the nine brothers and Nuoqiang fought against each other. It really grew dark, and the flood poured down on the earth from the north. The sister and her brother quickly hid in the wooden drum and drifted in the water. They followed Nuoqiang's words, and on the first day, they ate a rice ball, threw a cock and a needle out of the drum, but they couldn't hear any sound. They did the same for the second day, the third day… until the eighth day, with only one rice ball, one cock and one needle left. What should they do? The sister and her brother became very anxious.

洪水已整整淹了八天，九弟兄被击败淹死了，大地上万物也快要淹完了，苏琼十分着急，很快来找她的丈夫说："诺强啊，你已经淹死了他们九弟兄，但也淹死了世上的万物。现在，山上只剩下了一头猪，森林里只剩下了一只麂子，所有鸟类只剩下了一只'东香鸟'，竹子只剩下了一蓬，树也只剩下了一棵'真筒树'，人类就只剩下了两个孤儿，再淹下去，连我们都要完了。快放了洪水，驱散黑暗吧！"诺强听了也很着急。他很快去找来了豪猪刺穿了水闸，放出了光明。

再说姐弟俩在木鼓里摇摇晃晃，十分着急。这一天，他们吃完了最后一个饭团，犹豫了半天，终于丢出了最后一只公鸡和最后一根针。他们沉住气，静静地听着动静。突然，他们听到了针掉在地上的响声，也听到了公鸡的叫声，便急忙打开鼓皮走出来。大地已经恢复了光明，洪水已经退去了。但是，大地上什么东西也没有了，看不到草木，听不到鸟啼，到处一片荒凉。姐弟两个肚子饿得发慌，东张西望，可是什么也找不到。突然，他们发现凹子头冒出一股青烟，便朝冒烟的地方走去。

Eight days had passed since the flood drowned the earth, and the nine brothers were defeated and drowned, and everything was going to be drowned. Suqiong, Nuoqiang's wife, was very anxious and went to see him and said, "Nuoqiang, the nine brothers had been drowned in the flood, which also drowned the creatures on the earth. Now there is only one pig in the mountain, one deer in the forest, one bird named Dongxiang, a clump of bamboo, one tree named Zhentong, and two orphans left. And we all will die if it continues. Let the flood go and disperse the darkness!" Nuoqiang was very anxious too, and he quickly asked the porcupine to pierce the sluice and let out the light.

As to the sister and her brother, trembling in the wooden drum, they were very anxious. One day, they ate the last rice ball, hesitated for a long time, and finally threw out the last cock and needle. They kept calm and listened carefully. Suddenly, they heard the sound of the needle falling to the ground and the cock's cry, so they hurriedly opened the drum and went out. The earth had become bright again, and the flood had subsided. But there was nothing left on the earth, no grass and trees, no birds singing, and it was completely desolate. They were so hungry and looked around, only to find nothing to eat. Suddenly, they saw a puff of smoke from a col and walked towards it.

　　原来凹子头住着一个麻风鬼，他也饿得发慌，正愁找不到东西吃。姐弟俩走到他面前，恭敬地对他说："老爷爷，谢谢您，我们很饿了，请您给我们一点饭吃吧！"麻风鬼高兴地答应了他们的要求，立即拿上水筒说去接点水来给他们做饭。这时，姐姐看出这老人神情有点不安，就悄悄地跟在他背后，观看他的行动。老爷爷在凹子里一边接着水，一边自言自语地念着："水啊水啊，快快满吧，今天我的口福来了，两个小姐弟，够我吃一顿。"姐姐听了吓了一跳，原来不是给我们煮饭，而是要吃我们姐弟俩啊！她急忙折回来告诉弟弟，领着他跑了。

　　姐弟俩跑了几山又几凹，又见一个凹子尾冒出了一股青烟。他俩来到凹子尾，又见一个老爷爷正在煮饭。他俩恭恭敬敬地对他说："老爷爷，谢谢您，我们很饿了，给我们一点饭吃吧！"老爷爷一口答应了他们的要求，并立即起身拿着水筒出去接水。姐弟俩悄悄地跟在后面，只听老爷爷自言自语地念道："水啊水啊，快快满吧，我要赶快煮饭给两个小孩。"这样，姐弟俩才放心了。

It turned out that a leper ghost lived there, who was also hungry and worried about the food. The sister and her brother went to him and said respectfully, "Grandpa, could you give us something to eat? We are very hungry." The leper ghost agreed happily, and immediately took his water bucket and said he would fetch some water and cook for them. But the sister found that he looked strange and followed him quietly. The leper ghost said to himself while he was taking the water, "Water, water, come on quickly, I'm very lucky today, for the two kids is enough for me to have a big meal." The sister was shocked to hear that, and she realized that the ghost was not going to cook for them but to cook them. She hurried back to tell her brother it and they ran away quickly.

The sister and brother ran across a few mountains and again saw a puff of smoke from another col. They went to the col and saw another old man cooking. They said respectfully to the old man, "Grandpa, could you give us something to eat? We are very hungry." The old man agreed to their request, and immediately took the water bucket to fetch water. The sister and her brother followed him, and heard him speak to himself, "Water, water, come on quickly, and I will cook for the two kids." Hearing this, the sister and her brother felt safe.

原来，这位老爷爷叫董腊顺。为了繁衍人类，他才专门来接待姐弟俩的。姐弟俩吃了饭后，老爷爷叫他们在他身边住下来，并且叫他们白天做姐弟，晚上做夫妻，繁衍人类。可是，姐弟俩都不敢做夫妻。老爷爷便想了个办法。他修了两条路，叫姐弟俩各走一条路，去寻找自己的对象。姐弟俩走了一天，仍然是他们俩相见。晚上回来，姐姐说："老爷爷啊，无论走多远，走到哪里，都只见到和我弟弟一样的人，不行啊！"弟弟也说只见到和姐姐一样的人，说做夫妻不行。老爷爷只得另打主意，叫他俩各拿一扇石磨，从两边山顶滚下坡去，若姐弟能做夫妻，石磨滚到坡脚就合在一起。第二天，姐弟俩去滚石磨，石磨真的滚合在一起了。但姐弟俩还是不敢做夫妻。老爷爷只得又另打主意。第三天，老爷爷去找来了许多野芭蕉和"唐辣"①，叫姐弟俩到河里去闹鱼。两个人敲打着野芭蕉和"唐辣"，浆汁溅到他们的脚上、手上、身上，溅到哪里就痒到哪里。实在熬不住了，姐姐说："弟弟啊，今天的日子怎么过啊，董腊顺爷爷要叫我们做夫妻，天神也要叫我们做夫妻，算了吧，我们就遮着脸做夫妻吧。"姐弟俩就这样做了夫妻。

---

① 唐辣：像芋头一样的植物块根，可毒鱼。

It turned out that the old man was Dong Lashun, who was there to treat the sister and her brother and help them reproduce the human being. After the meal, the old man asked the sister and brother to live with him, and told them to be sister and brother in the daytime and husband and wife at night. But the sister and her brother dared not be husband and wife. The old man then came up with an idea. He built two roads and asked the sister and her brother to choose one to go and look for their mate. The sister and her brother walked away and looked for a whole day but only to see the other. At night, the sister said to the old man, "Grandpa, on matter how far I went and no matter where I went, the only human I could see is my brother, but we can't marry." The brother also said so. The old man had to try another way. He asked the sister and her brother to take a stone mill respectively, and rolled it from the top of two different mountains. If the two stone mills rolled together, they should be husband and wife. On the second day, the sister and her brother did as the old man asked them to do, and the two stone mills met at the bottom of the mountains. But the sister and her brother were still afraid of being husband and wife. The old man had to find another way. On the third day, he found a lot of wild banana and Tangla①, which could poison the fish, and asked the sister and her brother to catch fish. They beat the wild banana and Tangla, and the pulp splashed onto their feet, hands and bodies, where became very itchy. They could not bear the itch, and the sister said to her brother, "Dear brother, how can we spend the whole day like this? Since the Grandpa asked us to be husband and wife, and the god also thought so, then let's be husband and wife." Then the sister and her brother became husband and wife.

---

① Tangla, looking like a taro, is a plant root which can poison the fish.

<br>

过了几个月，姐姐感到身体不好，梦也多了。有一天，她竟梦着腰间夹了一个草烟盒①，心里很难过。她想今后怎样见人呢？真是羞愧难当啊！一次，姐姐想走到后面的山坡上寻死，可是走到半路上，她见到许多草，都成双成对。她又一想：连草都成双成对，人又为什么不行呢？她打消了寻死的念头，又转回来。后来她生了一个孩子，姐弟俩给小孩祝福，并给他取了一个名字。可是这个小孩天天哭，而且越哭越厉害。一天，姐弟俩出去找粮食，老爷爷在家领着小孩。任凭老爷爷怎么哄，小孩还是哭个不停。老爷爷抱着孩子哄着说："啊！啊！啊！别哭了，长大了做'董萨'（祭师），当'强仲'（祭品陈设师）！"

可是小孩哭得更厉害。老爷爷又哄道："啊！啊！啊！别哭了，将来长大了做官。"小孩还是照样哭个不停。老爷爷气极了，骂道："我把你剁碎，把你的肉撒到九岔路上去！"这一来，小孩就果真不哭了。老爷爷真的就把小孩子砍了，把他的肉剁碎，撒到九岔路上，又把他的肚脏洗了煮成稀粥。

---

①　这种梦象征怀孕。

南方民间创世神话选集（上）　Anthology of the Creation Mythology in South China(1)

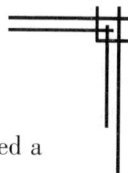

A few months later, the sister didn't feel well and dreamed a lot. One day, she was very sad because she dreamed a straw cigarette case tied on her waist①. How could she meet people in the future? She felt so shameful that she wanted to die on the slope of the hill. However, on her way to the slope, she saw pairs of grass and thought that why couldn't people be pairs? She then gave up the idea of death and went back home. Later, a baby was born and they blessed it and gave it a name. But the baby cried all the time. One day, the sister and her brother went out to look for food, and the old man stayed at home nursing the baby. No matter how hard he tried to calm down the baby, it cried continuously. The old man cradled the baby in his arms and coaxed it, "Don't cry, baby, you're going to be a Dongsa (Priest), or a Qiangzhong (a person who displays the sacrifices in the ceremony) when you grow up".

But the baby cried more seriously. The old man then said, "Don't cry, baby, you're going to be an official." The baby still cried all the time. The old man was so angry and threatened, "I'll chop you up into little pieces and scatter them on the road with nine branches!" Then the child really stopped crying. The old man did chop it up and scatter on the road, and cleaned its guts and cooked it in the gruel.

---

① This kind of dream symbolizes the pragnancy.

第二天，姐弟俩回来了。姐姐一进门就说："爷爷，请把小孩给我喂奶吧，我的奶已胀疼了。"老爷爷说："孩子刚睡着，你们先吃饭。"姐弟俩看了一眼睡着的孩子就吃饭了。吃完饭，姐姐去掀开毯子一看，原来盖着的只是一个木枕头，哪里是孩子！他们追问老爷爷，老爷爷只得如实告诉他俩："你们孩子的肚肠，刚才已经被你们吃了，你们孩子的肉已经丢在九岔路上，你们不信就去那里看吧！"

姐弟俩一口气跑到了九岔路口，原来那些肉每一块都变成了一个人，一大伙人在那儿坐着呢！

"我的孩子们，快回来吧！"姐姐一见孩子就叫起来。

"你是吃我们心肝五脏的人，哪里是我们的母亲！"孩子们骂道。

"我是你们的母亲啊！我没有吃……"母亲分辩着。

可是，不管母亲怎么说，孩子们还是不相信。最后，孩子们提出：如果能把木炭洗白，就认她是母亲。这时，天上飞过一只燕子，拉下了一泡白屎，恰巧掉在木炭上，木炭被染白了。可是孩子们又提出另一个条件：要母亲把竹筒接满水。可是接呀接，水半天也满不起来。这时，突然有一只小雀掉进竹筒里，母亲抬起来一看，小雀从竹筒底钻出去了。母亲才知道上了当，转回来追打小孩，但小孩们都远远地跑了。

On the following day, the sister and her brother came back home. The sister said, "Grandpa, I'd like to breast-feed my baby and it is full." The old man said, "The baby has just slept, and you have dinner first." Taking a quick look at the sleeping baby, the sister and her brother began to eat. After the meal, the sister went to uncover the blanket, but what she saw was not a baby but a wooden pillow. They asked the old man over and over again, and he had to tell them the truth, "What you had eaten was the guts of your baby, and its meat was scattered on the road with nine branches. Go and see by yourself if you don't believe me."

They ran to the road with nine branches in one breath, and saw a lot of people sitting there, for each piece of meat turned into a human being.

"Come back, my kids!" the sister said as soon as she saw them.

"You're not our mother but the one who ate our guts." The children answered.

"I am your mother! I haven't..." the mother argued.

But no matter what the mother said, the children still didn't believe her. At last, they proposed that if she wash the charcoal white, they would admit her to be their mother. Just at this time, a swallow flew over in the sky and shat a bubble of white feces, which happened to fall on the charcoal and made it white. But the children put forward another request that the mother fill the bamboo bucket with water. But for a long time, the bucket could not be filled. Suddenly, a little bird fell into the bamboo bucket and went out from the bottom of it. The mother saw it and realized that she was cheated and tried to hit the children, but they had ran far away.

小孩们顺着九条道路跑，他们走得很远很远，各走到一个地方，就成了世界上各民族的祖先。

姐姐失去了孩子，心里很难过，终于活活气死了。她死后，一个魂上了天，成了天鬼，另一个入了地，变成了地鬼。人们一直在纪念着她。

讲述者：殷江腊
翻译者：永生
整理者：东耳，永生

# 始祖宁贯娃的故事

从前，大地上一片混沌，没有平地，没有河流，没有海洋，没有草，没有树，也没有风，只有石头和水混在一起。

天上有太阳，太阳神有一对儿女，男的叫宁贯知恁，女的叫玛章维舜，他们就是景颇族的始祖。他们生了一个儿子，名叫宁贯娃。

宁贯娃渐渐地长大成人，决心整理好大地。他告别了父母，到大地上来做活儿。太阳神给了他力气。他用大石头锤地，用锥形的石头开沟，用麻蛇做量地的尺子。

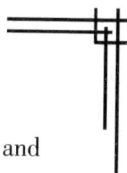

The children ran along the nine branches far far away, and each of them arrived in a different place, and became the ancestor of nations in the world.

The sister lost her child and she was so sad that she died of anger. After her death, one of her two souls went up to the heaven and became a heaven ghost, while the other went down to the ground and became a ghost underground. However, she was remembered by the human being all the time.

Narrator: Yin Jiangla
Translator: Yong Sheng
Collector: Dong Er, Yong Sheng

# Legend of the Ancestor Ningguanwa

Long time ago, it was chaotic on the earth. There was no land, no river and no ocean, nor was there grass or trees or wind, except for the mixture of stones and water.

There was a sun in the sky, and the God of Sun had a son, Ningguanzhinen, and a daughter, Mazhangweishun, who were the ancestors of the Jingpo People. They gave birth to a son named Ningguanwa.

Gradually, Ningguanwa grew up and decided to manage the earth. He said goodbye to his parents and went to the earth. With the strength given by the God of Sun, he hammered the ground with rocks, dug the trenches with stone cones, and measured the earth with the snakes.

　　宁贯娃用石锥开出很多的深沟，水就顺着这些深沟流出去，大地上有了河流。水流到最低处，汇集在宁贯娃敲得最重的地方——变成了海洋。宁贯娃用石锤猛敲大地，大地就变得凹凸不平了。凹下去的地方成了坝子和平地，凸出来的地方就成了大大小小、高矮不平的群山。凹得太低的地方积满了水，宁贯娃想把它戽干变成平地。

　　宁贯娃正忙碌哩，他的阿爹派歆哇鸟去叫宁贯娃。歆哇鸟飞到宁贯娃身边，对宁贯娃说："快回去吧！你阿妈死了！"宁贯娃听后只是一愣，便回答说："活路忙哩，阿妈死了就死了吧，母姓可以改父姓！"说完又埋下头忙着做活儿。原来宁贯娃是姓的母姓，后来才改为父姓的。宁贯知恁和玛章维舜再派歆哇鸟去催宁贯娃回家，这一次歆哇鸟一飞到宁贯娃身旁就说："快回去吧！你阿爹也死了！"宁贯娃听到他阿爹死去的消息大哭道："父姓不能改！"还没有把积水全都戽干，就急忙跑回家去。后来，没有排干的积水就成了湖泊。

With stone cones, Ningguanwa dug many trenches, which became rivers while the water flew down, and the lowest point where the water flew became an ocean. With the hammers striking on the ground, the earth became uneven, and the dams and plains came into being in the sinuses, and mountains of different heights and different sizes came into being in the bulges. Since there was too much water in the lower sinuses, Ningguanwa tried his best to dry them into plains.

Ningguanwa was busy with his work when his father sent a bird named Xinwa to ask him to go home. The bird flew to Ningguanwa and told him: "Go back home quickly! Your mother has died!" Ningguanwa was shocked to hear that and said, "I'm very busy, and since my mother has been dead, I'll be named after my father." Originally, Ningguanwa was named after his mother's family name. Since then, he was named after his father's. Again, Ningguanzhinen and Mazhangweishun sent the bird to urge Ningguanwa to go back home. This time, the bird told him that, "Go back home quickly! Your father has died too!" Hearing the news of his father's death, Ningguanwa cried out, "My father's family name can't be changed!" Without finishing his work, he hurried home. Later, the sinuses with much water became lakes.

　　宁贯娃哭着回到家里，看到他的父母都还活着，便惊奇地问道："哟，阿爹阿妈，这到底是怎么回事?"阿爹阿妈告诉他说："我们已经把你抚养成人，已经尽了自己的心，现在年老体衰，不久就要死了，还有很多话要嘱咐你，才派歃哇鸟把你叫回来。"宁贯娃伤心地哭着问："您二老不在了，我该咋办?"宁贯知恁说："我们死后，血肉会变成泥土，汗毛和头发会变成青草和树木，肠肝肚肺会变成各种宝藏。要繁衍这个世界就靠你了。今后泥土大地就是你的父母。做庄稼活路，要听鸟儿们的呼唤。一月砍地，三月撒种，五月栽插，十月收割。这样子孙后代才不会饿肚子。"宁贯娃抽泣着说："那阿爹阿妈的气息，要给哪个?"宁贯知恁回答说："阿爹阿妈的气息要交给清风。"玛章维舜接着说："太阳神的舞蹈——木脑是天上人间共庆的舞蹈，鸟儿会把它教给你的。"

　　后来，宁贯知恁和玛章维舜死了，他们的血肉变成了泥土，汗毛和头发变成了草儿树木，他们的内脏变成了各种宝藏，清风就是他们的气息。

Ningguanwa was very surprised to see his parents alive when he went back home with tears, and he asked them, "What on earth happened, dad and mum." His parents told him, "We have tried our best to bring you up, and now we are old and will die in the near future. We sent the bird to call you back for the purpose of telling you our wills." Ningguanwa was very sad to hear that and asked, "What can I do if you die?" His father said, "When we die, our flesh and blood will turn into earth, our hairs will turn into grass and trees, and our viscera will turn into various treasures, so it depends on you to prosper the world. In the future, the earth is your parents. You should listen to the calls of the birds to plough in January, to sew in March, to plant in May and to harvest in October, and then your descendants will not suffer from hunger." Ningguanwa sobbed and asked, "How about your breath? Who will take it?" His father answered, "It will be left to the breeze." His mother continued, "As to the dance of the God of Sun—the dance of the heaven and the earth, it will be taught to you by the birds."

Later, Ningguanzhinen and Mazhangweishun died, and their flesh and blood became earth, their hairs became grass and trees, their viscera became various treasures and the breeze took their breath.

宁贯娃遇到了龙王的女儿依若玛扎邦，他们打算结为夫妻。但是依若玛扎邦是龙女，身上有一股龙腥味。宁贯娃问过太阳神，按照太阳神的嘱咐，领依若玛扎邦从邦邦草前穿过。穿过了邦邦草丛，依若玛扎邦身上的腥味也就消失了。从那个时候起，直到现在，景颇人结婚时都要领新娘穿过邦邦草扎成的彩门，把还未穿过邦邦草门的新娘称为"有腥味的女人"——牡南侬。

宁贯娃摩甘和依若玛扎邦生育了很多的子女，他们变成了现在的各个民族。景颇族是麻堵（老四）。景颇人把宁贯娃摩甘和依若玛扎邦居住的地方称为中心地。各民族就是从那个地方分家分出来，分布到世界各地去的。

因此，景颇人认为景颇人的祖先是宁贯娃摩甘和依若玛扎邦。宁贯娃的父母是覆盖着大地的泥土，他们是太阳神的儿女。大地上的各民族都是兄弟姐妹。

整理者：木然脑都

# 创世纪

## 造天造地造万物

传说，造物主宁贯娃原来是居住在高高的太阳山上。

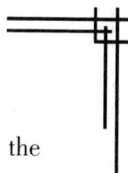

Ningguanwa met Nongruomazabang, the daughter of the Dragon King, and they planned to marry, but she had got a smell of dragon. Ningguanwa asked the God of Sun for help, and according to the instructions, he took her to walk through the Bangbang grass. The smell of dragon vanished after they crossed the grass. From then on, the brides in Jingpo Ethnic Group would be led to walk across the colorful gate decorated by the Bangbang grass, and those who haven't done it would be called Munannong, the fishy smell woman.

Ningguanwa and Nongruomazabang bore many children, who became the ancestors of today's different nationalities, and Jingpo Ethnic Group is the fourth. The place where Ningguanwa and his wife once lived is regarded as the center of the world by Jingpo Ethnic Group, and the different nationalities are the branches born from it and spread to the world.

Therefore, Ningguanwa and Nongruomazabang were regarded as the ancestors of Jingpo Ethnic Group. Ningguanwa's parents are the soil covering the ground, and they are the sons and daughters of the God of Sun. As a result, all the nationalities on the earth are brothers and sisters.

Collector: Murannaodu

# Legend of the Creation of the World

## Creation of the Heaven, the Earth and Everything

It was said that Ningguanwa, the creator of the world, once lived on the top of the highest Sun Mountain.

很古很古以前，世间本来没有天，没有地，也没有万物，一片混混沌沌。宁贯娃要造天、造地、造万物。他花了很大气力先造好了天，接着又不辞劳苦地来造地。他手持一把大锤，东边打打，西边敲敲，有时打得重，有时打得轻，打得重的地方成了平坝，打得轻的地方成了高山。后来，他又在高山平坝中开辟了九条大江。大地造好了，但是大地上除了宁贯娃自己再没有别的人，也没有什么飞禽走兽，他感到非常寂寞。于是他就照着自己的样子，用泥巴捏了很多很多的小泥人，有男的，也有女的。说来也怪，这些小泥人一放到地上就活了，而且很快就长得和他一般高，可把宁贯娃乐坏了。宁贯娃便高高兴兴地把他们一男一女地配成对合成双，让他们一家一户地过日子。接着宁贯娃又捏了很多鸡、鸭、牛、马、猪、羊、猫、狗、兔、猴、鹿、麂、狮、象、虎、豹和鱼儿、飞鸟。从此，才有野兽在林间戏耍，鱼儿在水中戏游，小鸟在天空飞翔。大地才充满了生机。

但是宁贯娃万万没有想到，与他同时应运而生的还有一个凶恶的魔鬼高佐洛雷。他只喜欢混混沌沌，不喜欢天地分明，更不喜欢世间出现万物。宁贯娃造天造地造万物时，这个家伙不知躲在什么地方抱头酣睡。后来，人们的阵阵欢声笑语把他从睡梦中惊醒。他低头一看，不觉为天地万物的出现而暴跳起来。他一纵身跳到大地上，大叫："谁人竟敢如此大胆，把我的世界变成这个样子！"这时，恰好碰上了宁贯娃。宁贯娃便说："哦，朋友，你问这个呀？"

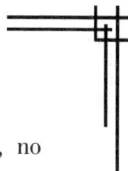

Long time ago, it was chaotic and there was no heaven, no earth and nothing in the universe. Ningguanwa had to create the heaven, the earth and all things between them. He tried his best to build the heaven firstly, and then the earth with endless hard work. Holding a big hammer in his hand, he stroke in the east and knocked in the west, sometimes heavily and sometimes lightly. The places he stroke heavily became the plains while the places he stroke lightly became mountains. Among the plains and mountains, he dug nine rivers. The ground had been built but Ningguanwa felt very lonely for there was nobody else, no birds or animals, except for himself. Therefore, he duplicated a lot of little clay figurines, male or female, out of mud according to his own appearance. It was very strange that the little clay figurines became alive as soon as they were placed on the ground, and soon grew as high as he, which made him very happy. So he paired them with a man and a woman so that each pair could live together as a single household. He then moulded a lot of chickens, ducks, cows, horses, pigs, sheep, cats, dogs, rabbits, monkeys, deer, suede, lions, elephants, tigers, leopards, fishes and birds, which enabled the beasts to play in the woods, fishes to swim in water and birds to fly in the sky, and the earth was full of vitality.

But a vicious devil named Gaozuoluolei was born at the same time as he was born, which was unexpected by Ningguanwa. The devil preferred the chaos to the heaven, the earth, and all the things in the world. He was just sleeping in an unknown place when Ningguanwa was creating the world, and later, he was waked up by the laughters from the earth. He looked down at the earth, and was very angry with the emergence of all things in the world. He jumped onto the ground and shouted, "Who on earth dares to make my world like this?" Just at that time, Ningguanwa came and asked, "Well, What's the matter?"

259

"这天地是你造的吗?"

"是呀!你看,天地这么一分,蓝天白云,大地苍翠,一派生机勃勃,不是比原来那景象好得多吗?"

宁贯娃兴奋的话语,自豪的神态,使得高佐洛雷更是暴跳如雷:"我要毁灭天地万物!"说着,他就"嗖"地拔出长刀,扭转身子,微闪双眼,仗刀作起法来。

高佐洛雷的疯狂举动,气得宁贯娃怒火万丈,钢牙咬碎。他岂能容忍恶魔肆虐,荼毒生灵,毁灭天地!"住手!"他大喝一声,举起长刀,狠狠向高佐洛雷劈去。高佐洛雷吓得连忙举刀相迎。于是两人便你来我往,吼声如雷,拼斗起来。整整斗了三天三夜,直斗得天昏地暗,日月无光。结果,宁贯娃被高佐洛雷砍伤了胸膛,只有用手堵住流血的伤口,登上云头,返回太阳山去了;高佐洛雷被宁贯娃劈去了半边身子,但是死到临头,这个害人精也没忘作恶,他虽精力不济,不能毁灭天地,却还能施法,使天河倒悬,大雨倾盆。于是,一瞬间,天水茫茫,大地被洪水淹没了,一切都被洪水冲走了。人类只有姐弟二人在高山上放牛,看见大水淹来,急忙杀了四头牛,用牛皮做了一个大鼓,两个躲进里面顺水漂流,才幸存下来。

"Is it you that made the world?"

"Yes! You see, isn't it much better than the old one since the heaven and the earth were separated from each other, with the blue sky, the white clouds, and the green and vital ground between them?"

Gaozuoluolei was very angry with Ningguanwa's exciting words and proud complexion, and shouted, "I'll destroy all the things in the world." He pulled out a long knife, twisted his body and spelled magic words with his eyes flashing.

Ningguanwa was furious with Gaozuoluolei's madness. How could he bear his indulging in wanton massacre, poisoning the creatures and destroying the world? "Stop!" Ningguanwa shouted and hacked Gaozuoluolei straightly with his long knife, and Gaozuoluolei had to fight against him in amazement. They fought with each other fiercely with roars like thunders for three days and nights until the heaven and the earth became darker and darker, and the sun and the moon lost their lights. As a result, Ningguanwa was cut in the chest and had to block the wounds with hands and climbed up the clouds and went back to the Sun Mountain, while Gaozuoluolei was chopped half of the body, but he didn't forget to do harm to the world before he died. He cast the magic words to turn over the river in the heaven to rain cats and dogs. Instantly, the whole world was flooded in the water and everything was washed away by it. Fortunately, a sister and her young brother saw the flood when they herded the cows in the high mountain, so they killed four cows and made a big drum with the skins, which floated on the surface of the water, hid in it and survived.

## 姐弟成亲

皮鼓漂呀，漂呀，也不知漂了多少天，后来忽然停住不动了。姐弟俩揭开条缝一看，是水退了，高兴极了，赶忙扯开牛皮，爬出大鼓，辨着方向，踏着泥泞，朝自己的家乡走去。走呀走，不晓得走了多少个白天黑夜，一路上竟没有遇到一个人。路过之处尸骸遍野，荒凉可怖，两人感到十分孤单。一天黄昏，他们走得又累又饿，正想找个地方歇一歇，忽然看见前面山坡上有个石洞，一个拱该①正站在洞口向四下张望。两人欢喜不已，蹦蹦跳跳地跑上前去叫了一声"奶奶！"然后说："奶奶，我们在你家歇一晚上行吗？"这拱该原来是达目鬼，它有很长时间没吃到人肉了，现在正想得口涎流淌，一见姐弟俩，高兴得拉着他们就往洞里走，嘴里还不住地念叨："行啊！行啊！住在我这里吧，我可喜欢小孩了。你们一定很饿了吧？我这就去背水来煮饭给你们吃，你们在家好好歇着。"说着，背起竹筒就朝山箐里走去了。

机灵的姐姐看出这个拱该像是喜欢又像是不怀好意，引起了警觉。因此达目鬼前脚刚出门，她就悄悄地跟在后面。一路上只听见拱该边走边情不自禁地哼道："去背水呀去背水，我要煮那两个小人吃！"姐姐听了吓了一大跳，急忙跑回来拉着弟弟就逃，等达目鬼把水背回来，两人已逃走了。

---

① 拱该：景颇语，老太婆。

## The Sister and Her Brother Got Married

The big drum floated in the water for many days before it stopped suddenly. The sister and her brother were happy to see from the gap in the drum that the water had subsided. They cut the drum open and climbed out of it and walked in the mud towards their hometown. They walked for days and nights, but they never met a human being, only to see the dead bodies along the road everywhere, horrible and desolate, so they felt very lonely. One day at dusk, tired and hungry, they were looking for a place to have a rest when they saw a cave in front of a hill ahead, and a Gonggai① was standing in front of it, looking around. They ran to the old woman with joy and said, "Granny, can we stay in your house tonight?" The Gonggai was originally a Damu ghost, who hadn't eaten human beings for a long time, and was thinking of it very much. She was so happy to see them that she took them to the cave and said, "It's Ok! Stay here with me and I like children very much. You must be very hungry, stay at home and have a good rest, and I'll go and fetch water and cook for you." Then, she took the bamboo tube on the back and walked towards the mountain.

The clever sister was a little curious about the Gonggai and found that she seemed to be happy and malicious at the same time. So the sister followed the Gonggai secretly as soon as she walked out of the cave. On the way, the Gonggai couldn't help humming, "I'll take back water and cook the two kids." The sister was so shocked to hear that and ran back to take her brother away. When the ghost took the water back, only to find that the sister and her brother had fled.

---

① Gonggai means an old lady in the Jingpo dialect.

姐弟俩又辛辛苦苦地走了很多个日日夜夜，人走瘦了，脚走肿了，再也走不动了。这时，他们多么想能有一间房子来遮风避寒，好好睡上一觉，养养精神呀！特别是弟弟，更是不想再走了。说来也巧，前面山头上果真有间房子。两人一口气爬到山顶，叫开房门一看，出来开门的是个拱该，她是治同鬼①。"奶奶！我们无家可归，你能收留我们姐弟俩吗？"姐弟俩同声哀求。见是两个累得精疲力尽的孤儿，治同鬼十分同情，说："进来吧，可怜的孩子，奶奶一个人也很苦闷，你们就跟我在一起生活吧！"她把他们迎进屋，安顿好后，又说："你们在家歇着，我去背水来煮饭给你们吃。"她刚一出门，姐姐又悄悄地跟在后面观察动静。在接水的时候，听见她轻声唱道："水呀快满，水呀快满，我要赶快回去煮饭给两个孤儿吃，他们饿坏了。"姐姐相信治同鬼不会伤害他们，于是和弟弟欢欢喜喜地跟着她生活起来。

日子过得真快，转眼间姐弟俩已长大成人了。治同鬼很为他们的婚事操心，总想给他们早日解决。但世界上，除了他们俩，再没有别的人可供选择，没法子，只得劝他俩结对成亲。姐弟俩怎么能够结婚呢？可是不成亲，不生育后代，等他们死后，人类不是就要绝种了吗？成亲也不好，不成亲也不好，尽管治同鬼多次劝说，姐弟俩仍犹豫不决，十分为难。

---

① 治同鬼：景颇神话传说中管理山的鬼，即山神。

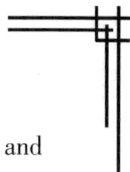

The sister and her brother walked hard for many days and nights until they could not move a step. They grew thinner and were so tired that a place to keep warm and have a good sleep was all that they expected, especially for the brother. It so happened that they saw a house in front of the mountain ahead. They climbed up the mountain without a stop and knocked at the door. Another Gonggai, a Zhitong ghost①, who was the God of Mountain, answered the door. "Granny, could you allow us to stay here for some time for we could go nowhere?" The sister and brother entreated. Seeing the two exhausted children in front of her, the God of Mountain was very sympathetic with them and said, "Come in, poor kids, and live with me since I'm lonely too." She took them in and settled them down, and said, "Just stay here and have a good rest, and I'm going to fetch some water and cook for you." As soon as the God of Mountain went out of the house, the sister followed her secretly and made observations. Hearing her humming "Water, water comes to my bottle, and I have to be hurry and go back to cook for the two hungry orphans", the sister was sure that the old lady would not do them harm, so they lived with her happily.

How time flied! Almost in an instance, the sister and her brother had grown up. The God of Mountain was very worried about their marriage, and wanted to solve the problem early. But there were nobody else in the world except for them two, and the God of Mountain tried to persuade them to marry each other since they had no choice. How could the sister marry her brother? However, would the human being extinct if they wouldn't get married or have children? To get married or not, and the sister and her brother were still very hesitated and perplexed though the God of Mountain tried many times to persuade them.

---

① Zhitong ghost refers to the mountain deity in the Jingpo legends.

　　"我们还是来问问天吧，看看天是不是也同意你们成亲？你们俩一个在东山，一个在西山，同时往凹子里滚，如果天同意你们成亲，就让你们俩滚在一起；如果天不允许你们成亲，就不让你们滚在一起。"后来治同鬼出了这么个主意，姐弟俩没有别的办法，也就同意按天的意志办。他们拜了天，请天来做主，然后姐姐上东山，弟弟上西山，同时往下滚，一连滚了三次，都滚在了一起。天意凑合，姐弟俩便高高兴兴地成了亲。

## 驾驭太阳的母亲

　　成亲后的日子过得很快乐，白天，姐弟俩一同下地劳动，晚上，弟弟弹起口弦，陪伴着姐姐在月光下织布缝衣。不久他们生了个儿子，取名叫娃刚。娃刚生得眉清目秀、白白胖胖，很是逗人喜爱。不过娃刚这孩子有个爱哭的毛病，一哭起来就要哭个够。哭不够，谁都哄不乖，你越哄他越哭，简直叫人心烦意乱。

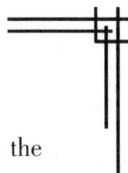

Later, the God of Mountain got an idea. "Let's ask the Heaven to decide whether you must get married. One of you goes to the east mountain, the other the west mountain, and both of you roll towards the valley from the top of the mountain. If you are allowed to get married, you two will meet, and if don't, you two will not meet." The sister and her brother had no other choice but to agree. They bowed to the Heaven before the sister climbed up to the east mountain and the brother to the west mountain. Then they rolled down the mountains simultaneously for three times, and every time they met each other. So they got married happily according to the Heaven's will.

## The Mother Reining the Sun

They lived a very happy life after the sister and her brother got married. During the daytime, they went to farm together, and at night, the brother played the chord while the sister weaved and sewed in the moonlight. Soon, they gave birth to a son named Wagang, who was born to be white, chubby and cute, with bright eyes and graceful eyebrow. But the little boy had a very bad habit of crying at any time for a long time. If he didn't want to stop crying, the more you coaxed him, the more he cried, which was very annoying.

一天，姐弟俩下地去了，不知为什么娃刚又哭了起来。治同鬼背他抱他，他也哭不停，喂他吃他不吃，逗他玩他不玩，放床上不理他，他哭得更凶。气得治同鬼火冒三丈，把他抱到九岔路口①，用刀劈成八块丢了。这一劈，哭声倒是没有了，但孩子也没有了。看着血淋淋的肉块，治同鬼后悔不已，内心深深自责，感到对不起姐弟俩，也不好意思再回家见他们，一个人远远地躲开了。想不到治同鬼刚离开岔路口后不久，八块肉体却变成了四男四女八个年轻人。他们的耳朵上都穿着洞，戴着银光闪闪的漂亮耳环，样子都长得和小娃刚一模一样。

那天傍晚，姐弟俩收工回来，见娃刚和治同鬼不在家，饭也没煮，火塘还是冷的，很惊奇："奶奶从来都不去哪儿串呀，今天会去哪里呢，怎么到现在还不回来？"一开始他们还以为是出外玩去了，等把饭做好，天也黑了，仍不见回来。姐弟俩这才焦急起来，赶忙分头四处找寻，可哪里还有治同鬼和小娃刚的踪影呀！当妈的急得像发了疯，她跌跌滚滚、哭哭叫叫地找了一夜。直到第二天红日东升时，才在九岔路口看见四对男女青年正互相依偎着谈情说爱。她赶上前去向他们打听小娃刚和治同鬼的下落，他们都回答说没看见。但是当她把他们上下仔细一打量，不禁惊叫起来："哎呀，你们一个个的样子都和我的小娃刚长得一模一样嘛！"

---

① 九岔路口：景颇族神话传说中的人、鬼世界的分界处。

One day, they went out to farm, and the boy started crying without any reason. The God of Mountain tried to calm him down with a hug or putting him on the back, but he didn't stop crying; she tried to feed him and he didn't eat; she put him on the bed and let him alone, and he cried more fiercely. The God of Mountain was so angry that she took him to an intersection with nine branches[1], and cut him into eight pieces with a knife. With the cutting, the crying disappeared and the child was gone, too. Seeing the pieces of blooding flesh, the God of Mountain was very regretful and deeply self-condemned. She felt sorry to see the sister and her brother, and fled far away. It was unexpected that the eight pieces of flesh turned into eight young men, four males and four females, who looked just like the little Wagang, wearing beautiful silvery earrings.

At dawn, the sister and her brother were very surprised to see that the baby and the God of Mountain were not at home when they came back home. The dinner was not ready, and the fire pond was cold. "The granny has never been out, and where has she gone today? And why hasn't she come back home now?" They had thought that the God of Mountain and Wagang were playing outside, but they hadn't come back yet when it was very dark outside and the dinner was ready. They began to worry about them and hurried to look for them everywhere, but could find nothing at all. The sister was almost mad and cried and searched for a whole night until the second day when the sun rose, she saw four pairs of young men and women sitting at the intersection with nine branches. She went up to them and asked whether they had seen her baby and the God of Mountain, but they all answered no. She couldn't help screaming when she looked them up and down carefully, "Ouch! You all look just like my little baby."

---

[1] It is said to be the division of the ghost world and the human world in the Jingpo legends.

　　"你是我们的妈妈？"看着这个年纪和他们差不多的人自称是他们的妈妈，年轻人你看看我，我看看你，谁也不相信这是真的。"嬢嬢，我们都不叫娃刚，也不知道谁是我们的妈妈。"他们中的一个很难为情地对她说。

　　"什么，你们不是我的娃刚？难道是我眼花看不真？"她揉了揉眼睛，再一个个地细细打量，可是越打量越觉得他们像娃刚，那音容笑貌，一举一动都和娃刚一模一样。难道当妈的还能认不准自己的孩子？不，没错，"你们就是我的娃刚！"

　　"嬢嬢，我们不可能会是你的娃刚，你想想，你的娃刚才是一个刚会走路的小孩子，而我们却是八个年轻人。一个小娃娃怎么能一夜间长成八个年轻人？"

　　"这，这叫我怎么说得清呢？可你们一个个都长得和我的小娃刚一模一样，能说不是我的娃刚吗？孩子们，我真的是你们的妈妈呀，走，快跟妈妈回家吧！"她紧紧拉着孩子们的手舍不得放下，眼泪又不住地滚落下来。"嬢嬢，你说我们长得像你的小娃刚，可我们谁也没有见过小娃刚，不知道他长什么样，单凭你说，还不能使我们相信我们就是你的娃刚。请问你还有什么别的证据来证明你真是我们的妈妈呢？"

　　孩子们的话使她张口结舌回答不出来。可也是呀，孩子们说的不是没有道理，如果没有足以使他们信服的证据，他们怎么会轻易相信这是真的呢？但是要叫她一下子拿出证据来，她无论如何也办不到。"要是治同鬼奶奶在场就好了，可她……"真叫她不晓得咋个整才好。

"You're our mother?" looking at the woman who seemed to be the same age as them and called herself their mother, the young people looked at each other and nobody thought it was true. "Aunt, we are not Wagang, and we don't know who our mother is." One of the young people said embarrassedly.

"What? You are not my baby? Am I dazzling and can not see you clearly?" She rubbed her eyes and looked them up and down one by one. But the more she watched them carefully, the more she felt that their voices and expressions and behaviors looked like her baby's. Could a mother mistake her child for someone else? No, never. "You're my Wagang."

"Aunt, we can't be your baby. Just think about it, your baby is just old enough to walk while we are eight young men. How can a baby grow into eight young men overnight?"

"Well, how can I make it clear? But every one of you looks like my little baby, and how can I say you're not. I'm really your mum, kids, and come and go back home with me." She held their hands tightly and didn't want to let them go, with tears falling down from her eyes. "Aunt, you say that we look like your baby, but how can we believe you since none of us have ever seen your baby, and we don't know what he looks like. We can't be convinced just because of what you have told us. Could you give us more evidence to prove that you are really our mother?"

The children's words made her dumb with open mouth. However, they were not unreasonable. How could they believe her easily if she could not show them enough evidence? But it was also a hard work for her to produce more evidence at one, and she couldn't do it anyway. "If only the God of Mountain were here, but she..." She really didn't know how to do it.

"嬢嬢，你看这样好不好？"一个小伙子从旁边的火堆里拣起块熄灭的火炭递给她，对她说："你说是我们的妈妈，那就请你来洗这块炭吧，如果你能把它洗白，说明你是我们的妈妈；如果洗不白，就说明你不是我们的妈妈。"

母亲认儿心切，既然孩子这么说，她也就毫不犹豫地接过火炭去小河里洗。洗呀洗，把河水都洗黑了，而炭却怎么也洗不白。孩子们见她不能把炭洗白，以为她不是他们的母亲，于是在她专心致志洗炭时，悄悄地离开了她，离开了九岔路口，走进"定塔门"①，来到"定塔嘎"②，在高高的蒙古利亚山定居下来，开始了和睦友好、幸福美满的人类生活。传说他们就是景颇族、德昂族、傈僳族、佤族等民族的祖先了。

当母亲发觉孩子们离开时，他们已经走得无影无踪了。她慌忙丢掉尚未洗白的火炭，也顾不得自己的丈夫，拔腿就追，谁知却追错了方向，来到了太阳门③外。但太阳门关着，无法进去。为了进太阳门寻找孩子，她就坐在太阳门前，边织筒裙边等着太阳门打开，哪儿也不去。据说美丽的彩虹，就是她织的筒裙布。

---

① 定塔门：景颇族神话传说中人类世界的大门。传说在此之前，人类和鬼是共同生活在一个世界里。
② 定塔嘎：人类世界。
③ 太阳门：景颇族神话传说中天堂世界的大门。

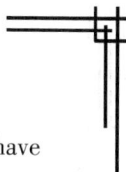

"Well, Aunt, what do you think about it since you have said you are our mother?" One of the young men took out an extinct charcoal fire from the fireplace aside and handed it to her, "Take the charcoal fire and wash it. If you can make it white, it means you are our mother, otherwise, you're not."

The mother was so eager to make them believe her that she took the charcoal fire without hesitation and washed it in the river. Nevertheless, no matter how hard she washed it and made the water black, the charcoal fire was still black. Seeing that she couldn't make it white, the children thought she was not their mother, and left her secretly while she was still working at it. They left the intersection with nine branches, crossed the Dingta Gate① and arrived Dingtaga②, then settled down on the high Mongolia Mountain, and began their friendly and happy human life. It is said that they are the ancestors of Jingpo, Deang, Lisu, Awa and so on.

The children had gone without any trace when the mother realized it. She hurriedly left the unfinished charcoal fire and set out to run after the children regardless of her husband. Unfortunately, she ran towards the wrong direction and went to the Sun Gate③, which was closed and she couldn't go into. In order to find her children, she sat in front of it and weaved the straight skirt, waiting for the opening of the gate and without going anywhere. It is said that the beautiful rainbows are the cloth she has knitted.

---

① Dingta Gate is the gate of human world in Jingpo legends. It is said that the human beings and the ghosts live in the same world in ancient times.

② Dingtaga refers to the human world.

③ The Sun Gate is the gate of the heaven in Jingpo legends.

天上一日，地下十年。宁贯娃回到太阳山治疗养伤后，仍然挂念着他造的天地万物。当他俯首大地，满目荒凉，心里非常难过，后悔当初没能立即杀死高佐洛雷。想再到大地上修补山河，创造人类时，他看到了娃刚的奇变和母亲寻子的一切情况，深深同情娃刚的母亲。于是他来到太阳门外，把事情的始末告诉了她，然后又带她回到大地上与孩子相认。

回到大地上，经过宁贯娃的解释，娃刚的母亲与孩子们相认了，乐得她笑容满面，热泪盈眶。可是，马上她又为应和谁在一起生活的事而苦恼，因为现在由娃刚变成的四对年轻人已成家分居，有了儿女。孩子们也为她应该和谁一起生活的问题发生了争执。都说应该和自己一起生活，你争我夺，互不相让。还是宁贯娃把大家劝住，说："孩子们，听我说，你们不要争。你们的母亲确实是个慈母，完全值得你们大家热爱和尊敬。不过她不能跟你们在一起生活，因为太阳现在还没有人驾驭，我想请你们的母亲去驾驭太阳。这样，她既能让太阳更好地为大家造福，又能天天和大家见面，一举两得，你们说好不好呀？"

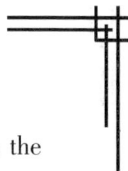

It was said that one day in the Heaven was ten years on the earth. Ningguanwa was still concerned about everything he had created when he went back to heal his wounds in the Sun Mountain. When he looked down at the desolate earth, he was very sad and regretted that he had not been able to kill Gaozuoluolei at that time. He happened to see the whole story of the transforming of Wagang and his mother's looking for her child when he wanted to repair the mountains and rivers on the earth. He sympathized with the mother, so he went to the gate of the Heaven, told her the whole story and took her to the earth to reunite with her children.

Back to the earth, Ningguanwa explained the whole story to the children, so the mother and her children were happy to see each other with tears in their eyes. However, the mother was troubled with a new problem. The four pairs of young men had got married, had their own family and children and lived separately, so it was difficult for her to decide with which one she would live. The children also argued with each other, tried to live with the mother and nobody wanted to give it up. At last, Ningguanwa tried to persuade them and said, "Listen to me, kids, your mother is really a good mother who deserves your love and respect, but she can not live with any one of you, for I want to ask your mother to rein the sun since it is out of control now. In this way, she can make the sun serve you better and you can meet each other every day, which will kill two birds with one stone. It's so good, isn't it?"

得以会见自己的孩子，对母亲来说已是心满意足的事情了。当看到自己的子孙已得繁衍，大家都能安居乐业，幸福、和睦地生活，她更感到无比的欣慰。现在听宁贯娃这样安排，心想："是呀，我怎么能坐享孩子们的清福呢？应该为孩子们造福，使他们生活得更美满才好！"于是她谢绝了孩子们的热情挽留，欣然接受了宁贯娃的封赐，跟着宁贯娃回到了太阳上。从此，她每天鸡叫起床，傍晚归家，终日驾驭着太阳在天空上飞驰，让明亮的阳光普照着大地，温暖着自己的子孙。

整理者：岳志明，杨国治

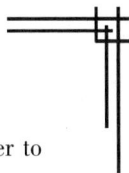

The mother was content to see her children and felt better to see that her children had got their own ones and lived a happy and harmonious life in peace. Hearing Ningguanwa's words, she thought, "How can I sit and enjoy the happy life when they are working hard? I'd better do something to make them live a better life." Then she declined the children's requirement and agreed to rein the sun. From then on, every morning the mother got up when the cock crowed, and went back home every evening, reining the sun in the sky and letting the bright sunlight shine on the earth and warm her offspring.

Collector: Yue Zhiming, Yang Guozhi